'The more you struggle to live, the less you live. Give up the notion that you must be sure of what you are doing. Instead, surrender to what is real within you, for that alone is sure.'
Baruch Spinoza

Lord Peter Wimsey: 'You would have to abandon the jig-saw kind of story and write a book about human beings for a change.'
Harriet Vane: 'I'm afraid to try that, Peter. It might go too near the bone.'
Lord Peter Wimsey: 'It might be the wisest thing you could do.'
Harriet Vane: 'Write it out and get rid of it?'
Lord Peter Wimsey: 'Yes.'
Harriet Vane: 'I'll think about it. It would hurt like hell.'
Lord Peter Wimsey: 'What would that matter, if it made a good book.'

Dialogue from *Gaudy Night*, Dorothy L Sayers.
Coronet Books, Hodder & Stoughton 1990, page 291.

Chapter 1

Wednesday 19 May 2010

The room is already full when Aurora arrives with Hannah. It is one of the long, narrow teaching rooms at the university which retains some of its original nineteenth-century features, coving around the ceiling and a small, plain, cast-iron fireplace, semicircular at its apex. Other than that the decor is unexceptional; bland walls and a dark, hard-wearing carpet. This is now covered over with brightly coloured blankets and floor cushions, as if prepared for an indoor picnic. The lighting is provided by an assortment of desk lamps from the possibly antique to the Wilko £2.99 variety, each making its own pool of yellow light. Blinds are drawn across the windows; after the warmth of the day, the night is chilly, the wind rattling at the glass panes. A huge screen is being rigged up across the fireplace end.

It had been Max who had persuaded Aurora to go when she mentioned it to him on her return home yesterday evening. He'd been solicitous, caring. *Repentant for messing up my evening.* 'Go on, it's your sort of thing, all that experimental drama stuff. You deserve some fun. Take Hannah, she could do with cheering up.'

She hadn't given him time to change his mind or find a design brief which absolutely had to be finished before he could be free to look after Oli. She'd rung Hannah immediately, who after a fraction of a hesitation had agreed. *She's making an effort to get out more. And she's looking better for it.* As they follow eagerly chattering clusters of people further into the room, Aurora puts a hand on her friend's shoulder. *A friendship wrought of adversity*, she feels awkward contemplating it. Those early weeks of motherhood had nearly sent her mad. *Mad*, she doesn't even like the word to form in her mind. *And it was Hannah and Rose who pulled me through. And I was there for Hannah when she was attacked*, she adds to herself quickly. *All this stuff with her father, though ...* She knows the bare minimum, doesn't ask for more details, doesn't want more details. In her job, she deals with the terrible fallout brewed in estranged and troubled families, and she manages it all professionally. *But with Hannah it's different. It's too close. It's as if knowing would infect me, infect me and Oliver.* She shakes away this notion before it can properly take hold.

A young woman with pink hair and piercings is in charge of getting everyone seated. She greets Hannah like an old friend, calling her 'hun' and asking after Ben. She points to a couple of large bean bags covered in corduroy, 'Go park yourselves over there, we'll be starting very soon.'

As they make their way to their seats through the already gathered audience, she hears her name being called. The beat in her chest gives a brief prance at hearing his voice. *Ridiculous.* She knows she's looking gorgeous in her caramel shalwar kameez, both Hannah and Max have commented. Only she hadn't needed them to tell her. She'd swept her shiny black hair up into a chignon and hung her Indian gold from her ear and around her neck. She smiles widely, turning.

Professor Aiden Haswell rises to his feet in one easy movement. 'Glad you decided to come.' His touch on her arm is brief, yet it imprints itself. He's wearing a silky shirt patterned like an abstract study in grey-blue. His feet are bare below white slacks. Not many men can get away with white trousers. Professor Haswell can. They set off his tanned skin. 'You've brought a friend? Haven't we met?'

Once again she is aware of the others in the room and Hannah standing awkwardly by her side. Hannah admits, hesitantly, to having been at Dr Shrimpton's seminar the previous week. Then Aiden introduces his companions, (the aforementioned) Dr Clare Shrimpton and Felicity Pritchard. They scramble up. Haswell offers wine and strawberries from a wicker hamper. Aurora inspects the two women. They are both tall, as tall as Aurora. Felicity is ungainly, she looks hot. She's tried to do something with her hair which is mousy, and brittle with blonde dye growing out, however, it only hangs wearily around her dull face. Clare, in comparison, is sparkling, all reds and silver against her Mediterranean colouring.

She smiles warmly at Hannah, they exchange pleasantries. Aurora has heard Hannah talk about her, describe her as beautiful, *and she's right.*

'The ascending star of the English department,' Aiden says. He hangs an arm around Clare's shoulder. It looks casual and his blue eyes are still on Aurora.

'Not if Professor Peer had his way,' says Felicity. She's moved closer to Clare, so the woman is flanked. Felicity snatches a glance at Haswell's hand resting on Dr Shrimpton's upper arm.

She'd like to see it gone too. Aurora accepts a strawberry from the bowl Haswell is holding. She takes a bite. It disintegrates sweetly on her tongue.

'Oh Harrison,' Clare is saying, apparently unembarrassed by the accolades. 'He's alright. It's all part of the legitimate rough and tumble of academia.'

'Where is he anyway?' asks Aiden.

'No one seems to know,' Clare replies with a mischievous grin. 'It's all rather mysterious.'

'And we know how much you love a mystery, my dear,' Aiden's fingers massage the top of Clare's arm.

'He wouldn't lower himself to come here, by all accounts,' mutters Felicity.

The discussion is brought to an end by Pink Hair speaking through a microphone and asking everyone to take their seats. 'We'll talk after,' Aurora hears Aiden's promise, as she and Hannah hurry off to sink rather inelegantly into their bean bags. Pink Hair then introduces, 'A man who needs no introduction, Dr Hal Denver.'

Some in the audience clap as he comes forward. He is wearing army-green shirt and trousers; his head is shaved to a snowy stubble which descends to his chin. 'Right folks, the art will speak for itself, so can we have the lights off and let's get this gig on the road.'

Once in darkness, the film begins to play. Aurora is aware of some of the background from the local paper. The coast around

Scarborough is slowly being eaten away where it is not protected, and about twelve months ago a good few metres of land collapsed down cliffs at Knipe Point not far south of the town. Houses had been built on the top of the cliffs. They were much extended static caravans and had been meant to be holiday homes, though a number were occupied all the year round. This, or some recent water-pipe work, could have been the reason for the landslide. Whatever, the three dwellings which had once had gardens running to the precipice were now teetering on its edge. One had to be dismantled. Of the other two, both were abandoned; one owner continued to fight with their insurers for compensation, the other sold their property to Dr Hal Denver, university lecturer and artist. He rigged it with cameras and said it would be a meditation on the inevitability of human destruction and decay. Then he waited. A year on and the metal and wooden structure hadn't budged. Most people had forgotten all about it.

The cameras were still rolling, however, or the ones which hadn't been nicked by local teens, who were later caught because one of them posted their escapade on Facebook. *Presumably a meditation on the modern justice system*, Aurora now jokes to herself. Dr Hal Denver continued to capture the footage from the cameras every now and again, and stored it for later use, but he too was moving on, he had a new exhibition to prepare for. Then, this Sunday, the house abruptly tipped over the brink and onto the beach below. Again the reason was obscure. The winter snows. There'd been a small seismic shift out under the waves. Martians had taken it up for inspection and then dumped it back, missing their target. Theories on the local paper's website chat-page abounded. The only certain fact was that it had gone and Dr Denver now had his film. And tonight is its premiere.

If she hadn't known the story, Aurora wouldn't have got it from the narrative. Interviews with the property owners are sliced in between the images of the building's abandoned and slowly degrading insides and outsides, which are becoming occupied by wildlife. Yet the people could have been talking about anything, any tragedy, any death. *And I suppose that's the point.* Aurora drains her glass. Her body is cradled by the bean bag and the atmosphere is warm, stuffy. She is tired, life is hectic. The music soundtrack of the film is lulling. She begins to feel she's drifting, drifting on a lilo in a tropical sea, drifting into sleep.

Then she's awake. Oli has screamed. *What's wrong? What's happened?* Her eyes are open, she's struggling to get off her bed, it's gone all soft and floppy, she can't get a purchase. Her heart thumps up against her sternum. There's another scream and she realises it's not Oli. She's deep into a bean bag and there's a rising mutter from the people around her.

'Lights.'
'Professor Peer.'
'Are you sure?'
'Can't be.'
'Get the fucking lights up.'

And someone throws the switch on the ceiling fluorescent strips, bringing into sharp focus the dazed audience, most staggering to their feet.

'Are you OK?' Hannah is sitting forwards towards Aurora.
'I'd fallen asleep. What happened?'

Hannah's face is chalk, the edges of her eyes are pink and the pouches of skin under them are more visible than they were earlier. 'There was a man, a man's face, in the window, as it went over.' She finds a scrappy bit of tissue and dabs at her nose and eyes. 'At least it looked a bit like a man's face. It was so quick.'

'You mean it was part of the film?'

'I don't think so. Not by the way everyone and what's-his-name, the artist, is behaving.'

They both get up. 'Are you OK?'

'I will be. I was finding it quite moving. Took me by surprise. And I think I recognised the face.'

Aurora hunts out a cotton handkerchief from her bag and gives it to Hannah to continue with her ministrations. Gazing round, Aurora can see a mix of reactions; others have clearly been dozing, some have been, like Hannah, affected by the film, others more bored. Now expressions are turning to either shock or curiosity.

Pink Hair has taken up the mic again: 'OK folks, well not exactly sure what to say, I guess we'll have to call it a night, um, yeah ... Maybe adjourn to the bar?'

'You need to get the film to the police,' someone shouts. There is agreement and disagreement, people are now questioning what they saw, or what others say they saw. Pink Hair and others, including Dr Denver, are urging everyone to leave, and they are gradually moving off.

Aurora scans the room, she thinks maybe she sees Aiden's shirt disappearing out the door. 'Do you fancy a drink, in the bar?' She finds she can hardly control her breath.

'Not really. You go if you want ... I'll ...' Hannah glances up and stops, then she shrugs, 'OK, a cold juice would be nice.'

Bother, I'd forgotten she's off the alcohol, maybe we oughtn't go. However, the tug towards Haswell is too great to ignore. She leads the way. 'Only I don't get many nights out, on my own.' Despite her best efforts, her enthusiasm spills out into her voice.

'Yeah, sure.'

Out in the corridor, the throng is dispersing, with a few heading towards the bar. Following them, they get to the threshold, a wave of music and the smell of beer hitting them. Aurora sorts through the crowd, there's some groups of girls sitting around tables, one holds numerous birthday cards. There's what is probably a rugby team with some of their cheerleaders, their table is awash with glasses, bottles and spilt alcohol. The few refugees from the premiere are huddled in a corner, determinedly having a drink. She ascertains after a few moments, *Aiden is not here.* Her interior balloon, which was bouncing, punctures.

'What do you want?' asks Hannah.

'No, nothing, let's not bother.' She walks off quickly.

Hannah has to scurry to catch her up. 'What's wrong?'

'Nothing,' she says curtly. They carry on in silence, stepping out into a damp, cold night, more young women in shorts and miniskirts passing them going in the other direction.

They reach the exit to the campus and have to wait to cross the main road. 'Is it something I did or said?' asks Hannah quietly.

The words hardly filter through Aurora's busy mind, *He didn't wait. Well see if I care. I don't care. God why should I care? I've got Max and Oli. Aiden Haswell, Professor Aiden Haswell, who's he?* Finally, however, Hannah's question does register.

'What?' Aurora turns and sees the shoulders and neck crushed down. Pity surges through Aurora, she gives Hannah a hug. She's a sparrow in her arms. 'No, no, of course not. But did you see that bar? Who'd want to go in there? It struck me I'm too old for it all.'

Hannah's response is as an exhalation of the air. 'Do you think we've just seen Professor Harrison Peer die, before our eyes?'

Chapter 2

Eight days earlier, Tuesday 11 May 2010

'Nah, it couldn't have been me, 'cos I wusn't there, love.' Jayson Smith grins, pleased with his logic. He is twenty-seven, though his looks and demeanour would put him in his late teens. He has a cherubic face, and the unhealthy pallor which suggests eating vegetables and going out in sunlight are rare activities. His pink tongue frequently lolls a fraction beyond his yellow, crooked teeth, as it does now.

DS Theo Akande has the urge to grab Jayson Smith by the grubby collar of his T-shirt to straighten him out of his slouch, then pull up his jeans which have slunk to his thighs, revealing less-than-appealing underpants. *And wipe the smirk off your face while you're at it.* The words form harshly in Theo's brain. *Where did they come from?* None of his family had spoken to him or anyone else like that. *Mum would have urged understanding, compassion for this little runt.* He remembers an old-school sergeant during those few months as a PC, after graduating university, twenty years ago, before being fast-tracked into CID. *He'd have said stuff like that, the white kids got it, not me, I'm too black.*

The chair back digs in through his linen jacket and Indian cotton shirt to the centre of his back. He wants to take a deep breath, but the fusty atmosphere doesn't encourage it. The interview room is square, painted a dull green and only has windows high up on its walls. It's the late afternoon of a fresh day in May, yet the outside doesn't reach the room's occupants. Theo wants to stretch, to go for a run up the coast path, instead he remains static, hoping the tension coming into his arms and neck isn't noticeable. *This isn't my show.*

He has let Harry lead the questioning. She now says firmly, 'DC Shilling to you, Mr Smith.' Jayson's mouth forms an 'Oooo', which would undoubtedly have been delivered with a mocking up-turn. However, Harry's level gaze silences him, he merely shrugs and folds his arms.

Next to Jayson sits the duty solicitor, a young man in an indifferent suit. He must be new, as Theo hasn't met him before. Since his sideways move from Manchester to Scarborough eighteen months ago, Theo has come across all the legal profession which trouble themselves with crims in this small seaside town. He's been told this one is an underling of the flamboyant Reggie Harvey who, in court, has a way of making the most hardened feel some empathy for petty offenders such as Jayson Smith. Theo has a grudging respect for Reggie Harvey's oratory and his commitment. Reggie's minion is keeping his head down, carefully taking copious notes.

On the watch for infractions of procedure. He won't find any. Harry, in a much more stylish (*and expensive*) suit, her blonde hair cut short and sharp, grazing her ferociously blushered cheeks, is working her way through methodically. *And she'll wipe the floor with you.* Had the occasion allowed it, Theo would have smiled as wolfishly as Jayson Smith.

* * *

The lilac tree is in bloom. It marks the edge of the back garden, the southern edge of Scarborough. Beyond is the scrubby dark-green shoulder of the cliffs. There is little human habitation on those cliffs between the lilac tree and the next town, some ten miles down the coast, only a few bungalows tenaciously holding to the crumbling sandy-earthed drop to the waves. Every once in a while a seagull rises into view on an updraft, cackling, enjoying the rollercoaster ride. Hannah Poole has opened the window and a cooling breeze slithers through, fingering the auburn nest on top of her head. She has not bothered to dress properly; is in jogging pants and sweatshirt which have become baggy on her.

This is her father's office. *The office of the great newspaper man Stan Poole*, she thinks sourly. *He would have wanted me to keep it as a museum to him.* She has not. She has tried to claim it for her own. Aided by Rose, she has cleaned and decorated it;

chased away the tell-tale odours of aniseed and unwashed flesh, the smells of her father in his final days. Most of his files are with CEOP, the Child Exploitation and Online Protection centre. The rest are with Lawrence. Hannah wonders what he is doing with them. *Does he read through them without a qualm? Does he? Is he able to separate off the man, the writer, from the deed?* Hannah doesn't know. Her father is rarely mentioned when she and Lawrence talk. *Our conversations have become vacuous, we no longer tell each other anything. Would we even talk if it weren't for Theo? Is he all that holds us together now?* Sadness accompanies this thought. *Lawrence thinks I've suddenly come up with this stuff about my father, he doesn't understand how it could have become so buried, so hidden, that I didn't tell him before. And it's hard for me too*, she admits to herself. *Now he's equivocal about believing what I say, anything I say, not just stuff about Dad.* It's insidious, the distrust, seeping in between them, a spring tide of suspicion slowly creeping in around the rocks until it overwhelms them.

The house is quiet around her; there is the background hum of a computer, the intermittent tick and creak of water and heating pipes, but no other human sound intrudes. *It can't last. Mother will return.* Val Poole has continued on the odyssey she started when her husband died. She visits various friends and cousins who resurfaced when she became a widow until she has outstayed their patience, then she goes back to her son's swanky ménage in York. *Stephen won't put up with it much longer, or his wife won't.* Veronica has started to defy her husband and leave panicky messages for her sister-in-law: 'Hannah, you must understand your mother can't stay here forever. You know I'd do anything for the dear, dear woman, but I'm not well myself. I'm exhausted.'

But I'm a traitor, ain't I? A traitor to the family. How's Stephen going to reconcile leaving our mother to my tender mercies?

Hannah runs her hand across the smooth surface in front of her. For a moment she expects it to be her father's desk. It was a large, heavy mahogany affair which her father placed to dominate all the offices he had in all the houses they occupied. In latter years, at its centre was the bronzed metal stand in the shape of a typewriter. This held the sleek and expensive Parkers her father loved, and was a gift from his son. Hannah had sold the desk on eBay and replaced it by a simple light wooden structure. She had taken the pens and stand as far as the charity shop door. They are now wrapped in newspaper in a box in the garage.

Her laptop has gone to screen saver. She can see her pasty face and her hazel eyes bruised by the shadows under them. She has already checked Facebook and Twitter, seen the updates from Steff and Rickie about their glittering careers in TV journalism in London and New York. Friends, or they used to be. *It's all such a long time ago since I was a part of their lives. Was I ever really a part of them?* She 'likes' and 'favourites' as something to do but cannot find the words to add anything of her own. *What would I say?* Physically she has recovered from the assault of a couple of months ago. *At least he pleaded guilty so I didn't have to endure a trial.* Yet in many ways she is still living in its gloom. She has not been able to practise as a counsellor. Even though she has submitted her final pieces of work and should hear if she has qualified any time now, she wonders if she will ever go back to it. She is anxious, low – OK, depressed – a lot of the time. She knows this is more to do with the distant rather than the recent past; still, the experience of being a victim again hasn't helped. Left to her own devices, she knows she would shut down, disengage, become trapped in the negativity of the large proportion of her thoughts and feelings. *You're no good. You're evil. You shouldn't have been born. A mistake. Stop breathing.* She twitches her sleeve loose over her increasingly bony wrist, fighting the impulse, the temptation.

Reach out, Hannah, ask for support. The words of her therapist, Izzie, have grown so familiar they sound as if they might be her own. Aurora from next door might have come round, only she's at work or got some kind of course or something. A young sparrow crash-lands on the telephone wire loosely hanging between pole and house. It swings unsteadily, flapping its wings to keep its balance, grimly gripping on. There's birdsong through the open window overlaying the distant thrum of the sea, a blackbird marking his patch with trills, peeps and whistles. *Ben.* She feels a softening in her belly. Their coming together appears vulnerable, the tender white head of a snowdrop pushing out through clods of dark earth. *I don't want to trample all over it with too many demands.* She knows what she's capable of, the stream of pleading and then accusative texts which she's sent in the past to people she mistakenly thought were fond of her. She cringes at the memory. *No, I'm too much, for anybody.*

* * *

Aurora Harris arrives hot, bothered and late. She has rushed back from work in York, at times driving too fast, picking up her fourteen-month-old son from his nan's on the way. She has had to quickly feed him before leaving him with Max, who was grumphing about being taken away from his design business before 5 pm, and hurrying over to the university buildings. *I knew I shouldn't have agreed to this. It's too much*, her voice in her head is whiney, it annoys her. *I didn't have a choice,* she returns, cross now both at the timbre of the voice and at not having a choice. *I need more credits to be considered for promotion and I need promotion so I can go part-time if ... when we have another baby. It'll be worth it in the end.* This kind of thinking has always got her through before.

Scarborough campus was built as a boys' school in the late nineteenth century. It has spacious rooms on the ground floor opening off a panelled corridor. Above and in the eves, what were once the sleeping quarters of staff and pupils are now offices or seminar rooms. More modern inserts have been added behind the orangey brick facade for a library, canteen and IT room. Aurora pauses for a moment in the impressive entrance hall which still has its ornate plaster mouldings in the ceiling and its wide-mouthed fireplace. She's not been in here before. It is very different from the ultra-contemporary university she attended. *It's quaint,* is her assessment. *Now where is ...?* A receptionist helpfully gives her directions down a corridor to a closed door painted a bright turquoise. A notice announces: 'New Developments in Family Law', assuring her she has reached her destination.

Aurora steadies herself. Her body thermostat has gone awry since she had Oli. Plus she has never quite lost all the weight she put on (*not that I was ever svelte*), which means even a mediocre amount of hurrying brings her out in a sweat. She can feel her ivory blouse, already limp from the day in the office, dampening around the chest area. Her legs are becoming uncomfortably clammy where they are encased in nylon tights, polyester lining and wool-mix skirt. She decides to keep her jacket on, though the suit as a whole is tight. She knows, however, that her dark straight hair, which she is growing once again to fall below her shoulders, is glossy, and her skin glows healthily from the recent sun. Both features are inheritances from her Indian father. She stands straighter, showing off her height and curves. Then she knocks and strides into the large oblong room set with rows of desks facing the front.

Eyes are upon her, mostly younger than hers. *Dark suits. White male faces feigning nonchalance.* She gains this impression from the periphery of her vision, she fixes her gaze forwards and fastens an upward curve to her lips. Momentarily stayed in what he was doing is a slight figure, a man in jeans and a shirt which could have been made from patches of curtains from the 1950s. She recognises the head of curly black hair and the tan from the publicity photo, but good studio lighting had softened the sharp pointed nose and given definition to the weak chin. Plus she'd expected the well-known Professor Aiden Haswell to be more substantial. He briefly consults a paper in front of him and then greets her by name, with what Aurora judges to be a genuine smile, and suggests she sits. She does so gratefully, in the far back corner by the window overlooking a sports pitch. She can hear the shouts from the two teams knocking about a football. She's reminded of the times she watched Max play footie in the early years of their relationship. She thinks about taking Oli along one time to see his dad at his five-a-side. *Max would like that.*

She draws her attention back into the room. Professor Haswell is giving information about the number of assignments and credits available during the course as he walks towards her. He gives her a folder, his hand gently (*deliberately?*) lingering in its contact with hers. And there again is the smile directed at her for a full moment before he retraces his steps. Aurora coolly regards the figure sauntering away. *What's your game, mister?*

CHAPTER 3

Tuesday 11 May

Hannah lifts her head. How quickly day fades into evening and a warm breeze turns into a draught. Then she notices the clock; she's been working solidly for a couple of hours. When she bombed out of journalism college over ten years ago, Lawrence gave her a room in his Highgate house as a favour to her father, his first mentor. *He rescued me*, is how she continues to characterise it. He also found her a job; copyediting and proofreading his writing and for his publishers. Despite all that has happened, he still wants her to work on his new book on Baruch Spinoza. *He trusts me enough for that.* She also has some work through the university; this afternoon she has finally completed proofing an article on DL Sayers by Dr Clare Shrimpton. *The lovely Dr Clare Shrimpton.* Hannah rubs at her tired eyes, aware that she herself is looking anything but lovely. She is certain she has smudged pen ink across her cheek. She is in need of a shower. *Can't be bothered.* She stands up and unbends, watches the sky become purpled, a dull contusion perforated by silver pins. The house is the last in Sea View Lane, which itself ends with a path down the precipitous cliffs. Hannah imagines rather than hears the tide pounding the soft sandstone at its base; hollowing, scooping, until the overhang topples in and another foot is reclaimed by the waves.

The doorbell startles her. She is reluctant to answer it. The few people she knows hereabouts wouldn't come round without checking first by text. *Even Ben? As a surprise? No, he's busy tonight.* She quashes a quiver of excitement. It is only the persistence of the caller, who leans on the bell-push half a dozen times for it seems like minutes, which finally persuades Hannah to investigate. At the top of the stairs she can see the front path through a long, narrow, stained-glass window. She can make out a human shape bundled up in a jacket with a hood. Again she hesitates. There have been burglaries recently, a 'spate' according to the local newspaper. *Don't be daft, Hannah, burglars don't announce themselves on your front doorstep.* This telling-off goads her down to the hall and she pulls open the door as her visitor lets off another volley of chimes.

'Yes?' Her irritation at being disturbed and then half-deafened powers through this one word.

'Hannah, you are in. Why the fuck didn't you answer me?' Maya Short's slight frame is drowned in the dark-green anorak, her elfin face is almost lost in the hood.

Maya in an anorak? No, a green waxed jacket. Maya in a green waxed jacket? Something is wrong, very wrong. Hannah holds tightly to the edge of the door. *Don't let her in*, a sensible part of Hannah's brain cautions. *Don't let her into the house, back into your life.*

Maya moves forward as if expecting the way to be opened for her.

As if we'd only seen each other last week. As if you had nothing to do with me being attacked. As if Ben hadn't chosen me over you. What are you expecting? To slip back into my bed with me because you've nowhere else to go? Hannah grips the door with both hands. 'What do you want?'

'I want to come in.' Without its usual heavy make-up, Maya's face is pale, vulnerable, her normally languid oval green eyes are squinting like a trapped bat's. Her voice falters, 'Please.' She glances down. Even so, she is alert to the momentary relaxation in Hannah's stance and uses it to gain entry into the hall from where she goes swiftly into the kitchen.

Hannah swears loudly, slams the front door and follows the younger woman, who is already making herself a ham sandwich. 'Maya, what do you want?'

'I want some Branston, haven't you got any?' She's opening and closing cupboard doors in her search.

'No. I don't like it. You know I don't.' There was a time, a very short time, maybe a year ago, when cooking and eating together with Maya had been laced with sensual pleasures.

'And no hidden bottles of wine, Hannah? Don't tell me you're sober? Ben's influence no doubt. He doesn't like his women to be pissheads. Oh well, no pickle then.' She sits on one of the hard-backed chairs at the kitchen table drawn up to the French windows leading into the garden.

The light in the kitchen doesn't allow Hannah to see into the dark beyond the glass, to see the patch of grass with its border of flowers and aspen tree at the side of the house. Maya's figure is stark against the black, hunched over her meagre repast, she reminds Hannah of a goblin perched on a toadstool. 'Why have you come here?'

'Because I need a place to stay. For tonight, then I'll be gone. I won't be any trouble.'

Hannah's guttural laugh takes herself by surprise, *when has Maya not been trouble?*

The spurt of noise from her hostess also catches Maya's attention, she turns on her most appealing smile, 'I promise, you won't even know I'm here.'

Slowly, Hannah runs herself a glass of water and takes a cooling few mouthfuls, then she sits at the table. She watches Maya's red lips and her delicate fingers as she devours her food. *I wouldn't be tempted to go with her, not any more, she's let me down too many times. Besides, I have Ben now. He chose me over her. Not that she was ever in the running, or so he says.*

'I did say I was sorry,' Maya says, wiping her chin with a man-sized handkerchief she's taken out of the coat pocket. 'I thought I was helping out telling him where to find you. What a nutter. I didn't know he would attack you.'

"Course you didn't.'

'I didn't.' She folds herself back into the jacket. 'Don't you ever put the fucking heating on?'

Not when I haven't a secure income and I've a loan for my counselling training. 'Maya, tell me why you are here.'

'Or what?'

'Or I'll phone your mum and Ben and we'll have a nice little party. I'm sure Rose would want to know if her daughter's got a problem, you know how she worries about you. And you've always said Ben's your one true friend, your protector since you were a kid, he'd help you out wouldn't he? *Not that he's as patient or as forgiving of you as he used to be.*

Maya looks sulky, she's maybe weighing up whether Hannah will carry out her threat. Finally she says quietly, 'Please, Hannah, one night. I've been an idiot, and yeah, you can say it if you want to, "again". I've been hanging out with this guy, we were partying, you know, at one of his mate's house, Jayson, what a twat he was, who spells Jason with a "y" anyway? And now, Jesus, there's cops all over the fucking house, looking for knocked-off stuff. I had to get out. Please, Hannah. Haven't you done anything stupid in your life which you just wanted to forget about?'

You know I have. Loads. 'Did you talk to the police?'

''Course I did, gave a statement and everything.'

Yeah right. Hannah considers phoning Theo. *He'd know what to do.*

Then Maya leans forwards and takes hold of Hannah's hands, fingernails digging into her flesh. 'Ben's an understanding bloke, isn't he, Hannah? Bet you've told him all your little secrets and he's been fine, hasn't he? Well you'd expect it of a psychotherapist. But he's also a man. Men, on the whole, don't like to be reminded that there's been a heap of lovers, particularly not one-night stands, before they came on the scene. I was just wondering, Hannah, how much you've really told him?'

You bitch.

* * *

'So, Mr Smith, I want to ensure we have your story straight,' DC Shilling gives a cursory glance at her notebook. They are back in the interview room after a break of forty-five minutes. Jayson Smith had been served a burger and chips and a high-energy drink, plus he'd had a smoke in the yard. After Harry had checked on the progress of the officers turning over the house where Jayson lives and been told they'd found nothing immediately of note, Theo had insisted they have a brief walk. They went out the back of the police station, down a snicket and into the graveyard, it was the best place he had found to get some air while at work. Here, behind high brick walls, the Victorians had laid out paths and flower beds for the dead. Headstones, crosses and weeping marble angels loomed in the dusk. The emergent tulips, made strange in the dim light, could have been deformed fingers stretching from the graves. Theo sensed a slight nervousness from Harry, which added to his own growing unease. A movement and a creak of a tree branch startled them both. Their steps quickened and they returned to their office somewhat out of breath. They eagerly downed hot frothy coffee, grinning at the ridiculousness that they could have been spooked.

Now Harry leans forward from her upright stance. 'You do understand the seriousness of the charges, burglary and handling stolen goods, Mr Smith? You'll be looking at prison this time. Do you have anything further to say?'

There is a momentary stiffening around Jayson's eyes and mouth, his gaze slides to his solicitor. The young brief has stopped writing, he does not look up. His client shrugs and slumps further down in his chair.

'Is that a no?' No response. 'I take it then, this is your story. The night of Friday, the seventh of May 2010, four days ago, you were with your friend, a Mr Gary Brook, drinking and watching videos. You were also with him and another who you cannot name between 6 pm and 8 pm on Sunday the ninth of May. That is correct is it, Mr Smith?'

A fraction of a nod.

You fool, Theo thinks, a little disconcerted by how pleased he feels.

'My problem is, Mr Smith, that on the seventh of May, a certain Mr Gary Brook was stopped by one of my colleagues for playing merry hell, in a stolen vehicle being driven up and down the seafront. Of course, Mr Brook gave a false name, but my colleague recognised him and his jacket-cam caught a clear profile of him. Didn't your friend tell you about this little incident, Mr Smith?'

Jayson snatches a glance at the youngster in the suit next to him who shakes his head slowly.

'Mr Smith?'

Jayson mumbles something.

'I'm sorry, I didn't catch that, Mr Smith?'

'No comment.'

Harry adds the words to her notebook. Then she snaps open a small laptop and clicks on the screen, 'Would you like to watch this CCTV from seven-ten pm on the ninth of May, Mr Smith, and tell me what's going on?'

Jayson doesn't look up. He rubs a hand across his brow which is becoming noticeably sticky. 'No comment,' he mutters.

'Well, let me tell you what is going on, shall I? You and a certain Mr Gary Brook are taking two black bin bags past a pub just down the street from the house where you are a tenant and you carry them round the corner. A few metres round the corner is a back lane leading to a house which has sadly fallen into disrepair, the yard of this house has been used over the recent past as a dumping ground by local residents. Do you know what we found in the yard, Mr Smith? No? Two black bags. One containing a TV etched with a serial number, matching equipment taken in the one burglary. In the other an old-fashioned video player. I didn't know people still had video players, did you sarge?'

'I did not, DC Shilling,' says Theo, smiling. 'I would say this make would be pretty rare.'

'These match exactly what was taken in two burglaries which took place between ten pm and three am on seventh to eighth of May. Now what do you say, Mr Smith?'

Jayson Smith suddenly launches himself forward and Theo also shoots to his feet, energy powering through to his forearms, ready to grab, ready to restrain. But the boy in front of him only thumps the table and screams, 'No fucking comment!' before tottering backwards into his seat.

'Good, fine,' says Harry slowly, deliberately, perhaps giving herself time to recover her composure. 'I think that's enough for now. You will be charged, Mr Smith, and I will be recommending bail is denied.' She stands up. 'Come on, out you go, back to your cell.'

Theo makes way for Jayson to exit. He watches Smith carefully, assessing whether he is likely to turn violent again. The young man's shoulders are drooping, he is worrying away at his bottom lip with yellowed incisors. Something is worrying Theo too. Even though there are no forensics to place Jayson at either of the burglaries, he has no doubt of the lad's involvement. However, having met him, he's clear Jayson Smith isn't clever enough to have planned and executed them so cleanly, he must have been led by someone else. *And where have the Peers' diamonds disappeared to?*

CHAPTER 4

Tuesday 11 May

After seeing Jayson Smith back in his cell waiting to be charged, Theo returns to his rented lodgings and finds Mrs White's bin is still out on the street. He hesitates. His neighbour is the keeper and distributor of the keys to the metal gate which guards the lane to the rear of the little terrace. It is here that the bins ought to be kept. She has already warned him more than once about leaving his bin out in front too long after the lorry has been. 'Makes the street look such a mess,' she'd said. 'And we don't want that do we?' He'd tried to explain about his irregular working hours; however, his job gave him no dispensation. She sniffed as she turned away saying, 'This used to be such a nice area and now we get all sorts.'

Theo is under no illusion: his black face is one of the factors bringing the area down according to Mrs White. Mrs McKenzie, the longest-term resident of the street and his next-door the other way, had invited him in for tea and shortbread fingers. She told him to 'pay no mind' to Mrs White, 'She has an acid tongue, but a warm heart.' *I've yet to experience the latter.*

He looks at the front windows of Mrs White's red-brick two-up-two-down. The heavy curtains are tightly closed over her flouncy nets. *She's in there*, the thought conjures up the image of a bloated toad in a dank cave. Theo knows she rarely goes out of an evening. *And she'll be alone.* He's met her only daughter on one of her brief visits which she schedules for after her own day at work. There has been no Mr White for some years. Mrs McKenzie had explained that the couple with their daughter (a bit of an 'afterthought' and, therefore, several years younger than her brother) had moved to the scene of happy family holidays when Mr White had become ill with emphysema. She'd gone on to describe the details of his long and lingering death, hinting this was perhaps a reason to forgive Mrs White's acerbic retorts.

It is a remembered injunction from his mother, though, which has Theo wheeling Mrs White's bin round back. 'Prove them wrong with wit and kindness,' she had always said (and would still sometimes repeat, if necessary) whenever the young Theo came storming in having received another verbal or physical insult. 'It's their ignorance,' she'd add, her soft Cape-Verde-mixed-with-Cardiff accent belying her strong intention, as she held him tight or dabbed his injuries with arnica. Theo's aware he'd been spared the worst kind of prejudice; being brought up as he was in a leafy suburb of Birmingham and going to a school where the teachers still had the time and the energy to care. The majority of the abuse was spoken and he'd found it easy to fight it with wit and kindness, making him popular with both staff and pupils. Even when he went into the police after college, tongues were bitten; he was a vital statistic they couldn't afford to lose. *I escaped lightly. Why do I feel grateful for that?* he thinks angrily.

Theo had decided he would ditch Mrs White's bin in the lane by her gate rather than manoeuvre it into her yard; then he notices the indoor light pooled across the concrete. It is coming from the back door into her kitchen, which has been left open. Once again he is hesitant. 'Leave it,' Lawrence would have said. 'She's not your responsibility.' He had been mortified when Theo had intervened in a drunken spat one time. They'd been walking through Scarborough on a Saturday afternoon, Lawrence having carefully selected some fish and vegetables from the market for their dinner and having found an acceptable white wine in the offie. A couple were occupying the centre of the pavement outside one of the town centre pubs. Their clothes were drab and inadequate for the cool weather, their hair was unwashed, both were painfully thin, but he was taller than her and he had hold of the jumper which hung round her. They were both swaying and his grasp might have been to steady himself, except he was yelling at her, his mouth inches from her face, gobs of his spit being caught in her thin mousy hair. Lawrence, with his London ways, was giving them a wide berth, muttering, 'No Theo, leave it.'

Only Theo couldn't leave it, he went over and suggested mildly to the man to cool it. This resulted in a gush of invective accompanied by sour breath and saliva being spewed in his direction. Then the no-longer-cowering woman shouted at him, 'Let 'im go you four-eyed black bastard, 'ees not done 'owt wrong.' And they both staggered off, reunited by a common enemy. It had taken some cajoling for Lawrence to forgive Theo. They'd been indoors by the time Lawrence had sighed and given him a kiss before sending him off for a shower claiming he could smell 'that reprobate's odour' about Theo's person.

No, I couldn't leave it then and I can't leave it now. He pulls the bin into the yard and leans in at the door, calling out for Mrs White. He steps inside. The kitchen is the long galley type, the same as his, only this one hasn't been redone since the 1980s and still sports heavy 'country-style' cabinet fronts. There's a pan bubbling on the stove, Theo lifts the lid, some potatoes almost boiled dry. He turns the plate off. Then he hears a faint groaning sound. He follows it through the overstuffed lounge-cum-dining room to the hall and finds Mrs White sitting on the carpet at the bottom of the stairs, her legs stuck out straight in front of her.

Dampening his irritation, he kneels, 'It's OK Mrs White, it's Theo from next door. Have you hurt yourself? Can I check you over?'

She looks up. Her face, normally so carefully made up, is smeared with mascara, lipstick and powder. Her grey hair is straggly, her eyes are raw with crying, her lips are slack. 'Go away,' she slurs. 'Don't want your type in here.'

He takes a deep breath. 'I'm not going anywhere until I know you're OK. Did you fall? Have you hurt yourself?'

She shakes her head and tries to get up. 'Go away.'

Theo gets a whiff of something alcoholic. She's futilely trying to get a purchase on the stairs behind her and make her legs and arms work in some kind of unison.

After watching her flounder like a portly beetle on its back for a short while, Theo squats behind her, grasps her by her armpits and levers her up to her feet. He keeps his hands against her shoulders until she finds her balance. 'Are you sure you haven't injured yourself?' he asks again.

'I'm fine.' With the help of the door jamb and then the wall, she manages to transfer herself into the lounge and onto a chair of faded, cucumber-coloured plush. She sits, back straight, settling her mussed hair with trembling fingers.

Theo perches on the edge of the sofa, reluctant to leave. He can't see any obvious damage and she doesn't seem dangerously inebriated, plus she's made him very unwelcome. *Even so, I don't want to leave her alone.* 'Can I call your daughter, Mrs White, to be with you?'

'Nooooo.' The long drawn-out cry this elicits alarms him. The already shattered face crumples over on the elderly neck into the heaving bosom. Theo shifts forwards and touches her shaking hands only to have his grasped by spongy, clammy flesh. Her voice quivers as she whispers, 'Please, she mustn't know, she mustn't. You can't tell her.'

'I won't, Mrs White, of course I won't, if you don't want me to.' He wonders if this is a wise thing to say and if he may have to go back on it some day. 'I just thought you shouldn't be on your own.'

'I'm used to it,' her tone is bleak.

'I can stay, for a little while, if you like.'

She looks up. Theo can see the battle going on as her head nods at the same time as her mouth forms a silent, 'No.'

He extracts his hand. 'Tell you what, I'll make us both a cup of tea, and once you've had that, you can see how you feel.' She doesn't object, so he goes into the kitchen. There are numerous teapots, cosies, tea sets and milk jugs in the cupboards. He takes out two china mugs, uses a teabag in each, shouts out whether she wants milk and, when no answer comes, adds it, before returning to the lounge. Mrs White is leaning back in her chair and he thinks she might be asleep, but as soon as he holds out one of the mugs she rouses herself and takes it. She sips.

'Lovely,' she concedes. She stares at the liquid in her mug, supping it noisily.

Theo's gaze travels around the room. The television in the corner by the window is small and square. Beside it is a dark-wood, open-fronted cabinet filled with china knick-knacks and photos. There are a couple of large studio ones of Mrs White's daughter; one of her graduation, the other with her husband and two children. There's a smaller, less posed picture of a man, probably in his mid-fifties, with his family, an expanse of lake in the background. Theo can see the resemblance to Mrs White in the fleshy cheeks and dome of a forehead. Behind these are several older ones; they seem to be holiday snaps with Scarborough as a backdrop. They all have a slightly odd, unbalanced appearance. The subjects – Mrs White's daughter as a child with or without her mother, once with a young lad with dark curly hair and sharp pointed nose – are not quite central. At first Theo thinks it's merely the poor skills of the photographer, then he notices in one of them Mrs White's outstretched arm is draped over a shoulder of someone who has been pared off.

'My husband wouldn't have photos of him in the house. He cut him out of them all and made a bonfire of the bits in the garden. He burnt the negatives too or I'd have got them redone.'

Theo looks back at her, crooking his eyebrow.

'My son,' Mrs White says slowly and deliberately, putting her mug down carefully on a side table. 'He carried on working and Mr White was a NUM man. He couldn't forgive him. I see him now, though. Sometimes.'

The miners' strike. For Theo, born in 1969, it's no more than a confusion of shouting men gesturing with fisted hands at ranks of mounted police on grainy news or documentary footage. But he knows from colleagues from Yorkshire and the north-east how it split families. Families like Mrs White's. He is going to ask for more of her story when she suddenly says savagely, 'I've been such a fool, such a fool. I should have known.' She sobs drily, briefly.

'Should have known what, Mrs White?' Theo asks gently.

'He seemed so nice, so genuine.' Her glassy eyes peer up at him, 'But I suppose all the aging idiots like me say that.'

'Tell me what's happened, Mrs White. Maybe I can help?'

So she does, and it's a tale he's heard before. Some guy turns up on the doorstep of an elderly and vulnerable victim, spins them a yarn, makes them an offer which is too good to be true and turns out to be exactly that. Could have been insurance, collecting for charity, a new roof; this time it is bootleg liquor.

'He loves his fine brandy,' she continues, her voice falling to a mutter. 'And I knew this was the best, the Courvoisier Connoisseur Collection,' she poshens her vowels for the phrase. 'I'd seen it in his flat. Only it wasn't, you see, wasn't even brandy, just some cheap alcohol mixed with water and food colouring. He said he could tell by looking at it. I couldn't 'cos I'm an old fool, a foolish old woman.' Her chin drops again and her reddened eyes seep. 'Paid thirty-two quid for it. I wanted to give him something nice, you see.'

Theo fishes in the nearby wastepaper bin for an old envelope and starts to take notes. Mrs White gives a fairly good description of the fraudster, she even remembers what kind of van he drove and has a few numbers and letters from the registration. But the liquid has been poured away and the bottle thrown out with the recycling. Suddenly, Mrs White lurches forward, says in a panicky voice, 'You won't bring him into it, will you? I can't tell you who he is. He wouldn't like that. He's a busy man. If you ask me any more, I'll say I made it up, a silly old woman's imaginings.'

Might as well throw this back in the bin, and Theo is on the brink of screwing up his notes. Instead he folds the paper and puts it in his pocket, says he'll see what he can do. He reaches for the mugs, with the intention of taking them to wash up. Mrs White puts her hand on his; it is cool now. Her voice is steadier and her faded eyes, still pink and sunk into deep wrinkles, hold his as she says, 'Leave them, I won't keep you any longer. You've done enough for me tonight already. Thank you, Detective Sergeant

Akande.' It's the first time he's heard her say his name and she says it carefully, purposefully.

'You're welcome,' Theo says automatically.

'Goodnight.'

He can tell she wants him gone. *Summarily dismissed*, antagonism stirs in him. He goes out through the kitchen. Then he pauses before leaving; the standard light Mrs White has turned on haloes her in her chair, she's picked up one of the photos, she's tracing her fingers across it and her lips are moving. *She's a lonely old woman, be kind*, the words are what his mother would have said. He closes the door quietly.

CHAPTER 5
Tuesday 11 – Wednesday 12 May
Hannah realises how frightened Maya is when she refuses to sleep in the guest room on the first floor and insists on staying up in Hannah's attic rooms. 'What's happened, Maya? Tell me.' Hannah holds the younger woman's shoulder tightly for a moment as they stand on the landing.

Maya's gaze darts about, she shakes her head. 'Nothing, nothing,' she says quietly. 'Only those police put the wind up me.' Then she turns on her smile: bright, neon, 'And you know me, Hannah, I hate to sleep alone.' She begins to climb the stairs, 'Come on Hannah, I'll keep you warm, since you refuse to put the heating on.' She laughs, 'And no hanky-panky, I get it, you're all Ben's now.'

There is something almost companionable as they get ready for bed. Maya finds a music station on the radio, 'Instead of the boring blah, blah, blah you listen to, trying to impress Ben.' Then after they both showered, she gives Hannah a pedicure and manicure, carefully painting her nails with a peachy-pink varnish she'd rummaged out of a bag Hannah had stowed in the bottom of her wardrobe. 'Have you looking nice for Ben.' And once they are both primped and preened in their pyjamas, Maya turns the volume up on some 1980s disco numbers and they dance around the bedroom until they fall back onto the bed laughing. 'There you go, Hannah, you do remember how to have a good time.'

Yeah, maybe.

As soon as Maya clambers under the duvet she falls into a deep sleep, her snores soft cat purrs. Hannah watches her for a while. *How vulnerable she looks, how adolescent. Though she's only five years younger than me. Am I beginning to look old?* She slowly slumps into a fitful slumber, only to be dragged out of it by Maya thrashing her arms around.

'What is it? What is it?' She sits up to avoid being hit and says loudly, 'Maya.'

Maya wakes, her eyes wide, she lets out a mewling cry, a wild animal caught in a trap.

Instinctively, Hannah pulls her into a hug, 'It's OK, Maya, you're safe now.' They lie there for a while, until the younger woman once again drifts back to sleep. It takes a while for Hannah to follow her, not least as she is turning over in her mind the oddness of the situation. *What is Maya afraid of? She's never afraid.*

Wakefulness gradually edges away sleep and Hannah is lying in her bed, warmth groping around the edge of the blind across the dormer window from a sun in a harsh blue sky. It takes a bit longer for her to realise she is alone in the room and this is not as it should be. *Maybe Maya has gone already?* And there's some relief in this thought. She glances at the alarm clock to see it is 7.30 am. *I could stay here all day and no one would notice.* She lets her glance travel around the room. There's some of the chaos left by Maya: towels and clothing across the floor; dirty cotton wool buds, emery boards and nail varnish bottles on the table. One bottle is on its side, a pool of sticky red collecting where its lid isn't on tight, its astringent smell lingering. *I'm safe here.* The danger lies beyond the door; an amorphous thing, covered in livid green slime, waiting to pounce, to trip her up, to annihilate her, at the turn of the landing. She burrows down into the bed. Then the pointlessness of rising begins to overwhelm her. *No one would notice whether I got up or not. No one would care if I stopped breathing.*

When she looks again, the time on the alarm clock has jumped forward sixty minutes. For an hour she's been wrestling with pointlessness and its constant repetition of: 'No one would care, no one would miss you, they'd soon forget.' *No. Izzie, Ben, they would miss me.* With an immense effort she sits up. The air itself cloys at her, attempting to transfix her in an existential aspic. *One thing at a time, Hannah, toilet, wash, clothes.* As ever, it is the deciding of what to wear which really delays things. Each time she reaches out for a hanger the words *wrong, wrong, wrong* rebound in her head. The alarm clock has gobbled another seventy minutes before she is finally dressed in a pair of light trousers and a peachy linen top. She can't check herself in the mirror; if she does so, she would have to start all over again.

She hurries past the thing on the stairs, letting her breath out when she reaches the hall. She steadies herself and then walks into the kitchen, *Lawrence would want me to have some breakfast.* It is then she realises Maya has not gone, she is talking loudly into her phone: 'I get it, I heard you the first time, no need to shout.' Pause, then, 'Yeah, whatever,' before she cuts the connection. She looks up, her mouth thin and taut. She sees Hannah, shrugs and says, 'My last-chance motel.'

Hannah begins to measure coffee into the percolator. 'I thought I was that.'

'You know sometimes Hannah, you can be amusing, when you let yourself.' She leans against the table by the French windows, rubbing her mobile against her chin as if considering her options.

Maya is wearing the jeans she had on last night and an ivy-coloured cashmere pullover Hannah recognises as one Lawrence had given her for Christmas once. *Looks better on her.* Behind Maya, Hannah can see the garden, the loose-lipped tulips in the borders Rose had helped her plant. The untrimmed lawn is strewn with dandelions and the white catkins hang on the silvery aspen branches; so many lolling woolly tongues waiting to clack. At the tree's base are clusters of pale-lilac yarrow flowers, or devil's nettle as Rose calls them, gathering them for one of her pain-relieving lotions. The sky is blue with a thin layer of cloud scraped across. A blackbird with a yolk-coloured beak is busy nest building in the hedge in the corner furthest from the house. It doesn't look dangerous, out there beyond the glass. She turns away, back into the room to find herself a mug. The machine is starting to gluck like a drowning chicken and there is the aroma of strong coffee. The milk container stands empty by the sink, next to a used bowl, glass and folded-over juice carton, remnants of Maya's breakfast. *Black coffee and no orange it is then.*

'I'll have to go back to Mum's. Hannah you can drive me, the buses are rubbish out her way,' Maya says brightly.

'You know I haven't got a car.' Slowly, she pours herself a coffee and takes a sip. It warms her, *tastes of normality*. Her breath comes more easily.

'Can't you borrow one? Ben's or what's-her-name next door?'

'Aurora, and no.' *I'd have done it for her once.* 'You'll have to get the bus, the fast ones to York stop on the A64, it's not far for you to walk from there. Or get a taxi.'

'Can't afford a taxi unless you lend me … No? It'll have to be Mum then.'

Her voice changes as she talks to Rose on the phone, it becomes softer, less confident, 'You know I don't like to ask, if it's not too much trouble …'

Hannah sits at the table, holds her mug in both hands, thawing them, hopes Rose won't be too long.

Once Maya is off her mobile, she swings into action. 'Hannah, you won't get very far on coffee and you need feeding up by the looks of you, I'll make you some scrambled eggs.' Which she does. They are surprisingly edible. It also means that, as Rose arrives, Maya is wearing an apron and serving up more toast, looking the model of domesticity, *which is no doubt the point.*

Rotund, yet muscular, her grey hair in a thick plait down her back, Rose Short is dressed in navy dungarees, her work clothes for the cleaning, gardening and care company she owns. She used to be a lone trader, but the enterprise has grown and now most of the grunt work is done by staff. And though Hannah first met Rose when she was cleaning for Hannah's parents, their relationship has transmogrified, it is more affectionate, more like an older sister to a younger one. Consequently, they give each other a big hug as a greeting, and Hannah feels the tenseness in her joints ease fractionally.

Mother and daughter also embrace with genuine warmth, although Hannah notices Rose asks few questions about where Maya has been and how she has washed up in the Pooles' kitchen. There is a carefulness about how they negotiate the space between them, *as if they are pieces on a chess board.* Maya has already decided her next move, she announces she will go to her dad's in France; he'll pay, he always does.

'Maybe,' Rose says, a tad stiffly.

Hannah sees her discomfort, she knows it to be a discomfort borne of guilt, guilt that she cannot provide as much for her daughter as the man she had a long-term affair with. He is a French doctor who Rose met when she was a nurse working for Médecins Sans Frontières. He is rich and, in his expansive Gallic way, relaxed about welcoming Maya into his large family. *But I think Rose is also beginning to see Maya isn't just a free spirit. She is unkind, and is wondering where she gets it from.* Then remembering Aurora and her struggles with doubt, *perhaps guilt is an inevitable part of motherhood.*

Maya, however, is unbowed by her mother's lukewarm reception of her idea, she chatters on about it while she (ineffectively) washes up. Then she is ready to go, her leave-taking is polite if perfunctory. 'Come on, Mum,' she says as Rose lingers, taking both Hannah's hands in hers.

'Have you plans for today?' Rose asks.

Hannah hadn't thought about it; she mutters about needing to get the proofread article to Dr Shrimpton.

'Maybe walk over and see her. It's a lovely day out there. And doesn't Ben work at the uni on a Wednesday? I'm sure he'd be pleased to see you. '

Would he? The question loiters after Maya has recaptured her mother's attention and whirled her out of the house.

CHAPTER 6

Wednesday 12 May

Theo is on his way to see Professor Harrison Peer and his wife Caroline, the owners of the video machine in Jayson Smith's haul and victim to one of the burglaries. DC Brian Chesters had taken the initial statement from them and it lists as stolen some rather expensive jewellery which weren't in those black bags. Theo had watched Smith salivating over the photos of the necklaces which had been taken for insurance purposes and were provided by Mrs Peer. Smith had claimed he knew 'nowt about them'. *It was the only time in the interview I believed what he was saying.*

He could have sent Chesters back to update them or even could have talked to them on the phone, but he is curious to find out more about the people who own the missing diamonds and, besides, it gives him an excuse to get out of the office. During most of his life, the turning of the year hardly impinged on him beyond dictating which part of the wardrobe he took his clothes from. In Scarborough, however, he's found he can no longer remain immune to the changing moods of weather and landscape. He has planted some pots up for his yard. His dad had been cock-a-hoop when his son had asked him for instructions after so many years of disinterest in gardening. Working the soil, the older Akande frequently claims, reminds him of his short childhood in Nigeria before he fled to Birmingham to join his brother. Though Theo suspects this is a way of idealising those difficult years, and that his father learnt his plant-husbandry skills on his plot at the back of their family home, at his wife's behest for some edible vegetables.

Driving out of the town towards Hackness, Theo follows a narrow meandering road at the base of a small wood. It's as if the gradations of greens are soaking into him, as if he can taste the sharpness of the acidic greens and the coolness of the darker hues. As he rounds a corner, he sees a vein of bluebells opened across a slope laid bare to the light, and the sudden detonation of joy catches him by surprise.

'You'll have to come now,' Mrs Peer had said. 'My husband has to be at the university this afternoon.' Her tone had struck Theo as imperious, *she is used to getting what she wants.*

It fits his image of her to find the Peers living in an elegant grey-stone Georgian property, part of the estate that used to own the whole of the verdant valley in which it sits. The entrance is through a rose-filled front garden. The large front door is opened by a woman who is too young to be Mrs Peer, and her precise English and accent tells Theo she hails from somewhere east of the Elbe. She leads him through the black-and-white-tiled hall into a square sitting room; offers him a coffee which he accepts; says, 'The professor and Mrs Peer will be with you momentarily'; and leaves quietly.

Theo saunters around the room. *There's some money here.* He'd been brought up not to be overawed by class or wealth and at university he'd found he could slip easily from clique to clique; his colour and sexuality categorising him before anything else. Still, he finds himself stroking the wood surfaces, the polished silver candleholders, the lush upholstery; leaving his mark. Being south facing, the windows conduct the warmth of the morning. They give on to walled grounds planted with vegetables and fruit trees; here, a man, with the same matt-black hair as the woman who let Theo in, is working at a patch of earth with a spade. In the room there are two substantial sofas and three armchairs, all covered in a muted floral design, arranged around the elaborately tiled fireplace. On a sideboard there are photos, including a black and white one of this room with two girls posed on a large ottoman. The taller one is sat particularly upright, her straight hair held back in an Alice band, her face long with a pronounced chin. The long face and pronounced chin are there again in a large-format wedding photo, though the woman's body has elongated to balance it somewhat. Here she is on the arm of a man who doesn't match her in stature and already has thinning wiry hair despite his youthful features. She is wearing a draped white dress with a long train and he is in a grey morning coat. They are both smiling.

The room door opens and Theo is presented with the couple as they are forty years later. Harrison's hair has diminished to white tufts about his ears and his skin has developed creases and blemishes. Caroline is wearing smartly tailored trousers with a blouse, both of which camouflage her widened waistline, her hair is cut short, a grey forelock atop her long face. She smiles, her husband does not, as she suggests they all sit. They take an armchair each.

'What's all this about, detective sergeant?' Mrs Peer asks. 'We've given our statements.'

Before Theo can respond, the young woman from the former Eastern bloc comes in with a tray of china cups of coffee and a plate of what are probably home-baked biscuits. She puts it down on the oak-and-glass coffee table set between the three of them.

'Thank you Marta,' Mrs Peer says. 'Professor Peer will take some lunch at midday, please be punctual, he has to leave by one. You can go now.' Then she turns back to Theo.

Her poker back and folded hands remind him of the girl with the Alice band. He takes up his coffee and a biscuit, both are subtly aromatic. Neither of the others follows his example. Unhurriedly, he replaces his cup and saucer on the table as he explains that they have arrested a suspect for the burglary at the Peers' house and have retrieved the video player, but, unfortunately, the jewellery is still missing.

'Easier to get rid of I imagine, detective sergeant. More portable. More valuable, those necklaces were my grandmother's, she wore them at her coming out, when she was presented to George the Fifth. I don't suppose we'll see them again.' She pauses before saying, 'It's most upsetting.'

'I wonder if I could take you back to last Friday night? The night of the burglary?'

'If you must.'

Harrison reaches forwards, for a biscuit, snaps it in half and puts a segment of it into his mouth. It is his wife who replies to Theo's questions, as it had been her who had done all the talking previously, according to Chesters. Her story is the same now as it was then. Marta and her husband had had the night off. They were with family in Sheffield until the following afternoon, Chesters had checked their alibis. So the Peers had been left with a supper of cold cuts to eat. They had cleared up and loaded the dishwasher before listening to a concert on Radio 3 and had gone to bed. They had only discovered the thefts when they got up Saturday morning.

'The back door was slightly ajar when I went down to the kitchen, but I thought we'd forgotten to close it properly, until I saw one of the small panes had been cut out. It was so neatly done, detective sergeant, I still didn't immediately realise what had happened. Then I heard Harrison making a fuss, some of his papers had been moved in his study. It's across the hall, he is so particular no one should touch anything. He thought it had been Marta, until he noticed the video had gone. After that we called the police.'

'And you realised the jewellery had disappeared?'

'Yes, yes, Harrison did. It had been in the little safe in his study. He saw it was unlocked and checked inside. Of course, the necklaces are normally in a safe deposit box, we'd only taken them out to have them revalued for reinsurance purposes, they were to go back on Saturday. Lucky thieves.'

'And you heard nothing?' He keeps his incredulity toned down.

'Nothing, detective sergeant, I'm not usually a heavy sleeper, but Friday night I didn't stir.'

'And you, Professor Peer?'

Professor Peer munches the last of his biscuit, he doesn't look at Theo. 'No, nothing, don't you think I would already have said if I had?' His voice is gravelly, he clears his throat with a higher-pitched mechanical sound. 'It's been very disconcerting, the thought of people being able to get into our house so easily, we've had to have a new back door fitted, the noise has completely disrupted my work.'

'The professor has almost finished editing his opus magnum for his publishers,' Caroline says, smiling again. Then her expression becomes stern. 'My family have lived here for generations, detective sergeant, one doesn't expect to be ... to have one's own home assailed in such a manner.'

Theo nods. The break-in had been clean, there had been no violence to the person, but still he understands the psychological damage is acute. It's the first time he sees the Peers as victims and feels a twinge of pity. 'And who knows the combination to the safe?' This had not been explored by Chesters.

'Only Harrison and I.'

'Really? Most people have it written down somewhere, in among telephone numbers in their address book?'

She shakes her head.

Theo is not convinced, 'Is there no one who could have found it out? The thieves must have had it.'

'Can't they do a safe-breaking thingy? With a stethoscope?' Mrs Peer's voice loses some of its confidence.

A talented safe-cracker roaming the North Yorkshire countryside? Hardly. He takes a different tack, 'The valuer came to look at your necklaces on Friday?'

'Yes.' She stops, then says, 'No, actually, I had thought it was last Friday, I was wrong, it was to be Friday this week. It was only when I rang to ask where our Mr Jameson was that I realised my mistake, and by then it was too late to return the necklaces to the bank. I didn't think for one moment they wouldn't be safe here for one night.'

'Why would you? Why would you?' Harrison murmurs gently. 'It's the least you could expect.'

'And Mr Jameson comes from where?' Theo asks.

'London, of course,' Caroline replies.

'I mean the company, what company does he come from?'

'Jameson's of Piccadilly, our Mr Jameson is the owner.'

'Could I have contact details?'

She smiles a thin smile. 'Are you checking up on us, detective sergeant?'

'Not at all. Only people at Jameson's knew the jewellery was in the house. We have to look at every angle.'

'No, no they didn't know about the jewellery being here. Didn't I say? I was going to ring them and then saw the entry in my diary for the following week. Anyway you said you'd got your suspect, you've charged the burglar.'

'We have a suspect.' *Only he doesn't know anything about your diamonds.* 'Even so, I'd like to talk to Jameson's.' Theo is alert to the change of story and wonders if it's significant. The atmosphere in the room is suddenly a tad cooler. Perhaps it's the cloud obscuring the sun for a moment.

Mrs Peer shakes her head reproachfully. 'I'll get Marta to pass the details on to your people, detective sergeant. Now,' she readies herself to stand, 'if you've nothing more to ask us?'

Professor Peer has already got to his feet. 'Goodbye, Detective Sergeant Akande, it's been good to meet you,' he says, leaving the room. It is up to his wife, therefore, to see Theo out. She almost shoos him through the tiled hall and into the garden, watching him until he is past the front gate before closing her front door with a clack.

CHAPTER 7

Wednesday 12 May

Student services is in one of the newer brick-built extensions jutting out behind the original nineteenth-century building. Hannah has found her way round to the threshold and here she halts. *I shouldn't have come.* She had emailed Dr Clare Shrimpton her article and she had responded within the hour, delighted, saying she had more work for Hannah to do.

'Come and meet me in my room at 1.30 to discuss,' she wrote. 'And stay for my seminar if you can, it'll give you a very clear idea of where my research is going.'

With a couple of hours before this meeting and Rose's assertions hanging in her ears: 'It's a lovely day' and 'Ben will be pleased to see you', Hannah takes the decision to go to the campus early. *A stupid decision,* she now realises.

The glass-panelled door in front of her opens. A young woman, with bright-pink hair to match her baseball boots and a stud in her tongue to match those in her ears and nose, is standing there smiling. 'I saw you out here, why don't you come in?'

She leads Hannah into a nondescript corridor. There's an open-plan office to one side with its door open, a closed door at the end marked 'Student Therapy Services'. Once they are in the office, Pink Hair perches on the front of the first desk and asks, 'What can we do for you?'

'I've come to see Ben Cartwright.'

'Have you an appointment?'

She shakes her head. *I shouldn't have come. He won't want to see me.*

Pink Hair goes behind the desk to tap a couple of times on a computer keyboard, 'He's had a cancellation, if you can wait ten minutes?'

Hannah nods.

'Take a seat, then, over there. If you wouldn't mind filling this form in while you're waiting.'

Hannah takes the sheet fixed to a clipboard and the pen and goes to sit on one of the couple of chairs in the passage. She clutches the metal clasp on the clipboard until it digs into her palm. The pain is good punishment, *for being such an idiot.* She closes her eyes, leaning back against the cool wall, *I should leave, now.* Before she can move a slight young man exits from behind the closed door, then walks rapidly away. Pink Hair materialises from the office, knocks, waits for the muffled response and then enters the therapy room, leaving the door fractionally open. Hannah hears the words 'waiting' and 'no appointment'. Once again she attempts to galvanise herself into slinking away, only the lass is now in front of her, assuring her Ben won't be long. She seems a little disappointed at not being able to take possession of a filled-in form, however she says cheerfully, 'It's no problem,' before going back to her desk from where she apparently sees all. Hannah is now jammed to her seat.

When he appears, she's certain that his expression becomes an extra-warm grin as he sees it's her, certain until the doubts seep in. *I shouldn't have come.* He beckons her into his sanctum, she begins to apologise for bothering him at work.

'No bother,' he says, shutting the door, then wrapping his arms around her shoulders, hugging her close and kissing her on the crown of her head. She tilts her face up to look into those chocolate eyes and to receive a more lingering kiss on her lips. 'You're just in time for me to take you to lunch. I don't have to be back here till one-fifteen. Let me tidy up a bit.' The window looks out onto an oblong of grass and a brick wall, which means it's not very light, but at least the blind doesn't have to be down to maintain privacy. There's a couple of two-seater sofas opposite each other, and Ben is putting a large cushion and a tennis racket into the corner where there's already a sand tray and a small basket of pebbles – the customary accoutrements of a therapy room. She watches him, admiring the lithe tilt of his slim hips as he bends and moves. He is wearing black chinos as usual, though his collared shirt is a pale terracotta; perhaps spring has prompted the brighter colour. His chestnut hair falls to his shoulders, curling slightly around his face. The recent sunshine has honeyed his normally pale skin. A low bookcase holds some titles she recognises from her own training and a pile of pocket wallets. He picks these up along with a leather case and his jacket from the back of the door, 'Shall we go?'

He has to take the paperwork into the office where he introduces her as his girlfriend, his hand resting in the small of her back. She can feel the heat rising up her spine to ignite her face.

'You're the lucky woman who has finally won Ben's heart. You should have said.' Pink Hair winks at Ben, 'You've not done so bad, have you?'

Ben smiles broadly at the teasing. Hannah wishes she were somewhere else or, *preferably, someone else, someone as sassy as Pink Hair.*

They buy sandwiches and drinks from the student bar and take them outside where they find a bench next to an exuberant clematis, which climbed the fence separating the campus from the golf course. They'd seen each other last at the weekend. On Saturday, a bike ride through Dalby Forest (truncated because Hannah felt tired), followed by afternoon tea and then a pub in the evening to listen to a local band they've come to know. Sunday was lunch with Ben's dad, brother and his brother's family. It had been friendly, if a bit stilted, though nothing like as torturous as Sunday lunch with Hannah's family used to be. And then the disastrous film, *The Girl with the Dragon Tattoo*. How could she have thought she could watch this kind of movie anymore? She'd had to walk out halfway through, Ben berating himself for not insisting they give it a miss. The sea's shushing through the sharp night air calmed her, but later as they wound themselves around each other in Ben's bed she began to cry, and became panicky. She had slept poorly.

Ben hadn't wanted to leave her the next morning. She had insisted he must go; Monday and Tuesday he has his practice in York. He had texted her regularly throughout the day, rung her

Monday night. Now, as he asks her how she is, he involuntarily looks towards her forearms, hidden by her sleeves. She moves them in towards her, not because there is anything to see, no recent scars anyway, but because she suddenly resents his inspection.

She assures him she is fine and explains what's brought her to the campus. They talk. She omits to tell him about Maya's visit. *I don't want to spoil the mood.* Ben had been brought up down the road from Maya; Rose had been a surrogate mother when his own died, Maya a little sister when he needed to escape the environment of sport and suppressed emotions created by his father and older brother. She could do very little wrong in his eyes, was forgiven much, until recently, when her error in judgement led to the attack on Hannah. *He wants to protect me from her*, she thinks, not entirely comfortable with the notion.

They finish eating and he pulls her close. She rests her head against his chest, can hear the soft thump of his heart. She closes her eyes, *I do feel secure with him, safe, I want to believe I can trust him.* The sun's heat begins to soak through almost to her very marrow.

'You'll be fine,' Ben had said, holding her face in his hands, kissing her on the nose. 'I met Dr Shrimpton once, on a work matter, she showed a great deal of understanding. And you're good at what you do, Hannah.' This buoyed her as she followed the corridors into the old section of the building and up the stairs to Clare's cubbyhole of an office. Into its crammed space is: a desk with computer; an ergonomically designed typing stool; a filing cabinet; several shelves of books; a poster on a patch of wall for the DL Sayers book *Are Women Human?*, with its cubist representation of a female face; an open narrow casement; and two low easy-chairs. It is on these that the two occupants of the room are seated, no longer speaking, their combined gaze pinning Hannah to the doorway. *I shouldn't have come.*

Then Dr Shrimpton's tulip-red lips smile widely, she jumps up, greeting Hannah and ushering her into the room. She introduces the other woman as her PhD student, Felicity Pritchard. Tall and broad, with a large, rather sallow, flat face and washed-out blonde hair scraped into a ponytail, Felicity acknowledges the newcomer with a curt nod. Hannah reckons she could be a little older than herself, in her late thirties, though the features are more timeworn than the body.

Following her perfunctory greeting, Felicity says she'll go and check everything is ready for the seminar. 'Thank you,' says Clare with warmth. 'I would appreciate it very much.'

As soon as the other woman has gone, Dr Shrimpton turns her glow on Hannah. This and remembering Ben's words gets her through the next ten minutes with the minimum of self-criticism. Clare wants her to copyedit a chapter she has written for a new book, *DL Sayers, the woman and her writing*. 'It's for a more general than an academic audience, I'd appreciate your input on its accessibility, Hannah. You'll do it, of course.' It's hardly a question, then neither is her, 'You're coming to the seminar. I am glad. I've got a few bits to get ready, then we can go down together.' There's the generous smile of that tulip-red mouth which matches the polish on her finger and toenails and the broad stripe which twists through her dress, around her shapely breasts and hips, to her neat ankles.

It is those lips which caress each sentence as Dr Clare Shrimpton delivers her seminar, 'Fiction, a creation of the self'. 'Reading is an intimate act between reader and writer. As readers we feel we have privileged access into a writer's mind. The writer's words are meant for us only, they lay bare to us another person's thoughts and emotions in a way which we do not experience even with our lovers. We curl up with a book, the cover is the jewelled lid of a magical casket, we have the key, we open it, the story revealed is revealed solely to us, solely for our delectation. This is the seductive nature of reading. Of course this is a fiction, a fiction we as readers want to believe, so we do believe it. Or is it? How much does a writer disclose in their writing? How much does a writer create, and recreate, herself through her storytelling? And what does this mean for us readers?'

Hannah suspects there are a number around the long oval table in the room who are there merely to be in the presence of Clare's splendour, rather than to listen to the presentation. *We're a motley bunch.* There is Felicity, who sits close to her supervisor, her bland face brightened by a tender flush. There are ten youngsters, all of whom look underage for undergraduates. *I must be getting old.* Most came in with practised reluctance close to the session start-time, their fresh, open faces studies in casualness. Though even they have been drawn irresistibly into attentiveness, on occasion entering something into a handheld device or onto a tablet. Only one of them has a folder with pen and paper, he is tall and slight, lost in a black hoodie. When it's not feverishly making notes, his left hand shakes or taps softly on the table. He reminds Hannah of a client she had for a short time last year, *Craig*. She remembers his extreme hopelessness and his profound deficit of confidence. *I never managed to reach him.* For a moment, her heart sags. 'We never know what we do,' she recalls her supervisor, Orwell Winters, saying. *Maybe I did enough to encourage him to stick with his studies and he is at university somewhere*. She does not entirely believe it. She brings her focus back to the room.

Dr Shrimpton is building her argument piece by piece. She is now talking about hunting for the writer within their words. The metaphor she uses draws from fairy-tale imagery: the reader walking into an enchanted wood. Does she reach a clearing where the writer lays out her wares, or is the writer seen dodging between closely set trees, just out of reach?

Near to Clare, opposite Felicity, is an older man, white tufts at his ears, his bald pate marked with brown liver spots. He is dapperly dressed, a daffodil-hued tie matching a handkerchief in his top pocket. He has his small notebook closed on the table beside him and his arms crossed. In amongst the young women is the only other member of staff, though he could be a mature student with his glossy curly hair, his patchwork shirt, jeans and sandals. Clare had introduced him to Hannah as Professor Aiden Haswell. He is relaxed, makes the odd note, and, Hannah observes, when once in a while Clare's gaze searches him out, she is rewarded with an encouraging smile.

Now Clare is turning to her preferred subject, DL Sayers. 'Not only one of the most prominent members of what we call the golden age of detective fiction writing, but also a highly educated woman who wrote about theology and women's rights and translated Dante. We find the thinker in her non-fiction, we find the woman in her fiction. For example, in *Strong Poison* we meet Harriet Vane, who has socially transgressed by living with a man out of wedlock, as Sayers did. In *Gaudy Night*, Harriet struggles with the question of whether a woman can marry and maintain her creative and academic freedom. A tension which did not (does not?) trouble men, but did exercise Sayers.

'Despite these glimpses of the woman, Sayers kept at least one significant part of her life completely concealed: she had a son. He was brought up by a family member and Sayers was part of his life as an interested and generous relative. She could not abandon him, yet could not bring herself to be completely open with and about him. Already we can identify her several selves. Firstly, the thinker arguing, as in her essay "The Human-Not-Quite-Human": "... the fundamental thing is that women are more like men than anything else in the world. They are human beings ... This is the equality claimed and the fact that is persistently evaded and denied." Secondly, the woman concerned about her creative freedom and independence. She brought a woman's – a marginalised – voice into the dominant discourse of the male crime writer. Fiction lends itself to liminal spaces, Sayers used it to step into herself. We can see that in the progression from her rather flimsy early novels to her tour de force, *Gaudy Night*. Thirdly, we have the hidden and unacknowledged mother.

Through her writings – both fiction and non-fiction – we can see the creation of the first two, and the almost complete absence of the latter.

'But the reader's, our, love of fiction is not just about finding the writer, it is also about finding ourselves. We read about our selves, the ones we have lived and created, the ones we wished we had, the ones we wished we hadn't, the Jungian "other" which lurks in our shadow. It is in giving them meaning, that the writer creates a bridge of understanding between an element of herself and a part of our self – this is, in essence, what makes reading fiction so beguiling.'

She breaks off, checks her notes and then, looking up and around, invites questions and discussion. One of the young women says she thought she had read a Sayers novel where Wimsey and Vane had children. Another says wasn't that one written by someone else after Sayers had died, 'A kind of homage.'

'Yes, indeed, though the writer in that case, Paton Walsh, does take inspiration from a short story by Sayers, "Tallboys", where Wimsey and Vane are depicted as parents, not unkindly ones, but quite distant ones.'

Then there's some to-ing and fro-ing over whether Sayers could be said to be a feminist and whether it is an insult or not. Hannah is caught by the idea of the other and the shadow, which had also come up in her counselling training. *Being unaware of your shadow, splitting it off, seeing it in other people and not yourself, that's where danger lies.* She thinks of her father.

The drumbeat from the emaciated boy is now persistent. It becomes louder as the older man from the front stands to speak.

'Professor Harrison Peer,' he introduces himself with a brief incline of the head, almost a bow. When he clears his throat it is a scooter engine turning over. 'A very interesting colloquium Dr Shrimpton, we are indeed lucky to have you and your expertise at our provincial university. Yes indeed. I was fascinated to note that you did not consider it worthy to indicate when you began to stray into social constructionism. Are we all disciples of Gergan? Is the human self merely a process, a complex interaction of changing concepts? How we are seen depends on which angle we are observed from? There is no reality, only continually assembled discourses which merely attempt to approach an event which we cannot hope to know for certain occurred? Normality and deviance are constructed within a specific social context?' Again the scooter tries to cough into life. 'Dr Shrimpton, I did just want to question a paradigm solely reliant on the so-called evidence of fiction. I believe the accepted definition of fiction is: "as derived from the imagination, as opposed to fact".'

In the brief pause, Clare visibly gathers herself, though her smile never wavers, 'A writer speaks through all their work, Sayers indicates this in *The Mind of the Maker* when she says—'

'Yes, in opposition to fact,' Peer interrupts. 'Fiction is in opposition to fact, I think we can at least all agree on that.' He looks round the room. Most eyes do not meet his, some are focussed on mobiles, the young man's finger percussion is becoming more elaborate. Only Felicity, her colour heightening, and Aiden, with a grin on his face, do not drop their gaze. Peer ploughs on, 'And it is only the most woolly scholarly activity which does not. Indeed, may I say shoddy scholarship? Yes, indeed, I think I may.' Peer completes his performance to the assembly rather than addressing Clare, 'My dear, you do right to defend your research, if it be correct to use that term in this context. For my part, I do not know how to teach my subject, which I humbly term philosophy, without becoming a disturber of the peace.'

There is a stillness on all sides of the table, even the drumming ceases. Everyone is watching Shrimpton and Peer as if this were the final serve of the final game in the final set of the final at Wimbledon. Hannah, who has been trying to make sense of the professor's arguments, is distracted by why his final words sound familiar, then Haswell provides her with the answer in unhurried tones, 'Spinoza also warned against the vain human ambition of making everyone approve what we love or hate.' *Baruch Spinoza, Lawrence had used that quote in his book*, Hannah recalls. *Maybe it's not important to reference sources when speaking?* Aiden is continuing, 'If there is one thing we can all agree about scholarship is that it should be up for debate, but that debate should be based on content and not on critiques of the scholar.'

Haswell's softly spoken contribution releases Clare from the spell which has kept her rigid and locked into a staring bout with Peer. Her smile is broad, her body animated, her voice resolute, 'Professor Peer, Harrison, I am most grateful that you were here to remind us of the importance of rigorous analysis. Now,' she is once more taking in the rest of her audience, 'I do believe we have to wrap up for today. Thank you for coming, for listening and for your various inputs.'

Haswell leads the others in some applause. Peer does not join in, he snaps up his notebook and walks in front of Clare to leave the room. The door is prevented from slamming by the fire-closer, yet Hannah feels his anger ricocheting through her.

Others are departing, giggling and chatting, the young man is carefully packing away his things. Aiden and Felicity have formed a little coterie around Clare. Only Hannah is iced to the spot, she looks at the sentence she has scrawled down: 'There is no reality only continually assembled discourses which merely attempt to approach an event which we cannot hope to know for certain occurred.' Its meaning leaches into her. Her brother Stephen's parting words three months ago repeat themselves in her head, *'It's not true, Hannah. If you continue to tell these lies about Dad, I will sue you for slander.'*

Clare pauses by Hannah's chair, 'I hope you found that interesting, Hannah, the old guard ramming his horns once again into the juggernaut of new thought threatening to sweep him away.' Felicity and Haswell laugh with Clare. She gives Hannah's shoulder a quick squeeze and bends forwards to say, warmly, 'Thanks for coming.'

It begins the thaw, which allows Hannah to leave, stiffly battered by the thoughts, *I'm wrong, I'm wrong, I'm twisting reality. It never happened. Bad girl, Hannah.*

CHAPTER 8

Wednesday 12 May

In contrast to the sparkle and colour of the countryside, the CID offices in Scarborough town are unappealing. The unimaginative concrete block with its lines of tinted windows sits on a road junction. The atmosphere is muggy with the drone of computers and photocopiers, only the occasional screech from a seagull cuts through the noise of the traffic stopping and then accelerating away. There's something particularly lacklustre about the place when Theo returns from his jaunt to see the Peers, and Harry fills him in on why. The CPS had been reluctant to agree to a charge of burglary for Jayson Smith because of the lack of forensics linking him to the scene. Then Reggie Harvey had turned up; his good humour and polka-dot bow tie a front for his shrewdness. After twenty minutes with him, Jayson Smith had changed his story. 'He's pleading guilty to handling. No burglary charge. And he's on bail.' She sounds tired and disconsolate.

She's annoyed she hadn't been able to get him to admit the burglary before Reggie got here. 'Who for? Handling for whom?' Theo keeps the irritation out of his own voice.

'Says, swears, he doesn't know.'

'How can he not know? That's bullshit. What's he take us for, gawbys?'

As he had intended, his use of his childhood Brummy slang raises a smile. 'He swaggered out of here, you should have seen him,' she looks grim again. 'If only I'd ...'

'You did a good job back there. We'll get Mr Jayson Smith at some point, he's not that clever.' *But whoever he's working for is, and it's them I'm interested in.* He asks her to check out Mrs Peer's story with Jameson's *of Piccadilly*, his mind adding in Caroline's upper-class tones. He doesn't think it will lead anywhere, but her shift intrigued him. *Maybe she didn't expect a small-town plod to notice.* This is the cause of a silent, gleeful, *Ha.*

He seats himself at one of the desks shared by all the detective sergeants. It is squashed into one corner of the CID office and screened off by glass sections that don't meet the ceiling. He takes off his jacket, soft leather with a ruddy tinge, a new acquisition, and slips it carefully over the back of the chair. He extracts the notes he took down at Mrs White's the previous evening, then brings up the daily log on the computer.

There's one report of some bootlegged Courvoisier Connoisseur Collection, this time being touted around a pub down near the harbour. Theo can picture the place, cavernous and gloomy with sticky carpets, pulls in the crowds with riotous karaoke nights which usually end in a brawl or two. He finds the name attached to the police report and calls PC Trevor Trench. Surprisingly he gets straight through to him. It sounds like he's chewing on something doughy. Theo looks at his watch, *what would you call snap coming between elevenses and lunch?* He knows Trench to be careful and reliable, if a bit leisurely. As expected he's followed procedure with statements taken, a description being circulated and reports being typed up. Nothing has come of this so far. 'Do you want me to bring the folder up?' Trench asks.

'No, I'll come down for it, thank you.' This will earn him some brownie points and he feels the need to be moving.

Trench is just wiping away the leftovers of sugar and jam from his mouth and fingers when Theo arrives. He pulls a buff folder from a wire tray which serves the cluster of desks and hands it over. Theo asks him what he makes of it; Trench grew up in the town, he is acquainted with its characters.

'We probably wouldn't have heard about it if one of the witnesses hadn't been the brother-in-law of a youngster who's just started as a special, she persuaded him to make the report. He said at least twenty bottles got bought, but I've not been able to find any of the disgruntled customers. Who's going admit to buying bootleg which turns out to be dodgy? If they didn't drink it anyway, probably poured it down the drain and threw out the bottle. The pub management denied all knowledge, obviously.'

Thirty-two quid times twenty, that's a tidy sum.

'Spoke to trading standards, customs and the coastguard, it's all in the report.'

'The coastguard?'

'Yeah, likely it came in on a yacht bringing in drugs. Counterfeit liquor, it's little more 'un ballast to the smugglers.'

Smuggling? In Manchester smugglers had been on trains or in vans. A brief, unbidden image of men in breeches with eye patches and three-cornered hats comes to his mind. 'And Scarborough's smuggling families are?'

Trench shrugs, 'Nothing's ever stuck.' He looks unhappy.

'Your hunch?'

'The Rattenburys. Got more going on dry land these days, officially, but I don't know.'

Theo takes the folder back to his desk, stopping on the way to put the coffee machine on. It is an expensive, elaborate one, a gift from Lawrence 'to your office'; a gesture, perhaps, towards accepting Theo's decision to stay in Scarborough, *for now anyway*. At least until he gets a chance at the DI job everyone assumes he's been shifted over here for. At first the machine had been regarded as overly flamboyant, and had been accompanied by continual ribbing. The soon-to-be retired DI John Hoyle would sniff the air and look at his ham-hands before saying loudly he'd not known he'd come into a poncy espresso bar and give him white instant any day. Now, however, it has been adopted as an office essential by almost everyone, with packets of specialist beans appearing on the tray by its side. Its aroma is also a welcome antidote to the ubiquitous staleness in the air.

With mug in hand, he begins to read through the file. As well as the brother-in-law, there're three other people who said they saw the bootlegger. Inevitably, the descriptions of the man do not tally. He varies from about five foot five to just over six, his hair fluctuates between mousy and white blonde and his age from mid-thirties to mid-fifties. Though everyone agrees his hair was short, he was white and sturdy, 'built like a builder'. Mrs White had him as taller than Theo but not over tall, so around five eight or nine maybe with light-brown hair and pale skin, blotched red, 'like he was outdoors a lot'. He was wearing jeans and a white collared shirt, plus heavy boots. The others don't remember much about his outfits; probably jeans, maybe boots, perhaps an anorak, green in colour. One of the pub punters saw him exit and get into a van, a plain white, 'normal-sized' transit, which Trench has taken to mean a short wheel base variety. Theo thinks he is probably right. In the narrow residential street where he lives, anything bigger would have looked enormous and would have been difficult to manoeuvre, both of which Mrs White would have noticed. There is no van registration from the pub witness, but Mrs White had given what she said was at least part of it. Theo opens a new document on the computer reporting system, types up his notes, adding a case number and cross referencing it to Trench's folder number, then he sends through a query on the registration number.

 He begins a background check on the Rattenburys. There's the family firm, 'builders and contractors', he reads off the website which features photos of Bert and his two sons, Robbie, the eldest, and Phil. Theo studies them, *None of them are a million miles away from the descriptions we've received, but they'd cover more 'un half of the town's men. Bert and Robbie are more 'builder-like'. Phil is more rangy, a bit taller, less squat.* He taps to a police database: Bert has had a conviction, a few years previously, for assault on a witness to him smashing up his car when drunk. He got a suspended sentence.

 Theo is distracted by the chatter of two DCs coming in with their lunch, they are followed by DI John Hoyle. 'Want a word, lad,' he says to Theo, turning immediately on his heel. *Expecting me to scurry after him like a puppy,* Theo thinks, taking his time standing, stretching and retrieving his jacket.

CHAPTER 9

Wednesday 12 May

After meetings with DI John Hoyle, Theo frequently feels the need to escape the confines of the concrete and tinted windows. And anyway he wants to talk to Suze who is absent from her desk. He knows where she'll be. He takes the back exit of the station and follows the snicket through a wrought-iron gate in the ten-foot-high brick wall and into the cemetery. The plots and borders have been tidied up recently by young offenders on a 'pay back' scheme. The grey crosses, many of them encircled by stone anchors, stand amongst trimmed grass, clumps of wax-white Our Lady's Tears and crimson azaleas. A cherry tree has shed its flousy blossom, it pools pink at the entrance of the renovated mausoleum where Theo finds Suze. It had been where she would come to smoke; now she's given up the ciggies (at her daughter's request), she's still often to be found here for her breaks.

She glances at the door on hearing Theo's step and smiles when she sees who it is. 'Just in time, sarge.' She holds up the flask in her hand made crooked by swollen joints, explaining her son had put the lid on and didn't know his own strength, as he self-consciously swaggers into teenhood. The warmth of the day is dissipated by the tiled walls delicately painted with forget-me-nots and ferns and her diminutive bent body is wrapped in a dark-green knitted shawl. But then she is always cold. He opens the flask for her and accepts a share in a spare cup she brings out of the copious flowered bag at her feet, along with a tin of dark, bitter chocolates.

'You ever work for Detective Chief Inspector Stokes?'

'It was about him was it?' Secretary to the senior officers, including Hoyle and manager of the civilian admin staff, Suze knows where Theo's just been. She probably has more than an inkling of what he's been asked to do. In addition, she comes from one of the sprawling Old Town fishing families and is married into the amusement king's clan; which means she is familiar with the interweaving of the local alliances, their relationships and feuds. 'Yes he was DI in Scarborough for a while, he and Hoyle got to know each other here. Scales off the same fishtail, those two, though Stokes has, or had, more gumption. He got on when Hoyle stayed where he was.'

'And yet they remained friends?'

'I think that would be putting it too strongly. They help each other out when it suits them.'

'Scratching of backs?'

'Clearing up of messes.'

'What kind of messes has Stokes been in?'

She shrugs her sharp, narrow shoulders. 'He transferred over from Durham, quite precipitous it was. He'd not long taken on a DI post there, so it was,' she pauses, 'unusual. It must have been ninety-five or ninety-six? I'd not been working here for long, was only in my early twenties, didn't really know what was going on. 'Course he's moved back now to retire to be near his daughter and grandkids.'

'Informal', 'unofficial', 'chat', Hoyle had used those words a number of times during their one-sided conversation. *I'm being played,* Theo thinks, then corrects himself. *Hoyle always gives the impression of being cleverly Machiavellian when actually he's a straightforward bully. He's enjoying yanking my chain 'cos he knows he can.*

The air is definitely chillier than he'd like. He folds his arms and asks Suze about the Rattenburys. Some of what she says he already knows, then she goes onto what he really wants to hear from her, the little details about the dynamics within the family. There's the patriarch, Bert, he of the road rage, who is slowly retiring, letting his oldest son Robbie take over. Mrs Rattenbury, Eunice, was once a formidable lady, however, since she's currently in the last stages of lung cancer, Suze moderates her comments about her. Then there's Phil, 'the quiet twin'.

'Twin?' Theo prompts. 'Is there another son?'

'A daughter.' Her tone could freeze the already cool air.

He looks round. Suze's face appears pinched in pain. He wonders whether he should suggest they go out into the sun, he touches her elbow, tentatively offering some physical support.

'Felicity Pritchard,' she says flatly. 'As she calls herself, though the divorce's come through.' Pritchard, the married name of Felicity Rattenbury, is Suze's maiden name. She mentions a cousin, one of the few from her sprawling family who couldn't bear the shifting of a boat beneath his feet and so had made a life on land as a chef. 'Good riddance to her. Thinks she's above us all, doing something up at the university. She's still a Rattenbury, s'far's I'm concerned.' She'll say no more. She takes up her crutches, allowing Theo to give her a modicum of assistance. They exit into the warmth of the day. They walk at her slow pace. She is almost her usual self by the time they reach the station.

Detective Chief Inspector Stokes (retired) lives in a neat semi-detached in a village just to the north of Scarborough. The conservatory at the back where Theo is taken by a neat Mrs Stokes looks out over fields; one contains horses, the other the uprights and boards to make jumps. Bill Stokes is a tall man who takes care of himself. His hair is overly black for a man of his age. His leathery skin has been darkened by the many cruises Theo sees evidence of in the photos adorning a glass display case in the room he has passed through. Other photos show a boy and a girl gaining adulthood and then with children of their own. However, the picture which has pride of place in the sitting room is one of Stokes himself in uniform receiving a medal from a minor royal. There are books and newspapers in the conservatory and the radio is quickly turned off, but Theo gets the impression Stokes has been busy waiting; waiting for him.

There are some brief preliminaries as Mrs Stokes serves tea and the DCI ascertains markers in Theo's career, his movement through the ranks from joining the police in Manchester. "Course we spent more time on the beat,' says Stokes. 'Not like you graduates. How a degree prepares you for dealing with the scum of the earth I don't know.' He sips from his porcelain cup, nods and mutters, 'Good man,' when Theo mentions some of the superiors he's had. Seemingly satisfied with what he's heard, once they are on their own again, Bill Stokes brings out a brown A4 envelope and hands it over.

'At first I thought it was a joke, didn't take much notice of it, some of the earlier ones have gone into the recycling.'

Carefully, using a clean tissue to handle them by the corner, Theo skims through the papers. 'You're a dead man 4 what you did.' 'You think you're safe, but you're not.' 'Your deeds will catch up with you in the end.' 'You've nowhere to hide.' 'You'll not get away with what you've done. Romans 1:18.' Theo searches his memory. His parents weren't regular churchgoers, it was his one white aunt who sometimes took him. His mother objected, but his father said the experience would put Theo off. The preacher had known how to launch fire and brimstone onto his congregation. Theo doesn't recall the quote exactly though thinks it is something about the wrath of god. He will look it up to be certain later. He studies one of the pages in more detail. Each letter of each word carefully cut out of a newspaper. Stokes is right, they are absurd, and yet, Theo senses the anger behind the painstakingly constructed sentences. *Someone has taken a lot of time to do this, a lot of time and effort. Someone who knows where an apostrophe should be and isn't about to miss one out.*

'So what did you do, sir?'

When Stokes laughs, his facial skin hardly registers it. 'Call me Bill, we don't need to stick to convention now I'm retired. What did I do? I did what all police officers have to do and I made enemies.' He grows serious, 'It's the last one which really worried me.'

Theo takes a look. 'You ruined my family. Don't think yours is safe.' Stapled to it is a small square photo of a woman with toddler and pushchair.

'My daughter and grandkids,' Stokes says. Each letter has its envelope clipped to it, the name and address appears to have been created by the kind of plastic stencil Theo hasn't seen since he was a child. The flap of the envelope and stamp are self-adhesive. The post marks are York and Carlisle.

'There's not much to go on,' Theo says. 'Unless there are fingerprints, and given they've taken all this care with everything else, that would seem unlikely.'

'You could get the forensics done, though, couldn't you?'

'With a crime number.'

Stokes holds Theo's gaze with his own for a moment, his pupils are flint grey. 'Hoyle tells me you're on the up in the force. I still have influence, you know, DS Akande, despite having retired.'

'And you wouldn't want me to use my influence unduly would you, Bill?'

Faint creases appear around the edge of his eyes and his lips firmly press together. After a moment he says, 'I don't want my wife, my kids, bothered by this. You can understand can't you, Theo?'

Bubbles in his gut begin to stir sourly. *He just expects me to roll over and do his bidding.* He tastes his own firmness settle on his tongue, a metal bit from a bridle. *I'm not going to be herded where I don't want to go.* 'If I were going to do any kind of investigation, they'd have to be bothered, I'd have to ask questions of them and others. I don't know any other way to do it.'

Stokes takes a deep breath and lets it go slowly, he sits back in his chair, a large wicker structure which creaks uneasily. 'You'd do the fingerprints first, see what they yield?'

Theo gives a non-committal wag of his head. 'I'd do what needed to be done to find out who is threatening you.'

There's another moment before Stokes responds, 'OK, get on with it.'

'You're reporting harassment?'

He nods, his shoulders sagging.

'Then perhaps you'll answer some questions.'

'I have no idea who might be doing this. I'm afraid I will have to ask you to go, DS Akande; one of the reasons I took early retirement were concerns around my health, and I am feeling too tired to deal with an interview now. I'll be glad to speak with you again in a few days' time.'

That metal bridle is jerked sharply into the side of his mouth. Pop goes one of those bubbles. Theo is terse as he takes his leave. He locks the folder into the boot of his car, decides to head home, grab his things and take a run up the coast.

Before he can go, his mobile rings. He sees who it is, decides on the formal approach, 'DI Wiltshire, what can I do for you?'

'Pippa, please.'

DI Wiltshire, a specialist in child abuse cases from York, had come in on a couple of investigations which Theo had been involved in. Initially they'd got on well, but the last time she'd thought he'd overstepped the mark. She'd threatened him with a reprimand, not that she'd carried it out and he suspects she never intended to, which irritates him. Not unpredictably, relations had cooled. *Now it's back to Pippa, which can only mean one thing, she wants something.*

She soon makes clear what it is, she wants to talk to Hannah Poole, 'You know her, don't you, Theo?'

'Yes, and shouldn't that exclude me from any interviewing?'

'It wouldn't be an interview, nothing formal, just a chat, plus I want you to arrange it for me.'

Which means not only is it informal but it is unofficial. What is she up to? Theo is intrigued. However, he is also aware of how vulnerable Hannah is and doesn't want her further traumatised. He says as much and Pippa says that's exactly why she wants him there. 'What's this about, Pippa?' Theo asks, not overly warmly.

'I'll fill you in, I promise, when we meet. Monday next week would be good for me. Text me the arrangements. And thank you Theo.' She hangs up. He snaps his phone shut. *Mrs White, Bill Stokes and now Pippa, all wanting me to run around for them, but nothing official mind,* in his thoughts he mimics the flattening of vowels in the local accent. He could do with talking to Lawrence, *he'd be sympathetic, he's getting better at listening.* He has a sardonic fascination with the prevarications and machinations of folk, *and he'd help me to laugh about it.* Only he's at some political do that evening. Theo would rather not think about the way his lover's focus – *obsession* – with the recent election is pushing him to one side. He tells himself, *he is coming up this weekend, to see me, we'll have time enough then.* His jaw unclenches fractionally. But he knows his run won't unwind him completely, he needs to talk, to a mate, one he can trust. He doesn't have many in Scarborough. He takes out his phone and dials, he'll see if Ben will meet him at the Mills pub where they can watch the dusk turn to night over the sea.

CHAPTER 10

Saturday 15 May

It's been a good day so far. She'd slept well and she and Ben had a relaxed breakfast before he went off to his Saturday five-a-side. Then Hannah sets off for her walk, which is becoming an almost daily ritual, *to keep me sane.* She pauses briefly by the front gate to look back. The house, paired with Aurora's, was the project in the 1920s for an architect enamoured by ocean liners. Though modest in size, they are graced with white rendering and curving lines which echo the cruising decadence. The building looks benign today in the sunshine, though there've been times when Hannah has felt the presence of troubled souls. She'd heard stories of witches who had been hung on this promontory, and had formulated the notion that the turbulent spirits belonged to them – or to those who had done the hanging.

But it had more to do with me and Dad. She turns quickly into Sea View Lane. Where its tarmac ends, a chalky path heads down the cliff to a tussocky outcrop, then round the old lido (now filled-in) to the gothic Victorian Spa buildings and eventually the South Bay beach. The tide is far out, so low it gives the illusion that you could walk across the entrance of the harbour from the far end of the beach to the lighthouse standing below the castle headland. The sands are a tawny lion pelt, the stunted ribs of a wreck stick out from them, a skeleton of some wretched prey. The green manes of stranded mermaids are combed out across the rocks below the sea wall along which Hannah walks, the brackish weed perfumes the air. In amongst it, oystercatchers and gulls root about while a cormorant hangs its wings out to dry. Day trippers are beginning to take over the south beach, their brightly coloured T-shirts and wind-brakes semaphore in the haze. Nearer at hand, dog walkers shout after excited and snarling pooches while children screech peering into rock pools. All sound is sucked up into the enormous blue of the sky.

Hannah finds her sense of well-being is threatened by whirling thoughts: *What does Pippa Wiltshire want this time?* The DI had been the first to talk to her after her father's activities began to be investigated. There'd been several interviews since and she had attempted to marshal her memories into something coherent she could tell the police. Yet each time she's given her statements she's been barraged with doubts: *you liar, Hannah, you fantasist, how can you make all this up and spew it all out?* She hears her brother Stephen saying much the same thing to her, using more expletives and adding the accusation that she is destroying her family. *Should I have said yes to the meeting? Could I have said no? Theo said I could. Did he want me to?* She stops, makes an effort to look outwards. *Breathe, breathe, Hannah*, she instructs herself. *Notice the orange legs of the oystercatchers, the black cape of the cormorant. At least Theo will be there Monday*, it's a comforting thought. She smells the salt on the fresh breeze which undercuts the sun's warmth. *Breathe, breathe.*

 She turns away from the seafront and takes the steps clambering up through the cliff gardens. A squirrel hangs acrobatically from a branch by its hind legs while raiding a bird feeder filled with seeds. Hannah pauses to watch and to laugh to herself. New leaves unfurl – red-veined dragon's feet – on a young straggling sycamore. She thinks about Lawrence coming today. On sunny days like this, she remembers, they might take a picnic to one of the London parks or to Hampstead Heath, eat Lawrence's finely prepared pastries and drink his expensive wine, most often commiserating over the lack of someone special in their lives. *Now I have Ben and he has Theo, there appears to be less to talk about. And he doesn't want to hear what I want to say, about Dad.* Sadness brings a chill to the warm day as she thinks about the incomprehension she sometimes sees in his eyes. And then there's a wave of hot anger, there's been distaste there too, she's certain of it.

 Nearing the top of the cliffs, Hannah slows her pace, these thoughts about Lawrence leaden her soles. On the Esplanade, with its elegant, tall, creamy Victorian houses now split into apartments with bays and balconies, she finds people again. A little girl in a push chair, a toddler of maybe two, is crying, bending and twisting against the harness which is keeping her in the seat, her face red and scrunched up. Her sudden scream skewers through Hannah's lungs, the distress is hers, the fear and the pain of her younger self which was never attended to. She knows this, she and her therapist have talked this through. Even so, she turns and tries to run, though she doesn't have enough breath for it. Panting and stitched in her side she stumbles home.

It has become a tradition for Hannah, Ben, Aurora, Max and Oli, along with Theo and Lawrence if they are around, to meet for lunch about once a month after the five-a-side is over. Today Hannah is hosting it and she's been preparing for a picnic in the garden. Over the previous few days she's made quiches, as well as some brownies and a lemon drizzle cake. Initially she'd planned to buy it in, she is no great cook and it had all felt too great an effort. However, after Theo's phone call about DI Wiltshire, she hadn't been able to go back into the office which had once been her father's. Standing in the kitchen she'd picked up her mother's once much-used, now discarded, *Delia Smith*. She'd found the whole process of purchasing the ingredients, then measuring, mixing, moulding and baking them, absorbing, as well as tiring, giving her less time to think and helping her sleep.

    She's relatively pleased with the results; though they are hardly as sumptuous as the photos in the recipe book, she knows they taste good. She's put them out on the counters in the kitchen along with some green salad and a feta and tomato salad. There're plates, glasses for the drinks and the local baker's crusty French sticks. There're drinks: wine and beer, plus juice for her. She now knows that, like her parents, she is unable to take her vices in moderation. *Not half bad, Hannah, not half bad.* She's opened up the doors into the garden and got the plastic chairs from the shed. After her rush home, she's had a shower and changed into creamy cotton cut-off slacks and a silky green top, her curls are shining and she's applied mascara and a light-brown eye shadow which has gold flecks in it. She's managed to look at herself in the mirror, and feel mildly pleased with the effect, when the doorbell goes. It's Aurora with Oli.

Aurora is taller than Hannah and her fuller figure suits the fifties-style dress patterned with geranium flowers she is wearing. Her skin is already deeply tanned and her long black hair is caught up in a large-toothed clip at the back of her neck. Oli is in a striped top and shorts; he walks competently and is tackling running. Comfortable in his neighbour's house, he makes for the garden, finds 'his' ball which Hannah has put out for him and amuses himself chasing it round.

His mother accepts some wine and sits with Hannah in the plastic chairs, her eyes trailing her son while she talks. There's the usual catch-up on what the two women have been doing during the week. Hannah asks about the course Aurora had reluctantly signed up for and is surprised to hear it described more enthusiastically than she'd expected. She hears some of the passion which presumably initially shaped Aurora's career. Her career before Oli. Hannah didn't know her then, but she does know Aurora to be a smart, dedicated solicitor who says she remembers being ambitious. Only now she feels pushed into chasing promotion, because Max's business is less than secure. Hannah feels a little sorry for Max, he undeniably has a quirky flair for design, yet ongoing well-paid contracts continually elude him. Aurora mentions her tutor on the course, once, twice, three times. On each occasion bringing her hand up to her lips and then brushing back a wisp of hair which isn't there. Aiden Haswell, Hannah can picture him, his dark curls, his laid-back demeanour, the smiles for Dr Shrimpton. She can see Aurora is charmed, for some reason she wants to caution her.

The warning is not given as Aurora asks Hannah for her news. 'I got my results,' she says awkwardly, though she's grinning. 'I've finally done it, I've qualified as something, as a counsellor. My case study was marked as a distinction.'

Aurora bounces up and gives her a huge hug, then clinks glasses. 'So today we celebrate.'

'Oh, I don't want a fuss.'

'You haven't told anyone? Ben?'

'Yes, yes, of course, he knows.'

As if picking up on what she hasn't said, Aurora asks: 'Lawrence?' Then sitting down, she continues, 'Honestly Hannah, why ever not? He'd be proud of you. He'd be happy for you.'

Would he?

Aurora laughs, lifts up her glass in toast and then tosses back the rest of her wine, 'We're all so proud of you. You've done brilliantly.'

Considering. The words hangs in the air between them. *Considering what my father did. Considering his death. Considering being ostracised by my family. Considering the attack on me. Considering I'm a complete fuck-up when it comes to everything else.* 'I thought I might talk to Orwell, my supervisor, about returning to counselling.' She says it hesitantly, very hesitantly.

'Yes, you must, after you put in all that work.' Aurora has said it before, so doesn't have to repeat it – she doesn't want Hannah disappearing off back down to London – 'I've got used to you being here, next door.' Instead she asks Hannah whether she's thought more about her birthday. 'Midsummer, Rose wants you to come along to the rite. I thought you'd enjoyed the Awakening in February.'

'There had been something.' She knows Aurora finds moments of peace in the observations of the turning of the year organised by Rose and Ben. She also knows Aurora goes to repay the support Rose has given her. But Hannah finds it hard to stop being cynical, *give myself permission not to be sceptical and just let go.* 'I'll see, I'm not a great one for birthdays, mine especially, and thirty-four is hardly a significant one.'

'Maybe you don't want to celebrate yourself, but others might want to celebrate you.'

Izzie had said something similar once. It's not a notion Hannah wants to absorb right now. She changes the subject to Oli, a topic which never fails to captivate her friend.

It's not long before Max, Theo and Ben arrive, loud and ravenous. Max, the tallest and broadest of the three, his white-blonde thatch still damp from a shower, and his florid colouring high, goes immediately to Oliver, picking him up and tossing him into the air. The youngster squeals. Hannah watches to reassure herself the little boy is enjoying himself. Ben gives her an ardent hug and kiss, she can smell the familiar coconut soap and shampoo he's used in his ablutions. He's eschewed his dark colours for light-coloured knee-length shorts, a yellow polo shirt and sandals. Hannah notices how these flatter the muscles of his legs and arms. Theo has similar attire, his shorts are blue and his polo shirt burgundy (he's chosen his red-framed glasses today). He is looking similarly toned, though he is slighter than both his friends, his dark face less round, more sculptured.

It's apparently been a close match and as ever they nearly won. Aurora looks heavenward when she catches Hannah's eye and they both laugh. There is much exuberant chatter of what might have been and what nearly was.

Into the melee, Lawrence arrives from the train. He and Theo embrace. Then he comes to her. She grins, allowing herself to be enveloped in his arms and supported by his bulk. It could have been like old times. *Almost.* He's brought a bottle of Pimm's with him and has loaded up with fruit on his way from the station, so, shedding his jacket, he starts to prepare it, exclaiming with surprise at Hannah's new-found culinary talents. Lawrence's white skin is unaffected by the sun, his carefully trimmed beard follows the line of his square chin. There are steel filaments in the dark hair flopping across his forehead. He's brought news of the political earthquake, the coalition cemented in a rose garden two days before. He was there. Hannah can tell how pleased he is to have been present; seeing it on the TV would not have been enough for him. She can tell he is equally pleased to be a political prophet; in this case a prophet of doom and the downfall for the Lib Dems, as Clegg will have to go back on election promises over student fees. She becomes wrapped up for a moment by his humorous storytelling: the fat robin and the blue-tit he'd noticed nest building behind the politicians aping the odd coupling on the lawn. *Like old times. Almost.*

They pile up their plates with food and take them to the chairs in the garden. The talk is disrupted by the necessity of feeding and entertaining Oli. At one point, Max asks Hannah what she thinks of a local history guide she has been copyediting. He is doing the page and cover design and has put the work her way. She knows he finds the author somewhat eccentric and difficult to please. She's finding the text entertaining and says so. 'I'm on to the chapter about smuggling in the seventeenth century.'

Lawrence quotes a couple of lines from Kipling's *Smuggler's Song*: 'Watch the wall my darling as the gentlemen go by.'

'There wasn't much need to watch the wall when the whole flaming village was involved,' she says. 'And the Rattenburys were a sprawling family, everyone married to everyone else, so no one would betray them. They used fear and threats too, mind you. And were into a lot more than smuggling, a bit like the mobsters today, people got themselves tangled up, in hock to them.' She's aware of Theo leaning in, but it is Aurora who takes up the thread.

'Didn't you say there was some scandal somewhere out on the Hackness estate, a woman abandoned by her lover with an illegitimate child.'

'Yes, and you'd like this, Aurora, she eventually inherited shedloads and set up a trust for female descendants who are, what were the terms used? "Misused and forsaken." Or so the story goes.'

'I'd like to see that in the courts today. Max you've forsaken me, my wine glass is empty.' She laughs and the others join in.

After lunch, Max goes to change Oli's nappy and to try to settle him for a nap in the dark snug across the hallway. Theo, Ben and Aurora are tidying up a little. Hannah wanders down the garden. The air is cooling. The light-green catkins on the alder are turning paler, white tongues ready to clack. She feels his presence before he announces it by speaking, 'Well done, Hannah. I'm delighted for you. A qualified counsellor. Do you get a special title or letters after your name?' He puts his large fleshy hand on her shoulder, it is a warming and tender touch.

Much to Hannah's embarrassment, Aurora had insisted on toasting her success during the meal. 'I don't think so,' she now says, smiling. What did some psychotherapist say about embarrassment? *It's curdled delight.*

'How are you, Hannah? You look tired.'

She laughs, 'I thought I was looking pretty good today.' She's told Lawrence nothing of the fractured nights: of the nightmares; of the choking; of the cold; of the helplessness; of the despair; of the pushing Ben away, because she doesn't know it's him, trying to comfort her.

'You are, apart from around the eyes.' Despite the smiles there's a tenseness in his body. 'We've not talked, not properly, not since ... since Stan died. And I'm sorry. I know it's my fault. I should have been ...'

She turns to face him. His eyes are screwed shut. Gratefulness knocks against resentment. *You can't even look at me?*

'... been better at listening.'

Resentment knocks against disbelief. *Is this Theo's influence, him telling you to say this?*

'It's been hard for me to think about you being hurt in that way. I didn't want to believe it. I am sorry.' His thumb rubs at her skin. She eases into his embrace and feels his breath on her neck. *Like the old days. He's always been there for me.*

'I know you say Stan did some awful things.'

Say? Her spine stiffens. Her scalp prickles.

'He could be ... he did do .... I've read in his diaries, he was ashamed of some of what he did. He appears quite down about it in a few of the entries, depressed even, said he almost felt like he was another person sometimes and he couldn't always control him. Jekyll and Hyde. That's how it seemed to him. He did tell me he loved you ... and Stephen. He loved both of you.'

He put his cock in my mouth when I was a baby and jerked himself off.

'At least you knew your father, for good or ill, you had a father.'

Later he invited his pals to look at photos of me and rape me. He shared child porn online.

Lawrence continues, as if musing to himself, 'Parents, there's a special bond between parents and children, it can't ever be broken. There's love there despite everything.'

No. 'No.' The sharpness of her tone brings him round. 'No, you're wrong, Lawrence, some parents, some children ... it's not love. Not what I would call love.' He looks sad and suddenly she knows what this is about, *his father.* The half-recalled, half-fantasised father who had abandoned him and his mother when he was a toddler. The father who his mother had told him was dead. Lawrence thought he had found a substitute in Stan.

'Stan, he did regret it, I know he did,' Lawrence said with some force, straightening up.

'I fucking don't.' She pulls away, feels queasy and shaky with the movement. She wants to be held, to be safely held. She looks at Lawrence, his arms crossed, his mouth set. *Not by you, not by you anymore.*

CHAPTER 11

Monday 17 May

DI Pippa Wiltshire has been putting on weight, Theo can tell, and the turquoise trouser suit she is wearing is both tight and unflattering. When he first met her, she'd drunk camomile tea in the incident room, now it's strong coffee, a chocolate bar is always near at hand and she's even snagging a quick smoke on the way from the car to Hannah's front door. The term *'self-medicate'* comes to mind as he watches the rotund Pippa bowl up the path. *Or maybe 'self-barricade'. The job's getting to you.*

She'd arrived late, giving no time for discussion before leaving the police station, and she had been reticent in the car. He is, therefore, none the wiser as to her purpose, which makes him tense. This is sharpened because the interview – *informal chat* – involves Hannah. Since moving to Scarborough, he's had to question acquaintances before, Max Harris for one during the Dr Greene case, *before we were friends. The hazard of trawling in a small pond, as Suze has told me often enough. But this is different. All this 'informal chat' business. And this is Hannah.*

Recollections of Saturday afternoon filter in. *Hannah had been on good form, we'd all had a good laugh, at least, until the end.* He'd known as soon as Lawrence and Hannah re-entered the kitchen, *something was off.* They were turned, ever so slightly, shoulder to back, and their expressions were grim. However, it was a habitual spat between Aurora and Max which ignited the tinder in the air. Oli had not settled and Max was all for letting him 'enjoy the fun'. Aurora was having none of it. In truth all three were exhausted. 'It never stops, I have two children, and the bigger kid is more trouble. I have to do everything,' was Aurora's sparked complaint, as she polished off the last of her wine and corralled her family towards the door. Lawrence orchestrated his and Theo's exit at the same time.

It was only once they'd got back to Theo's house that he'd admitted some of the discussion in the garden. A misunderstanding he'd called it, 'I wanted her to know, about Stan, his regret.' *The expression chosen carefully.* 'I thought it would help.' He had been genuinely upset by it. 'I'll put it right. I'll call her and put it right.' Theo had believed him. He had wanted to believe him.

There's a lurch somewhere inside Theo when the door is opened and he sees Hannah. Two days earlier, her auburn curls were glossy, her petite figure was flattered by her green top, her face had a bloom to it. Now her hair is scraped back off pinched, pale features, her eyes are more pink than hazel, she looks as if she hasn't slept and her increasing thinness is emphasised by a sweatshirt which swamps her. She manages a stiff curving of the lips and lets them in. Theo is glad she takes them through to the dining room, a room he's never been in. It is stuffed full; not only with a large, heavy table and upright chairs but also other furniture, all in the dark, fussy repro style Theo knows Mrs Poole favours. To sit, DI Wiltshire has to squeeze in past a sideboard. On its top surface – once highly polished, now marked by the rings left by bottles gathering dust – are numerous photos in frames with their faces down.

When her offer of hot drinks is declined, Hannah takes the chair at the head of the table nearest the door. Theo sits on her right opposite Pippa, who begins by thanking Hannah for seeing her again. Her voice is modulated, coaxing. Theo is reminded, *she does this work for a reason.* He starts to relax.

'Why? Why do you want to talk to me again? I've already said everything.' Hannah's tone is sharp. Theo is immediately on guard again.

'I've recently begun to liaise across force boundaries, Ms Poole,' Pippa continues calmly. 'It's given me a broader picture, it's one I think you can help me with.'

'How?'

Pippa reaches into her bag and takes out a file followed by two clear evidence bags. One contains a buff folder of what looks like sheets of paper and pages torn from magazines. The other holds an A5 address book, its blue cover is faded and warped. 'You recognise these?'

Hannah's gaze slides over them. She folds her arms. She nods.

'You found them in amongst your father's documents after he died. You told me you thought they were connected with a paedophile ring he was involved in.'

'I was guessing, I was making it up. You must know the rest of my family deny anything ever happened,' the sharpness in her voice and her pose makes her seem brittle. Theo wants to tell Pippa to leave her alone.

'I'm aware of that,' the DI says gently.

Hannah lifts her chin, 'And it's not going to help me is it? Raking over it all again. My father will never stand trial.'

'It could help others.' Pause. From the file she takes two colour photocopies, one is of a patch of blue forget-me-nots, one is of a silver-coloured Rolls-Royce. 'These are copies of a couple of pages in here,' she indicates the buff folder in the plastic sleeve. 'They were stapled together. What do they mean to you, Ms Poole?'

Again the sliding gaze. The arms hug tighter, there's a slight tremor in her shoulders as if she is cold.

Stop this, Pippa, can't you see it's too much for her? Theo holds himself still.

When Hannah speaks, her voice is steady, firm, *it's as if another woman – no a child, a woman-child – is talking not her.* 'My daddy gave me a dress, it was forget-me-not blue, to go to the party with him. It was for kids who'd been very sick and I was going to help him give out presents. He'd chosen me over Stephen, I was so proud. Mummy did my hair up, with a bow, a blue bow. Mr Fix-It was there with his gold Mr Fix-It necklace and a big man with whiskers, he said he was a policeman, so it was all going to be OK.'

Pippa leans forwards. 'What happened, Hannah, what happened?'

Hannah also shifts to the centre of the table, 'I don't know, but my lovely blue dress got torn and Mummy said I'd done a very bad thing and I never saw it again.'

'What was the name of the policeman?'

'He never said, he was very important, he had gold braid on his uniform, he was in charge of everyone there, so it made everything alright. Didn't it?'

Pippa shakes her head, it appears to be an unconscious movement, her focus is still on her questioning, 'How old were you Hannah?'

'Eight. It was two days after my eighth birthday.'

'Twenty-third June 1984. And where was this?'

'We were living in Leeds when I was eight.'

Pippa sits back, her arms stretched in front, her fingers tapping on the file, her mouth in a flat compressed line.

Theo slumps in his chair and finds he has been holding his breath, the air tastes stagnant as he takes it in. There's a touch on his hand and he looks away from Pippa to Hannah. She's chewing at the knuckle on her other hand, enough to draw pin pricks of blood. He gives a squeeze of the fingers which have reached out to his and what he hopes is a reassuring nod and smile.

Pippa is upright again. 'You're sure, Ms Poole?'

Hannah glares and snaps, 'Of course I'm not fucking sure.' Her voice is scratchy, thin. Theo sees wetness around her eyes.

Pippa takes a moment and then says evenly, 'The date, though, we can be pretty clear about that?'

Hannah shrugs, drops her gaze.

Another slight pause, then, 'OK, you've been very helpful Ms Poole, very helpful.' She tidies away the photocopies into her file and puts it with the evidence bags into the leather case at her feet. She is quick and precise in her movements.

She's got what she wants.

'Have I?' Hannah's words are strained, there is a pleading in her tone.

'Yes. Thank you. Here's my card, if you think of anything else.'

Pippa stands up. 'DS Akande I have a train in half an hour, I'd be grateful if you could drop me at the railway station in time for it. However, I think it would be best if you spent some time ensuring Ms Poole has what she needs.' And then she exits the room.

'Have I? Have I really been helpful?' Hannah screams at the closed door, before bringing her forehead down hard onto the surface of the table.

Ow. Theo knows the force is deliberate. He expects tears. None come. He moves round so he is crouching by her side and puts his arm around her shoulder, until slowly she allows herself to be held.

'Don't you have to get going? For the DI's train?' she mutters into his shoulder.

'She can get the next one.' *Give her time to explain what this was all about.*

'I don't want to get you into any trouble.'

'You won't. Shall we get out of here?' *And the wreckage of your family.* She lets herself be guided into the kitchen which is lighter, airier and warmer. He makes them both tea and a sandwich each.

She doesn't eat or drink much, however colour does begin to seep into her taut cheeks and her body becomes a little less tense. 'Did I do OK? I'm not certain what I said, it's all a bit hazy. Does that sound weird?'

'No. And you were terrific, brave.'

She shakes her head. 'What was she after, DI Wiltshire?'

He shrugs. 'I was merely the chauffeur.'

'And the sweeper-up-er, the caretaker,' she says with a ghost of a smile. 'What's your hunch then?'

'She's got the scent of something, for sure, but she's not told me anything more than she has you.'

It's now forty minutes since the DI left them and Theo imagines her pacing up and down outside. Hannah must have sensed a change in his posture, she gets up to rewarm her tea in the microwave and dig out a biscuit. 'You should go.'

'I want to make sure you're OK.'

'If you go now, before she gets too mad, maybe you'll get something useful out of her and you could tell me. You would, wouldn't you, Theo? Tell me?'

'If I could, I would.'

She looks dissatisfied, then retrieves her mug and leans up against the cabinets behind her, cradling her hot drink to her chest. 'You'd better go.'

'Will you be alright?'

She nods.

'Are you sure?' Her words flung at Pippa come to his mind, *'Of course I'm not fucking sure.'*

After a breath, she says, 'No, not really. But I won't hurt myself, if that's what you mean? Anyway you can't babysit me until Ben or Aurora are free this evening. Maybe I'll give Agatha a call, you know my friend from counselling training? Yes, I will, I'll phone her.'

You've said that to make me feel better. He gives her another hug and kisses her on the forehead as he leaves.

He steps outside into the air, it smells clean. He saunters down to the gate and out onto the road. No DI Wiltshire, only another cigarette butt to accompany the one she'd discarded on the way in. Lodged under the wiper on his windscreen is a scrawled note: 'Got a taxi, Pippa.' He scrunches it up. 'Bloody hell.' His shout startles a seagull which screeches and flaps his wings in Theo's direction like some manic morris dancer. *You're right mate, you're bloody right, the world is run by cowardly tossers*, Theo thinks sourly. His anger isn't just about Pippa, perhaps it isn't about her at all, it's about all those who abuse, who betray trust and misuse power. He climbs into his car and thumps the door behind him.

The partial registration number Mrs White had given him had matched any number of vans in the local area, none owned by the Rattenburys. Still, it suited his mood to have a visit to *kick over some stones and have a look-see*.

'Rattenbury's Builders, no job too small' has a yard and warehouse with a tiny office attached on the industrial estate off the road to York. The solitary sign of life is in the cluttered office where a chunky young woman with a flat wan face sits behind a desk. She has an iPod plugged into one ear and a pile of invoices in front of her which she could be sorting into lever arch files. She looks startled at Theo's entry into her space and even more unsure of herself when he explains who he is and says he wants to talk to one of the Mr Rattenburys. She gets up slowly, pulling up her jeans which have sunk low over her backside revealing an overstretched black thong, opens a door in the rear of the room and yells, 'Granddad, there's a detective here to see ya.' Then she returns to her seat and continues with her work.

Ignored, Theo glances around. In the small room there are three filing cabinets, the desk with a computer pushed to one side and a noticeboard on the wall covered by a job planner. It reveals that, as well as working in Scarborough, Rattenbury's has work across the northern half of England. And it is Phil who does the travelling. Since the beginning of the year he's been twice to Cumbria, once to Liverpool, once to Darlington and twice to Northumberland. Theo is leaning closer to take in the other details on the planner when Bert Rattenbury enters through the door from the warehouse.

He is two spheres, held up by short legs – the top one bald, the other with a beer-gut straining at his belt. He's wearing dark trousers and a denim shirt, the sleeves rolled up to reveal an intricate artwork in black, orange and yellow tattooed into his skin. He quickly looks Theo up and down and then holds out his hand to be shaken, asking what he can do for him, adding he's always happy to help the police. He says to the girl to get into the warehouse to check off some stock against the delivery note.

When she looks at him blankly, he says, 'Oh get off home with you, you can finish your filing tomorrow. And remember to call in on your nan sometime tonight.'

Once his granddaughter has rapidly grabbed her things and left, Bert smiles indulgently, 'Work placement from school. Got some crazy idea she's going to be a pop star, they all do at her age, don't they? Now,' he wheels the vacated chair round for Theo to sit on and finds one for himself under some unopened post, 'What's this about detective? A colleague of yourn, Trevor Trench, he's been round here. My Robbie knew him at school, they never did see eye-to-eye. Yon Trevor was asking about smuggled brandy? I said it sounded like something from one of them costume dramas my old lady's so fond of.'

'I know, Mr Rattenbury, but it is happening today and it's poor-quality bootleg.'

'Now that is a crime.'

'People are being ripped off, and there's always the danger of poisoning.'

'I still don't see how I can help. If I knew anything, I'd be the first to come forward.'

'Your vans, you've two registered to the firm? I don't see them around?'

'They're both out.'

'Could you describe them?'

Bert huffs a bit at this, then obliges: 'Royal blue they are, with Rattenbury's Builders in gold lettering.' His voice warms and his face softens as he continues, 'My grandson did the design for them. Does it all on computer, he's good on computers, gone off to college to get a qualification in it.'

'And you don't have occasion to hire other vans?'

Bert smooths over his crown, perhaps expecting there still to be some hair. 'Mebe, on occasion.'

Theo reels off the dates the dodgy brandy was hawked around the pub on the seafront and to Mrs White.

Bert smiles. 'One of them's the date Trev was interested in. I told him, I couldn't be certain, without looking out the paperwork.' He glances round the office as if this was a job beyond his ken. 'I think I did say I'd try and do it, but what with Eunice and everything. She's my wife, detective, she's been very poorly, you probably know that.' His eyes are sad when he brings his gaze back to Theo's. 'She's pulling through, though, she'll pull through, see if she don't,' he adds quietly. 'If I remember right, Trevor checked where my lads were for that first date you mentioned. Phil was away, and Robbie was keeping me company sitting with Eunice.' Bert glances at his watch, 'I'd like to get off, if it's all the same to you. Our lass has had a carer for a few hours today, 'cos none of us could be with her. I want to get home to her sooner rather than later.' He stands up.

Theo would like to stay and rifle through those filing cabinets himself, not to mention the computer, even the very accomplished crims often leave a trace. However, he is being ushered through the door.

'Goodbye,' Bert says with a friendly slap on Theo's back. 'Hope you find out whoever it is, it's not good for the town, this sort of thing.'

Outside the cloud has thickened. Theo is wearing his short Burberry trench coat over his camel-coloured suit. He stands with his hands in its pockets, *What have I learnt?* The breeze brings with it only the smell of traffic fumes. This arid stretch of metal boxes on a branching treeless road could be anywhere, it bears no hint of the cliff and sea not half a mile away. *Nothing much.*

He'd thought about not going back to the police station at all, but then wondered if the forensic report on the letters to Stokes had come in. It has not. He is about to leave when he realises the CID enclave is no longer empty. DC Harry Shilling has entered quietly and is sitting at the desk she uses. She is leaning on her elbows, her shoulder-length hair obscuring her face. She roots around in one of the drawers. Extracting a packet of tissues, she takes one out and uses it to dab at her eyes, still behind her blonde curtain. Then a loud sob escapes, she lays her forehead on the desk top and her shoulders droop.

Theo goes over to her, closer so he can hear her weeping. He says her name, has to repeat it before she quickly sits up straight, her skin pink, her eyes red and panicked. This dissipates a little when she sees who it is, even so she wipes furiously at the tears which are still dribbling down her nose, and mutters that she must be going. Theo asks her to stay, to tell him what's wrong. He puts out his arm and when it makes contact with her sleeve, he holds it. She tries to pull away, but not with any great determination, and then collapses back down on her chair. Theo would like to pull one over for himself, but is afraid if he moves she will flee, so he perches on the corner of the desk. He asks her again what's wrong, what he can do to help. She shrugs. There's silence. She continues to try to control the flow of tears, the tip of her nose is a port light against the paleness of the rest of her face.

'Is it DI Hoyle?' Theo guesses.

She turns sternly towards him, 'What have you heard?'

'Nothing,' he holds up his hands. 'I know he can be, is sometimes, a little harsh, that's all.'

She nods.

'Especially if you cross him,' Theo adds cautiously.

'You have heard something,' there's pinching at the bridge of her nose. 'What?'

'I know you stood up for yourself when DI Hoyle was making some personal remarks about how you looked.'

She shakes her head, 'I shouldn't have risen to it, now he knows how to rile me.'

'You were right, he was wrong, DC Shilling. If he's continuing to pass comment because of it, then you should speak to someone.'

'He's, he's,' she choked over a sob. 'In my last appraisal he said I wouldn't go the extra mile when the job required it.'

The extra mile? Hoyle doesn't go the extra half-centimetre.

'I went to, I went to HR and asked for a review and they made him take it off. But now, now he's, he's ... It's like everything I do is wrong, needs redoing.' She gives a watery glance towards Theo. 'He's just told me a case won't go to court because I messed up the evidence trail. It was that lass ripping off her employers by giving refunds for goods which had not been returned and pocketing the money. I went bloody cross-eyed with those receipts getting the link with her, I know I bagged them properly, I know I put the right reference codes on, I know I did.' She sits up straight, Theo sees some of her steeliness reasserting itself.

'You have to get some support, go back to HR. This is bullying.'

She shakes her head. She's been giving her face vigorous wipes with a handful of tissues; apart from the beacon of her nose, there's now little evidence that she's been crying. 'It would only make things worse. I'll just keep my head down. He's retiring soon.'

Theo is about to remonstrate when his mobile rings, he looks at the screen, not a number he recognises. In this moment of his inattention, DC Shilling slips from his hold and darts out, the door shutting gently behind her.

'Damn,' Theo says under his breath, but decides to let her go. He answers his phone. Mrs Caroline Peer announces it is she. Her accent makes Theo's toes scrunch. 'I thought I should tell you, Detective Sergeant Akande, you can stop looking for the thieves of my diamonds.'

'I can?'

'Yes, my husband, I am very sorry to say, has decided to leave with them.'

'What?'

'He's gone, left me, and taken the jewels. He presumably felt I owed him something. The burglary was staged, by my husband, and now he's gone. So you see, detective sergeant, you do not need to look for anyone else.'

She cuts the connection before he can say anything further. When he replays it in his head, it gives him the impression he's been caught in an Oscar Wilde play. *'In a handbag?'* He cuts off his own smirk, *it's not funny. Harrison Peer run off? Is this for real?* He remembers the obvious fondness of the couple, *it doesn't make sense.*

CHAPTER 12

Monday 17 May

She feels the rage surging through her, a tidal bore of filthy water, borne on an ancient current, gaining strength from the inundation of the present. *Hit. Hit. Bad girl. Punish.*

'Not yourself, Hannah,' Izzie's voice comes through the confusion, lucid, reasonable. 'Hit out. The anger needs to be out there, not turned on you.'

It takes a huge effort for her to grasp the handle and lift it. She knows it to be a plastic tennis racket. It could be made of lead. She brings it down on the floor cushion. She can't get any force behind it. *Weak. Stupid.* She drops it. Sits on the edge of the sofa. Curls over on herself. The stinking flood seeps from the edges of her eyes.

'It's OK, Hannah, you've done really well. Take a break.'

Take a break? I haven't done anything. Not managed even one satisfying thwack. I'm tired, so tired of holding it all together. She's not sure whether she says it or thinks it. The room is warm, becoming stuffy. She knows it so well, has been coming here week after week for (she calculates) *eighteen months*. It's narrow, a square window in the end wall, built over a garage detached from the bungalow in whose garden it sits. She knows its walls painted with a hint of lavender, the large-format photos of the local coast, the one image of peacocks against the backdrop of an Indian temple. She knows the hardwearing texture of the sofa she is perched on. She knows the woman who is sitting opposite, waiting. Hannah can see the short, bare toes painted with silvery-purple varnish in flat leather sandals below the hems of creamy slacks. She can't bring herself to glance any further up, would like to metamorphose into the worm she feels she is and slink away under the door to bury herself in the sludge in the drain outside.

'Do you think you could look at me, Hannah?'

No. I know you hate me, despise me. I don't want to see you despising me. The urge to cause herself pain is becoming overwhelming again. *Stop it. Stop it.*

'What's going on? Can you say a little?'

No. A pulled-in breath, *I know Izzie, I know she doesn't despise me.* She is able to bring her gaze up to Izzie's chest level; she's wearing an oatmeal blouse over her rounded bosom and a necklace of chunky beads in wood, glass and metal. 'Can't you see the evil? It's coming out of me like a slime,' the words are spoken in a whisper though they rebound loudly about her head.

'I understand that's how you feel right now and I want you to know that's not what I see. You are not evil. Evil things were done to you. You took on the shame, the anger, the cruelty of those who did those things to you, you absorbed them like a sponge, because you were little and didn't know where your boundaries were. You don't have to keep them, hold onto them, now.'

Another in-breath and she peeks at the familiar face. It's round with pale skin, and freckles over the strong nose, silver and wheat hair cut to a bob. Izzie smiles kindly. *She is unswervingly kind.*

Hannah says sharply, 'Why don't you ever tell me to shut up? Tell me I'm lying?' There's some of the tidal bore back in her voice.

'You're not lying and I want to hear what you have to say.'

'Stephen says I'm lying.'

'We've talked about the reasons your brother might have for saying that, and the fact is he can't know, he wasn't there.'

'I expect Mother will have to come home soon,' the knot at the back of her neck makes an extra twist. 'I wish she'd stay away. I don't like her, I don't love her. Isn't that an awful thing to say about your own mother?'

'It's how you feel.'

'Ben says I can move in with him when it happens. But I'm not sure I want to. I like the house, we moved so much when I was a kid, this feels like somewhere I could settle, nothing bad ever happened there. I like having Aurora next door. And Ben, I don't know, sometimes I think he's only with me out of pity.'

'Maya said that, didn't she?'

'Yes. I know, not to be trusted.' *She'd wanted to keep me away from Ben.*

'Her motives anyway.'

'She's doing her penance now, or,' Hannah is faintly amused, 'that's how she sees it, working at the miners' convalescent home, near Peasholm.' *Surprisingly.* 'Ben persuaded Rose not to pay for Maya to go to her father's, and Rose persuaded Maya's father not to either, so she's having to earn her way over there. She'll spin it to her own advantage, no doubt. Ben says it'll do her good to grow up a little, like he's being all rational, but really he's cross with her for duping him and with himself for being duped.'

Izzie says: 'You came in angry about Lawrence. What's happened with your anger, Hannah?'

When she stops talking, she feels it, the deep crevasse opening up within her, the thin crust covering it drops away and she falls through into sadness and loneliness. Grief, not just for Lawrence, for the loss of Lawrence, but for the parenting she'd never had. 'I realise now I wanted him to be a replacement mother, maybe I pushed too hard to have him be what he couldn't be. But then, it wasn't just me, was it? He believed he could be, a substitute, for me, and now he's not so sure, 'cos of having to accept stuff he doesn't want to think about. We were both deluded.' It's as if a sharp hook of ice has jabbed into her stomach, winding her. Now she's caught there, splayed in mid-air. She scrabbles to get purchase, 'It was real though, our friendship, he did care, he still does in his own way. It's like all this, it puts the skids under everything, nothing is as I thought it was, yet some of it must be.' Images come to her mind: Stephen holding her up as she tried to roller-skate, another of her intense and short-lived passions when she was a girl, and them laughing, laughing, *so I almost wet myself.* 'It wasn't all bad, my childhood, it couldn't have been.' The hook turns more securely into her gut, she crunches over, the pain physical.

Izzie leans forwards and supplies tissues. 'Let it come, let it come,' she murmurs.

After a while, the tears and sobs ease, Hannah blows her nose, wipes her eyes. She can hear the din caused by a lorry thumping along the road at the end of the garden outside. She can see through the square window the tree branches stretching to the sky. They're greening, perhaps even as she sits here. With a breath she pulls herself upright, 'I wanted to say, DI Wiltshire sprang a surprise visit. You remember, she was the one who came right at the beginning, when all this started?' The first of several who came to tease out a story, *a story which makes sense out of something which doesn't make sense, until I end up with a narrative, of sorts.* She tells Izzie what happened. 'I presume Theo was there to mop up the emotion afterwards,' she concludes. 'He looked very uncomfortable.'

'She sounds clinical, this DI Wiltshire. How was it for you?'

'I was churned up, obviously, when she showed me those images again, this memory came, I don't know if it's true even.' *Everything on the skids.*

'Did you cut?'

She shakes her head. She'd been tempted, a razor across the forearm, a clean score, letting the evil out, releasing the pain. It had become a compulsion. She knows every day she doesn't do it is a *small* victory. *But it's always there waiting, an addiction.* She has the sense of being in free fall again. She clutches at anything, 'I rather like clinical, sometimes.' She is reminded of a poem written by a woman undergoing cancer treatment, the poet used the rhythm of medical terms, and Hannah's mind does the same with the words used to her by police officers:

oral,
vaginal,
anal,
penetrative,

non-penetrative.
Not a pretty poem, but precise, clear, no-nonsense. 'It gives me distance. I need that too.' She pauses, she still can't find anything solid under her feet. 'Only you can't put it back once it's out, can you? You can't unsay things, you can't unknow things. I wish it were different.' There's a moment's silence and they breathe together, Izzie and her. 'Do I? Probably not.'

CHAPTER 13

Tuesday 18 May

His reception this afternoon is decidedly chilly. 'What do you want DS Akande? I thought I'd made myself clear on the phone yesterday, there is no need for further police involvement.'

He'd been brought here by a last-minute decision to take a left rather than a right turn. He is now beginning to regret the impulse. He'd expected to find a sorrowful Mrs Peer ready to talk and, possibly, say something useful. Instead ... *Hard, brittle, armoured.* These are the words she is currently evoking for him. He has not been offered coffee or biscuits this time, not been allowed beyond the black-and-white-tiled hallway. Marta had asked him to wait there while she went to find her mistress. Theo had heard Caroline's exasperated, 'Why did you let him in?' before she appeared through a door to the back of the house, gardening gloves on and secateurs in hand.

'We still have burglaries to investigate,' Theo says calmly.

'Not here, you don't, he staged it all, Harrison, and now he's gone. There is no connection with those other unfortunates who really were burgled. Shouldn't you be spending precious police time going after the perpetrators of those?'

Professor Peer dreaming it all up and wielding glass cutters? Theo can't imagine it. *And the MO is so similar between the break-ins, it doesn't make sense.* 'Your husband had professional glass cutters, did he?' He can't keep the scepticism out of his voice. He can see it annoys Mrs Peer.

'Not to my knowledge, but it wasn't beyond his capabilities to get some.'

'And use them?' *They'd appeared close as a couple. But appearances can be deceptive.*

'I still don't see why you're interested in my troubles, detective. My diamonds have gone. My husband has gone. Isn't it what you'd call a domestic?'

'Perhaps he had help and that person is our burglar.'

'If he had help, I know nothing about it,' she begins to move towards the door.

She's tall, her arms are held out at an angle, those secateurs snap-snap. He can't avoid taking several steps backwards.

'You'd have to ask Harrison,' she adds. 'If you can find him.' There's a bitterness to her tone.

'I'd like to speak to Marta and her husband,' Theo says firmly, though he knows he has lost too much ground, he is practically on the doorstep.

'It's really not convenient. I will be in touch with your people when it is. I wouldn't want to be obstructive to the police, but now is not the time.'

As she closes the door, does Theo see a hint of tears in her eyes? *Maybe it's her way of grieving. She's probably embarrassed.* The wooden panels of the door against his back, he looks down the wide-bottomed valley. The air here is damp, with an underlying scent of turned earth and manure. The daylight is fading. There is a faint green tinge to the sky, as if it has been brushed on by the lush pasture below. A thin, silvery crescent hangs, fragile, above a mushroom of shadowy trees on the brow of the hill. *Maybe she doesn't know more than she's saying. Maybe.*

* * *

Dr Shrimpton is beautiful: her lips are molten-magma; her eyes lava; her tawny fingers flash with gold and gems as she talks animatedly. Over her shoulder, through the window of her office, the pale blue is rent, revealing the slender curve of the platinum stratosphere. They had met to talk about the editing Hannah has done on the chapter Clare has been working on. However, the conversation has ranged far beyond: to Hannah's appreciation of *Gaudy Night*, the DL Sayers novel she'd been reading; to whether writers always end up writing about themselves; to why the crime genre is not given the literary standing it deserves. It had been fun, Hannah had enjoyed stretching her intellect to keep up with

Clare's. She even thought she'd perhaps done a pretty good job. Now she is aware of the clock ticking and of Ben probably already arriving back from work, waiting for her. She is about to take her leave, when the other woman reaches out with warm fingers to touch her hands, briefly.

'I wonder if I might ask you something, Hannah?' she asks, uncharacteristically hesitant. When she receives assent, she continues, 'I expect with your training you have a deeper understanding of people. It's what it gives you, isn't it, insight into human behaviour?'

Hannah is uneasy. She knows some people attribute therapists with special, even magical, powers to see into them, *but Clare wouldn't be thinking this, would she?* 'I think it's more a case of having the insight to realise what you don't know, you can't predict.'

Clare looks faintly dissatisfied. 'Professor Peer,' she says quietly. 'Sometimes I could, ugh, you know ...' Her fingers twist round her dainty wrist as if it were a neck. 'Professional rivalry is one thing, but he makes it all so personal. And you saw what he was like, he can't be argued with.'

'He did appear to be very much in earnest, to take it all very seriously.'

'Of course it's serious,' Dr Shrimpton bursts out. 'It's our lives. What are we if our work isn't taken seriously?'

'There's no danger of that – in your case, I mean.'

Clare leans forward. 'I don't know. I've written articles and now I've got this chapter accepted, I'm ready to start on my own book, I feel ready. But the obvious publishers to go to, they publish Peer and he is on their review panel.'

'He can't have that much power, if they see the quality of your work, of your writing ...'

'And with your editorial assistance ...' Clare bestows one of her luscious smiles.

Hannah's cheeks sizzle, she wants to deny, she wants to simper, she forges on, 'The others would overrule him, surely? Quality trumps everything?'

Clare shakes her head, sadly. 'It doesn't always work like that.' Then she bounces up and paces to the window, talking to the gash in the darkening sky, 'He hasn't been around for the last few days, no one seems to know why. I keep thinking, keep hoping, maybe he's shuffled off ... you know, gone.' She turns back. 'Isn't that awful of me?'

As awful as me wishing Mum would shuffle off her mortal coil? Clare is looking expectant, Hannah is wary of answering, *what if my response isn't good enough? Shows my ignorance? Disappoints her?* She chooses her words carefully, 'I can understand it's a difficult situation, but in the end you can only focus on what you can do. Produce an excellent proposal and submit it. Right now you don't know how the publisher, or Professor Peer, will react. Until you do, there's no point in letting it tie you up in knots.'

'I know Peer won't let me in, I'm certain he'll do anything ...'

Hannah sees the squirming lack of confidence, the nervousness, the fear, as if they are tying themselves around Clare's body, the tentacles of a mythical beast. She stands too, says clearly, 'What you're scared of is rejection and the scare will stop you trying. It's got nothing to do with Professor Peer, he's merely a symbol. You're getting in your own way.'

Dr Shrimpton is suddenly still, she makes another ugly guttural sound, her mouth slack. Then she shakes her head, snaps herself upright, laughs flatly. 'An interesting theory, Hannah, I'll think on it, but believe me this has everything to do with Professor Peer.' The room has grown gloomy, she turns on a lamp to pool light onto the desk and thumbs some folders of papers. 'I've got marking to do tonight, I'd better get organised.'

I said the wrong thing. Hannah collects her bag. She's shattered, from the effort of remaining alert and upbeat for the afternoon's discussion. She's also worried she's forfeited any future contact with Clare. The other woman briefly looking up, smiling and saying, 'Thank you Hannah, for listening,' only minimally assuages her concerns. However, as she walks down the corridor, the thought of seeing Ben begins to lift her mood, as does the persistent, *if wrong-headed*, notion, *I'm not mistaken about you Dr Shrimpton, am I? It's you, not the professor, who is stopping you.*

* * *

Aurora doesn't normally stay after class and go to the bar with Professor Aiden Haswell and a few of the other students. However, she'd been late arriving, *again, and all because of Max and his precious business. He doesn't value what I do at all. Well, he can have his TV interrupted by our little chap wanting feeding or changing.* She orders herself a glass of white wine, sips it and realises it's far too rough to be palatable. *Never mind.* It reminds her of being an undergrad when volume was more important than taste and she feels some of the carefreeness she did then.

The bar's decor is basic and it's rather cheerless on this mid-week night, only a few students playing pool, one eye on the sports programme on a big screen on the wall. She nudges onto a padded bench with two of the youngest members of the class, hardly out of their solicitor exams. They now eschew suits and ties each Tuesday evening for jeans and brightly coloured polo shirts, perhaps inspired by their tutor's vivid garb. Opposite is a man who must be ten years older than her, in his late forties. He has a habit of using fifty words when five would do, and acting as if any listener should be interested in every one of them. At the other end of the table is a woman; closer in age to Aurora, mousy and quiet, she has nevertheless told a fair few of her classmates about her acrimonious divorce and her need to 'move on with her life'. Between her and the pompous bore is Aiden with his pint of real ale. For the moment he is listening politely to his dull neighbour make some laborious statement.

He's smiling at me, Aiden is smiling at me. She returns it with a generous curve of her lips. She notices the sparkling blue intensity of his eyes under his unruly dark curls. Finally, when the man opposite pauses to sip his half a lager, she is able to ask Aiden about his research. It is clear from his teaching that he is interested in how religion and culture intersects with what is written into law. She expects him to talk about this. Instead he says he is gathering people's stories. There is a pause, *they're all looking as blank as I feel, even Mr Know-it-all.*

Aiden continues, 'We academics dress it up as something complicated, but research is really about stories, people's stories.'

'Any particular people's?' she asks tentatively.

'I've been spending time at the miners' convalescent home, listening. I don't know what, but it'll build into something. It'll reveal itself to me.' He smiles broadly.

He's winding us up. Isn't he? 'I remember going to the Big Meeting,' she starts. Then encouraged by his genuine look of interest she goes on to describe the hot July days when her parents would take her to Durham. To watch the parade of miners holding aloft their brilliantly patterned banners. To hear (and not understand until she was older) the fiery speeches from the hotel balcony. To eat too many freshly fried doughnuts on the green field called The Sands by the river. 'That's where they'd met, Durham, my parents, while they were medical students. They thought it romantic to go back.'

'Of course it was Scargill who did it for the miners,' says the older man, as a prelude to his treatise on how the unions would have ruined the country if Thatcher hadn't come along. The two youngsters slope off, not waiting for him to finish, and the woman starts to fiddle with her phone.

Aurora plays around with suitable reposts in her head. She is uncomfortably warm. 'I think you'll find ...' she tries to intervene and fails.

Then Aiden motions with his head towards the door while holding her gaze. He finishes off his pint quickly and yawns loudly, interrupting his student's speech, 'Time to depart. See you all next week.' His movement out of his seat is smooth, fluid.

Aurora follows him, fearing it's more of a scurry than an elegant departure.

'There's no point in engaging with people like that,' he says as they walk together down the corridor towards the front door. 'He's made up his mind and it's a waste of time trying to change it.' They exit the building into the night-time coolness. He stops, begins to say goodbye, expecting her to go to a car. When she says she's walking, he says, 'Good, so am I.' There's a short exit road to the main one, as they saunter down, Aiden says, 'Thank you for your description of the Durham Gala, it brought the day alive to me. I used to go as a child, my father was a pit man. It was a very special occasion for us.'

Aurora is startled, she'd had Aiden down as coming from a family of academics, now she can detect the northern in his accent.

They've reached the road junction and he's turning left, while Aurora is going to cross over to go straight ahead. They say goodbye and she waits at the crossing for a break in the traffic. He halts after a few paces and turns back. 'There's the premiere of a film by one of my colleagues, back up here, tomorrow night, it's all very experimental. I hope you come, I think you'll like it.' Then he's gone.

Be still my beating heart, Aurora laughs to herself as she imagines herself dancing airborne around that slender sickle moon. *Just like in a Bollywood movie.* The lights change and she crosses the road. She decides she won't go the next evening. *Two nights out in a row, not likely Mrs Harris.* Even so, she's glad of the cool air on her skin and in her lungs and would have preferred a little longer to compose herself before her front gate comes into view.

CHAPTER 14

Wednesday 19 May

The three of them sit round the desk in the DS's enclave. There is activity in the incident room beyond the glass partition. Eyes fixed to computer screens. The arrhythmic clicking of inexpert typing. A discussion about what really happened on a previous night out. Theo can identify the bravado in the voices, not the actual words, but he's heard much of it before: the amount of alcohol consumed; the liaisons which did or did not come off; the early-morning realisations. He'd had similar conversations, in the past, with friends, never with colleagues. He briefly envisions genders being immaterial to the banter, only the resulting picture remains awkward. He brings his attention back to the folders in front of him.

'What we have are three ongoing investigations. There are the burglaries which took place on the seventh of May. There're the two incidents of a man selling counterfeit, probably smuggled, brandy. And there's these threatening letters sent to DCI Stokes.'

'And you think they're somehow connected,' DC Brian Chesters' gelled-up hair and large ears give him the air of an excited whippet, however, his tone and demeanour suggest incredulity and a lack of zeal.

I do, but I can't exactly say why. The only connection appears to be that they have all stalled. 'Let's go through each one and see what surfaces. The burglaries. Chesters?'

The DC does straighten in his chair and glance at the report he's brought in with him, though he speaks without enthusiasm, 'Two burglaries in one night, in Scalby and the Peers in Hackness. Only now Mrs Peer is saying it wasn't a burglary, and her old man made it look like one then made off with the chambermaid.' He smirks at his own joke.

'Keep to the facts, Chesters. And we'll keep it in for now.'

'Because that's sticking to the facts?' Chesters' manner is acerbic, perhaps he's still smarting from recently missing his sergeant's exam by a few points. He shrugs. 'Same MO, carefully executed, glass cut from a back door or window to gain entry. Owners were away from their home for the Scalby incident. The Peers were asleep in bed and their housekeeper and gardener were away. No useful forensics, though it is likely the same glass cutter was employed, it's high-end, used by professional builders, glaziers and the like. Expensive TV and electronic goods taken from the first, an old-fashioned video player and diamonds taken from the Peers.' He takes a moment skimming over his report, then adds, 'A white van sighted parked around the corner from the property in Scalby, probably a standard transit of the short wheel base variety. No registration available.' He looks up at Theo, leans back and folds his arms.

Theo holds his gaze for a moment, the folded arms remind him of Hoyle, *don't take him as your model for police work, me lad*. He turns to DC Harry Shilling, she has her report resting on her knee and he can see she has made a few pencilled annotations as Chesters was speaking. He also observes the make-up hiding shadows under her eyes, and that her cheeks are more fevered than ever with blusher. However, when she talks she's as clear and exact as usual. The diamonds have not been recovered. She'd checked out Mrs Peer's story with the valuers and they confirmed it. 'They also confirmed the necklaces were insured, wouldn't say for how much, except it is a lot. But now it seems Professor Peer has gone off with them, I'm not sure how that will change things.' Only the TV and video recorder have been recovered, from the black rubbish sacks Jayson Smith was seen hauling round to a back lane nearby. 'He has no alibi for the nights of the burglaries, though nothing puts him at the scene either. He does not own, nor does he appear to have hired, a white transit van. He's got previous, though it's all been petty, and he's always the gofer, never the chief. He has been charged with handling.' The disappointment seeps into her tone. She rallies a little when she adds, 'A white van has been associated with the counterfeit brandy incident.'

'There must be hundreds in Scarborough alone,' says Chesters, a tad harshly.

Hoyle's influence again. 'Still, it's worth bearing in mind,' Theo says peaceably.

'Trench has the Rattenburys down for the brandy,' says Shilling. 'They fit descriptions given.'

'Yes, all three of them, as do most of the builders in the town,' says Chesters. 'Anyway, Trench and Robbie Rattenbury have hated each other since school, Robbie nicked Trev's girlfriend and then married her. And the Rattenburys don't own a white van.'

'Felicity owns the house Jayson rents,' there's triumph in Shilling's voice. 'A neighbour told me this morning when I, er, happened to be passing.'

She won't let it go with Jayson. Theo feels a ping of excitement, 'Now that is interesting. What else do we know about her?'

'Not much. Nasty divorce, suggestions of violence, her on him. But no charges. Lives with her twin brother Phil. Doesn't have a job, owns one rental property, probably supported by the family firm. Spends time caring for her dying mother Eunice. Doing a PhD in English at the university, same department as Professor Peer. Supervisor is Dr Clare Shrimpton.'

'The Rattenburys have form as a family,' butts in Chesters, maybe now feeling he has some distance to make up. 'Daddy R for drink driving and for intimidating a witness. And there's always rumours not all their money comes from legit businesses.'

'Rumours,' Shilling imitates Chesters' previous flat tone.

He shrugs.

Theo shifts in his seat, he wants to jump up and move about, there isn't room. 'We're getting some connections. The Rattenburys to Jayson through Felicity, and maybe to the Peers through Felicity again.'

'Felicity helped the professor stage a burglary so he could make off with the family diamonds to start a new life?' Chesters is obviously unconvinced.

'We can't discount it.' *But is it likely? Don't they live in two different worlds?*

'If she did, should we even be interested? Mrs Peer is adamant it's no longer a crime.'

Theo has to agree with Chesters, yet he's unwilling to let it drop completely, just yet. He allows a break. The walk to the gents and back does him good. He thinks over what he has found out about Stokes's career. Detective Chief Inspector William (Bill) Stokes retired two years previously at the age of fifty-six after an exemplary career spanning thirty-eight years. Born and raised in Consett, a steelworks town in County Durham. He joined the local constabulary, thus avoiding employment in the vast industrial plants which dominated the town and redundancy in his late twenties. Instead he rose to detective sergeant by the time he was thirty-one and detective inspector only four years later. Then there was the move to North Yorkshire and, following that, he progressed around the country as he progressed up the promotion ladder. Several times in his career, Theo has had to face-out the accusation of being fast-tracked (because he's a graduate, black or gay, depending on who is feeling aggrieved at the time) yet Stokes had out-paced him. Having passed his forty-first birthday a few months ago, Theo is only just looking at his first DI post. *When Hoyle finally goes.*

Theo has made sure it is Chesters who gets the coffee for them all, which he does with good grace. Once they are settled again, Theo gives the potted working history for Stokes, including a recent case which had been spectacularly thrown out by the judge because of undue pressure put on a suspect. The resulting furore in the press had possibly led to Stokes's retirement.

'Plenty of suspects, then,' Shilling mutters.

'You can't make an omelette without cracking eggs,' retorts Chesters.

Theo continues with a summary of the report from the lab on the letters. The printer paper used could be bought in any high street. The cut-out words come from newspapers, undoubtedly tabloids, probably the *Express* and/or the *Daily Mail*. There are no fingerprints apart from those left by Stokes himself when he handled the pages and the envelopes.

Chesters is more attentive than he was before, his eager akin-to-a-whippet has re-emerged, 'Postmarks?'

'York and Carlisle.'

'Local and Cumbria, then,' says Chesters.

Cumbria? Ping. 'Phil Rattenbury has worked away in Cumbria.' He regrets the comment as soon as it is out of his mouth.

Chesters' gaze is less than deferential, 'And his connection with Stokes?'

None, there is none, I'm letting a preoccupation get in the way. He rapidly shifts onto handing out tasks. Stokes had never been on the force in Cumbria and his sojourn in Scarborough was short and a long time ago. However, someone he did have dealings with may have moved to either area. It is grunt work to sift through prison and probation records, but Chesters is quick to pick it up. 'Check for recent releases, recent relocations, anniversaries of sentences or crimes. These letters have all been sent in the last six months; something, some event, some reminder, set the writer off. Harry, investigate this link between Felicity and Jayson a bit more. We know he can't have been acting alone.' She's pleased. *To be given a second chance.*

They leave and Theo becomes more aware of the traffic outside – accelerating and decelerating for the lights – and the movement of people beyond the glass partition. *And me? What should the soon-to-be DI Akande be doing?* He smiles to himself. On Sunday, Lawrence had taken him to a preview at the Lowry in Manchester. It had been a glittering affair, Lawrence a feted guest. Theo had enjoyed the occasion, mixing with the artistic, both known and unknown, more than he had the art. It was a world his lover opened up for him and which he appreciated. Afterwards, over dinner, he'd told Lawrence the applications for Hoyle's position were soon to be requested and he'd decided to go for it. He'd expected some opposition with Lawrence once again asking him why he was so settled on Scarborough and why he didn't seek a transfer to the Met. But instead Lawrence was supportive and encouraging. He even said he would look for some writing work which would give him reason to base himself more often up here. Theo doubted it would happen, *but it's a nice thought.*

Theo looks down at his notepad on his desk. He's written 'Rattenbury' in the centre of the page, doodling intersecting lines sprouting off each letter to form an untidy web. *Tunnel vision, it's dangerous in policing.* He'll make some phone calls, get a fuller picture of who is known to be smuggling counterfeit alcohol and how they do it. *But first,* he stands, *I'll drop in on a jeweller's in town and find out what someone might do with some stolen diamonds.* He crumples up the top sheet of paper on his pad and tosses it into the bin.

CHAPTER 15

Thursday 20 May

'You'll like this one, DS Akande,' DI Hoyle had said. 'It's some bloke making what he calls art. Can't see it meself. You'll have more appreciation, with your education.' *He makes it sound like a disease.*

Dr Hal Denver had been in at seven that morning, he had left with the desk sergeant a memory stick and a brief explanation of what had happened the previous night. Having gathered the basics from the latter, Theo snaps the stick into a computer. There are various files: one contains the whole film; the others stills from when the house went over the cliff. They are grainy, indistinct, *worse than when CCTV was on tape, which was over-used until it got mashed.* Even so, he can make out a face at the window. Dr Denver has included on the stick, for comparison, a photo of Harrison Peer which looks like one from a book dust jacket. But Theo doesn't need it, he hasn't forgotten the professor from his encounter with him, *and the face could certainly be his. Looks squashed. Battered maybe?* He reads through Dr Denver's account again. According to the timer on the recording, the house toppled between 11.05 and 11.20 on Sunday night. *Mrs Peer called me Monday evening to say her husband had taken off.* He'd not been given the chance to get the details of the story, *was he with her Monday morning? Or was he already gone?*

He takes Shilling with him to the Peers' house. She's never one to chatter, *not like bloody Chesters.* However, her quietness is unnerving. After he fills her in on what he knows, he expects some questions, instead she merely stares out the window. He asks her if she's OK and the only response he gets is, 'Fine.' He's not convinced and wonders whether Hoyle has continued with his bullying. *It seems probable, the DI is not one to give up once he has the scent of a victim.* He decides it's not the moment to delve, he wants Shilling composed.

This time Mrs Peer opens the door. There is something slightly off-kilter about her appearance, the skin around her taut mouth is damaged porcelain, her lipstick red dye running into the cracks. She doesn't want to let them in. It is Theo's firm insistence which means they are finally seated in the lounge, Caroline distractedly pulling at a thread unravelling from the sleeve of her hip-length cardigan. The room is as ostentatious and as neat as before, making the contrast with its mistress more palpable. A large vase of cut flowers stands on the sideboard. *The wedding photo's still there though*, Theo notices. *Pushed back behind.*

'What is it you want, DS Akande? I don't suppose either of us has all day.' Her clipped haughtiness is undiminished.

'I was wondering when you last saw Professor Peer?'

'What's it to you?' When she receives no response and Theo doesn't glance away, she shrugs, 'Sunday afternoon, around three o'clock. He said goodbye and I went upstairs for a nap. I've not been sleeping since, since the break-in, or what I thought was …'

After he's sure she's not going to finish her sentence, Theo asks, 'You knew he was going then?'

'He'd said he was going to London, to do some work, at the British Library. I'd asked Marta to book the train and a hotel for him. He was to spend a few days. But he left me a note, for when I woke up, explaining he'd gone. Permanently.'

'And he admitted taking the diamonds?'

She nods.

'May I see this note?'

'I burnt it.' She clasps her hands on her lap.

'Did anyone else see it?'

She shakes her head, 'Who would I show it to? My humiliation at being misused and forsaken.'

Misused and forsaken?

Shilling takes up the questioning, could Mrs Peer be definite the professor had taken the train and gone to London? Does she know where he is now? The shrug Caroline gives remains unfinished, her shoulders hunch. She asks again for an explanation. Harry glances over at Theo.

Passing me the buck. 'We have reason to believe,' he begins slowly. *Have we? A grainy image on a film. Could it all be fabricated?* 'It's possible Professor Peer never left Scarborough ...'

'I doubt it detective sergeant, what would he stay here for?'

His work? His position at the university?

'He was always destined for higher things,' Caroline continues, as if picking up his thoughts. 'He should have gone to a far better establishment years ago, got the recognition he deserved. He'd had offers. He stayed for me. I imagine it finally got to him, he wanted more.'

'And the diamonds?' asks Shilling.

'Apart from his salary, paltry as it is, and book royalties, he had no money of his own. All this,' she gazes round. 'Is mine. In any case, I controlled the finances. He preferred it that way, or I thought he did. Apparently I was wrong.'

Theo suddenly realises he asked the wrong question. 'When did you last hear from your husband, Mrs Peer?'

She looks into the far corner of the room before replying, 'Tuesday morning. He texted me, to apologise, for the "inconvenience" he's caused me.'

'May I see the text?'

'I deleted it.'

It'll be recoverable. 'Then could I take your phone, to be analysed? And would you give us access to your financial records, to see if the professor has withdrawn any money?'

She stiffens. 'Absolutely not. I can tell you he hasn't, he has those diamonds, what would he need further funds for? DS Akande, I am going to ask you to leave in a moment, and I will expect you to do so, but first I want you to tell me what this is all about.' She has frosty eyes and she's not going to be the first to blink.

'A Dr Hal Denver, from the university, has given us some film which appears to show someone who looks like your husband trapped in a house as it falls over a cliff.' *Yeah, sounds daft.*

'What? You're suggesting my husband has died in a house which has plunged down a cliff, in Scarborough?' For a moment, Theo thinks she might start yelling, then she laughs, stiffly. 'Harrison is not dead, I can assure you. He is very much alive. He has gorn off, not gorn over.' Her laugh sounds even more as if rictus has set in. Then she becomes serious, angry, 'It's some kind of joke, a sick joke, no one at that place appreciates him, they'd take any opportunity to poke fun at him. Especially that hyena in her red swirly petticoats. She's put Dr Denver up to it, somehow. Dr Clare Shrimpton. You talk to her.'

Theo leans forwards, saying quietly, 'It's imperative we locate Professor Peer.'

She gets to her feet, 'It's time you and the DC were going.' She flaps her hands in a shooing motion.

Theo stands up, as tall as he can make himself, says firmly, 'We just want to be sure he is safe, Mrs Peer. And, of course, if there has been any wrongdoing by Dr Denver, or Dr Shrimpton, we will investigate it.'

She falters and then inclines her head, 'OK, detective sergeant, I will text my husband and tell him to contact you direct. How about that? Have you a card?'

He hands one over. He also asks her to send him details of the professor's travel plans and hotel. He's not sure he gets agreement before he and Shilling are tersely ejected onto the front step. The warmth of the sun envelopes them and he realises how chilly it has been inside.

Theo rings the council to be told the landslip at Knipe Point had been reported by a resident the morning of Monday the twenty-first of May, but no one is immediately available to say more. He sends a message to Trench to follow up both with the council and the residents, then takes the road to the coast.

In truth, the impetus is only partly to do with the investigation, he also wants a whiff of the sea before he becomes enmeshed with the schemes of humans again. A small road leads them into a green sloping park, with embellished static caravans widely spaced across the grass. Low picket fences demarcate gardens. Late narcissi, tulips and hebe bushes hide the stands on which the trailers are perched. Some have patios. Others trellises hung with clematis or budding roses. Each plot raucously declares its permanence.

Shilling parks where the road loops back up the slope. The sea is now before them, a bolt of crinkled indigo silken cloth unfolding. The sky is a paler pennant stretched to where the two are pinned together. A breeze plays with the warmth of the sun, batting it away and then huffing it forwards. Theo takes a deep breath. The scent of mown grass mingles with a heavier, earthier smell. This begins to predominate as they move forward. There is one more complete dwelling, shutters at its door and windows. Then the land drops sharply away, a gaping mouth which has lost its top lip. They both stop. Perhaps Shilling too has the sense they will inexorably topple into the yawning maw. Tape and plastic barriers have been set up, but even these have started to slither with the sandy soil; orange fluorescent teeth strung with dental floss, which have been knocked crooked by a giant's fist.

Inching carefully forwards, Theo sees a few straggling bushes are clinging to the landslip, but mostly it is a clean sweep down. At the base no beach is visible, only waves nestling into the curve of the cliffs.

'Any evidence washed away,' says Shilling, sounding as if her throat is parched.

And any body already being pulled apart by the tides or smashed on rocks or being eaten. He remembers the coastguard giving him details of the sea's power to destroy a person during the case of a missing girl, *Vicky*, last December.

The walk back to the car feels like a scramble. *I'll get Trench up here to talk to the residents.*

Shilling pauses before getting in the passenger side door, 'Not many close neighbours and some of these are only occupied weekends or holidays, I don't suppose we'll get much from a house to house, or should I say, caravan to caravan.'

He agrees, however adds a not altogether forced, 'We might get lucky. Someone with a telescope.'

It has the desired effect, she grins.

'You're going for it, sarge?' Harry has perked up even further.

He's treated her to pizza and chips in the university canteen. *Or maybe it's the conversation we're having, about who'll succeed Hoyle?* 'He hasn't announced he's going yet.' Telling Lawrence his plans is one thing, it wouldn't be wise to say too much to a DC. He believes Shilling is basically trustworthy, *but rumours get started back at base in all sorts of ways, and then spread quicker than a shoal of snipefish, as Suze would say.* And today he doesn't feel as convinced as he did on Sunday; today he concludes he's being pushed forward to make the candidate list look good, not because he has any hope of getting it. The thought tastes of the mouldy centre of a fresh-looking bread roll.

'If Hoyle doesn't do it soon, I'll do it for him,' Shilling mutters.

They've had a brief interview with Dr Hal Denver who hasn't been much more forthcoming than his initial statement. He hadn't spent time up at the house at Knipe Point – 'It would have undermined the whole aim of the project.' He'd sounded exasperated. He had kept most of the footage he'd edited out to make the earlier sections of the film and he promised to download them so they could be reviewed at the station, 'Though there's nothing untoward in them.' He insisted the final scenes were untouched and he hadn't seen them until the night of the premiere. 'I wanted the final demise to take its own course, in the film as well as in reality. It adds to the raw nature of the art.' He and his students had also done some beachcombing Tuesday. 'There'd been tides, we didn't find much, certainly not a body.'

Still, he agreed with Shilling to contact students and collect back together as many of their finds as he could.

At Theo's behest, Denver retrieved the sign-in sheet from the premiere, 'Not everyone registered, by any means, and some of the names are illegible, others won't tell you a lot.'

Theo scanned down the list and picked out a Mickey and Minnie Mouse and a Daffy Duck. However, there were a couple of entries which were of particular interest: Dr Clare Shrimpton, Mrs Peer's target for disdain. And, next to hers, Felicity Pritchard. He also noted Hannah and Aurora had been there. *Good, I'll get some sense out of them.* He took the decision to allow himself to talk to them, despite their friendship, and without Shilling.

While he was doing this, Hal had been rocking from foot to foot. Finally he'd said, 'I don't think I can help you anymore, detective sergeant. I didn't know Professor Peer, not to speak to or have anything to do with.'

Theo had allowed a pause to lengthen, as if he were considering something deeply. He noticed the lecturer's eyes flicked around and how he fidgeted, *you're not so laid back now are you?* Then Theo'd let him go, tossing after him, 'I may need to speak to you again.' It gave him more pleasure than he wanted to admit to himself to see Dr Denver falter slightly on his swaggering exit.

Dr Shrimpton had not been available until the afternoon, hence the visit to the canteen. Theo checks his watch, it's nearly time. They make their way to the reception. It is a fine wood-panelled hallway with a large stone-mantled fireplace behind the modern welcome desk and its computer. Summoned by the receptionist, Dr Clare Shrimpton comes down the solid dark-wood stairs in the corner. She is tall, curvy, wearing a dress printed with blocks of primary colours which pinches in at her waist and then floats to her feet. Her raven-wing hair is twisted up onto her head, held by an extravagant gold comb. She has a firm handshake and a warm smile. *A hyena?*

She leads them back up the staircase which creaks at each step, along a passage and up again into what was once a corridor of bedrooms in the eaves. Some of the doors are open revealing people at work, mostly crammed behind computers. Theo notices only one door has a plaque on it: 'Professor Harrison Peer, English Department'. He stops, puts his hand on the handle, the door is locked. 'Can we get this opened?'

'I suppose so, what …?' Then a long 'Oh' trails out through her red lips. 'Clues?' she says with curiosity. She turns, 'I'll call the vice-chancellor's office, you'll need official permission, but shouldn't be a problem.' She leads them into her office. With the three of them seated, knees practically touching, the room is crowded. She has offered them coffee, which they've refused, and is now attentive, her manicured fingers interwoven. Her skirt material has fallen back to reveal on a tanned ankle a discreet tattoo – a coiled grass-toned snake with a diamond pattern down its back.

Theo begins by asking her to recount her experience of the premiere. She does so in some detail, estimating maybe thirty in the audience. Denver had stuck with twenty, *perhaps wary of fire regs?* 'It all started out so jolly,' she says, her voice careful and calm. 'Hal has a way of creating things which shake up what you'd expect of academia. It's his mission, and he does it so well. I was absorbed by the film when suddenly I saw, we all saw, well, I can't really say what we saw. A man's face at the window.'

'Professor Harrison Peer?'

'I suppose it looked a bit like him. But it couldn't be, could it? What would he be doing there? And he's gone to London.'

'He told you?'

She shakes her head, 'I think his wife rang in and told one of the secretaries, word gets around a small campus like this, you know?'

'When did you last see him?' asks Harry.

'Friday afternoon, about four-ish, I was coming back from a meeting and he was locking up. I said bye, have a good weekend, he said goodbye, turned and walked down the corridor to the stairs. Bit strange he didn't mention his trip, he usually likes to make a thing about his research at the British Library. As if we don't all have readers' tickets there,' sarcasm in her voice. Then she catches hold of her bottom lip with a white tooth. 'He did go, didn't he? Like his wife said?'

Theo holds her gaze, asks, 'How did he seem to you as he left?'

'We only exchanged au revoirs, nothing more, but he didn't seem any different. DS Akande, why are you asking these questions? You have located him in London?' Theo doesn't give a response; however, this is answer enough, shock infuses her face. 'It can't have been him in the house, it can't have,' she says quietly. 'Are you sure you don't want a drink? I think I could do with one.' She braces herself for movement.

Theo shakes his head. 'What about you and Professor Peer? Do you get on well?'

Dr Shrimpton sinks back, she looks down at her hands as they grasp at her knees, 'We are colleagues. We don't always see each other's point of view. That's how it is in academia.'

Hyena? 'You fell out?'

Her lipstick-glossy mouth twists slightly at the side. 'I wouldn't say that.'

'What would you say?'

The snake stretches and arches as she taps her foot. 'He could be forceful at times. For him, his work was paramount, nothing could get in the way of it. Not even the students.' The twist comes again, maybe this time an attempt at a smile.

Theo notes the past tense and wonders if it is significant. 'What could he be forceful about?' He is feeling very warm now, considers taking off his linen jacket, only he doesn't want to break the flow. He keeps his focus on the woman in front of him. *Anxious or excited?* Theo can't tell.

Finally she parts her hands and holds them palms towards him. 'None of us academics want to accept it, but we do actually want to sell our books, we do want people to read them. Academic publishers don't have the same marketing budgets as commercial ones, but they rely on the same tactics as them. We pretend it's all about the ideas, the theories, but it's not.' She lets her hands fall to her brightly patterned lap. 'Haven't you noticed the high proportion of young female professors with flowing locks presenting BBC4 documentaries these days?'

Theo brings an image of the professor to mind. Harrison Peer couldn't hope to compete with what Theo sees in front of him: the lovely figure, the lipstick, the tattoo, the flamboyant dress sense.

'Women are still judged by their looks before their skills or thoughts, and I hate it.'

So why do you play up to it?

She looks sad, 'Harrison hasn't achieved the acclaim he thinks he deserves, academically I mean. His next book will make his name. Or so he believes. As long as his publishers don't decide it's all a bit old hat and go for the new kid on the block.'

'You?'

She shrugs. 'No harm in making a call, opening a discussion with them.'

Harry stirs herself, looks up from her notepad. 'He was bullying you, to hold you back?'

'I suppose he has tried.' Dr Shrimpton smiles pleasantly. 'I'm not such a pushover.'

Another reason for the professor to have taken flight, being shoved off the podium just when he'd written his 'opus magnum'? Or, the notion comes to him, *propel him over the edge, psychologically? Could this be an elaborate suicide attempt designed to have revenge on his colleagues as well?* Theo takes Clare back to the film night, had she gone alone? She shakes her head and names Professor Aiden Haswell and Felicity Pritchard, 'My PhD student.' And their responses to what happened? 'We were all startled, of course. Felicity appeared particularly upset, gave out quite a shriek, which surprised me, she's not usually very ... very demonstrative. Then she had been jumpy all evening.'

'Jumpy? Why?'

She shrugs. 'I got the impression she was a bit uncomfortable, in the environment. Her background is very different and she doesn't relax easily. Maybe it was being a third with Aiden and me, we're not an item or anything, only I suppose she could have got hold of the erroneous end of the stick. I did wonder if I should have asked her along, she didn't seem to be enjoying it much and then really became quite distressed … Aiden was very good with her. He was most cheering, convinced it had been some kind of arty pun or other. I know you're having to investigate, but that's what you think isn't it? ' She looks from Theo to Harry and undoubtedly doesn't get the reassurance she seeks. She sits back. After a moment, she glances at the clock. 'I'm sorry, I'm going to have to get ready. I've a supervision in ten minutes.' Her voice has lost its bounce.

Theo nods. They all stand up as one. A human mandala. He catches the heavy perfume Dr Shrimpton is wearing, it reminds him of when too many incense sticks are lit at once. He asks her where he might find Professor Haswell and Felicity Pritchard. He is told the former will be teaching for another hour and the latter would probably be in the library as she finds it hard to work at home. He also has her smooth his way to an authorisation to access Peer's room, organised for the end of the afternoon.

Chapter 16

Thursday 20 May

It's not as if the sea greets her like an old friend. The sea is totally indifferent to her existence and this is what is comforting. Hannah leans on the railings along the perimeter of the old South Bay lido. Several feet below her is a concrete path. Level with it, the cobalt water slips and slaps languidly against its rim, the breathing skin of a huge slumbering creature. Gulls – black-headed, Mediterranean, herring – are white beetles clinging to its swaying back. A yellow buoy, a yellow kayak are gashes in its hide. It smells of seaweed and the Saharan-sand-laden breeze. Its head is buried in the grey fret fringing the horizon. *What if it wakes?* Hannah knows the answer. *It will engulf our petty human concerns.*

That morning there'd been an email from Lawrence, the first communication from him since her picnic, five days ago.

Sent: Thurs 20/05/2010 05:55
This message will be sent via
LawrenceFielding@LawrenceFielding.co.uk
To: HannahPoole0676@gmail.com
Subject: Biographical piece
Dear Hannah
I realise I have been tardy in getting in touch with you. I know you were upset when we left after your picnic. I had no doubt been clumsy, hadn't chosen my words judiciously, though I wonder if I can ever get it right for you again. I find it hard to let go of the Stan who was my mentor, who was an accomplished journalist. That was the Stan I knew all these years. It's as if you expect me to deny he existed in order to stay friends with you.
I've had a request to write an article about Stan and his place in the changes which overtook local newspapers during his career. It could lead to a more expansive piece of work. I think it would be a fitting memorial to the Stan I knew. However, I do not want to

embark on such a project without hearing your opinion of it. So please let me know your thoughts as soon as you can.
Love as always, take care, L x

Hannah had taken some comfort in the time the missive had been sent. *Perhaps he's lost some sleep over this.* She'd read through Lawrence's words again. *Am I asking him to take sides? Is it unfair of me?* The notion could have drawn her into a funnel of self-recrimination and self-doubt. She tried to hold herself steady, *he doesn't realise how hard it is for me to keep a grip on firm ground. How his judgement still matters to me.* She imagined scales of justice, Stan's two faces – the mentor and the abuser – held one on each side. *Do they come to rest level?* A chill gripped her aching shoulders. She stomped up and down the carpet a few times and then spent forty-five minutes typing and re-typing a response she felt she could send.

Sent: Thurs 20/05/2010 10:18
This message will be sent via HannahPoole0676@gmail.com
To: LawrenceFielding@LawrenceFielding.co.uk
Subject: Re: Biography
Dear Lulu
OK it's difficult for you, trust me it's not been a stroll in the park for me either. I guess we're just going to have to be patient with each other. I don't want my father to destroy our relationship as he has destroyed so much else.
I understand the argument that it is possible to separate the person from his or her work. I don't buy it, Lawrence, not anymore, not after all this. It's all been hushed up and denied for so long, to have you push it to one side too would be too hard. I'm not asking you to ignore Stan the newspaperman and what he meant to you, I'm only asking you to paint a rounded, honest picture.
H x

She hadn't been able to sit still once her email had disappeared from the outbox. She didn't know how long Lawrence would take to reply and she knew if she waited indoors, she would have to fight the temptation to send ever more desperate messages to prompt him to get in touch. *To check he still cares.* She now understands her impulse to prod and prod for some reaction, any reaction, for even anger is better than silence. Silence is laden with condemnation. Silence is the accomplice of pain and fear.

However, the waves are not having their usual calming effect. Her mind races through a variety of possible things he might say, mostly brutal and un-empathic. *He's my friend, it's tough for him, but he doesn't want to hurt me, not deliberately;* she attempts to quell her anxiety with this approach Izzie has urged her to adopt. She doesn't entirely bring it off. She turns away from the lilting blue and stamps up the rickety cliff path.

She cradles her mug of coffee, the rustic ceramic warms her fingers. She hesitates briefly before clicking on Lawrence's email.

Date: 20/05/2010 12:58
This message will be sent via
LawrenceFielding@LawrenceFielding.co.uk
To: HannahPoole0676@gmail.com
Subject: Re: Biography
Dear Hannah
It's very possible you cannot slice the creator out of the creation, and it would not be my intention to brush anything to one side, but I do not feel equal to the task you set me. I write about politics, culture, philosophy, I am no crime writer. There are questions of evidence, admissible or otherwise, contempt, libel, maybe of any of Stan's associates. I haven't dealt with any of that since my training. I wouldn't know where to start. Perhaps it would be best if I didn't try. Maybe I should refuse the commission. I too value our friendship.
L x

All volition has skulked away, she would cry if she had any energy left. *He does care.* Then it occurs to her. She presses reply and types quickly: 'Didn't Spinoza give writers the mission of Janus? Aren't you meant to be able to hold opposing views and creatively present them to the rest of us? I want you to try, you are the only person I trust to tell the story, to get it right, in all its complexity. You've always told me in whatever you're writing it's about finding the story and telling it as credibly as you can.'

He wants evidence? Why can't he believe me? Am I so untrustworthy? Has he known me to lie, or, at least, lie successfully? She searches through the 'w' section in her card index box, then adds DI Pippa Wiltshire's details. He'd have to believe her. She takes a deep breath. He's not saying he doesn't believe me, she chides herself. She finishes with, 'Hxx' and presses send before she can delete the whole thing.

CHAPTER 17
Thursday 20 May
Theo is grateful for Hannah's invite to dinner. The afternoon had been long and exacting. Dr Shrimpton had taken him to the library and introduced him to Felicity Pritchard. Tall and big-boned, she had some of the stockiness of her father. Her face was pasty, the smile which appeared on Clare's approach quickly became a grim line once her supervisor had left.

She hadn't been unhelpful exactly, merely not giving more than was strictly necessary. She'd met Professor Peer a few times, but didn't know him. She didn't know where he was now. She'd been caught up in the film and had been convinced she was seeing the professor going to his death; however, now she believed it'd been a stunt, 'like Professor Haswell said'. She knew there was debate between Dr Shrimpton and Professor Peer, she didn't think it was particularly serious, happens all the time in academia. She began to gather her books, said she had to get back to look after her mother.

Then Harry asked, 'And you didn't see Professor Peer after about four pm last Friday?'

Felicity's frown deepened. In the background there were loud yelps of laughter from a group of students gathered around another table. A flush crept up from Felicity's neck as she replied forcefully, 'No.' She looked from Shilling to Theo and back again, 'I know what you're up to. If there's trouble, point at the Rattenburys. With Suze Pritchard working for yous, spreading lies about me, she got me into strife last time.' She stood up.

'I was only trying to ascertain Professor Peer's last known movements,' Harry said, a shade defensively.

'The last time I see him was ages ago, two weeks ago, at Dr Shrimpton's seminar.' She strode off.

Theo watched her go, his curiosity piqued, though his attention was quickly drawn back to Harry. She was hunched over the desk they were sitting at, her chin resting on clenched fists. 'Made a hash of that one too,' she muttered.

'Not at all,' he chuckled, before realising she was seriously upset. *What's wrong with her? It isn't like her to be so easily flustered.* 'You did great Shilling.'

'She stormed off.'

'Exactly. The question is, why did you get to her? Now come on, let's see if you can work the same magic on Professor Haswell.'

However, Harry remained subdued, *cowed. And it would have taken more than a few questions from a couple of dumb local police officers to ruffle Professor Teflon*, Theo later reflected. Haswell had more the appearance of coming from a surfing beach, with his flowered shirt (*silk*, Theo noticed) and sandals, than from a lecture theatre. He was of the mind that what had happened in the film was a prank played by one of Denver's more techie students, 'Digitally patched in Harrison's face to the film, somehow. Harrison'll turn up, like an out-of-circulation penny.'

'Where do you think he's gone?' asked DC Shilling, hesitancy still in her voice, though she'd thawed a little in the beam of Haswell's smile.

He did become more serious, as he answered, 'I understand he's left his wife, poor woman, after all those years of supporting him. Peer likes to think he lives on a higher intellectual plane where other people's feelings take second place.' Haswell also down-played the friction with Dr Shrimpton. 'Clare can take care of herself. As can Harrison. It's merely healthy academic dialogue.' He had last seen the professor at a meeting several days before his departure, witnessed by Shrimpton, on the Friday. There didn't appear to be anything else to ask and a quick check of his watch told Theo they had to get on, so he and Shilling took their leave. Haswell's expression brightened again, 'Drop in any time, detective sergeant and detective constable, always happy to help the police.' There was something boyish about his demeanour, which, along with those coal-coloured curls and the sharp pointed nose, struck Theo as familiar.

This thought was rapidly filed away as he and Harry were shown into Peer's office. It was slightly larger than Dr Shrimpton's, though not as spacious as Professor Haswell's, which was in the newer block. Its small window gave onto the front of the university: the car park and sports field. Inside was neat and ordered. Along one wall there was a case of books, a shelf given over to those by Professor Harrison Peer or (as Theo checked the chapter listing) contributed to by him. Opposite were two filing cabinets (locked) and in between a desk (drawers also locked). The estate manager, who had let them in, said only the professor had keys to his cabinets and desk. Theo thought this unlikely but foresaw the official paperwork which would be required if he were going to push it. The computer was also username/password protected. *We're not going to get into any of this without warrants, and a warrant won't be issued without a verifiable crime.*

The only thing available for a flick-through was an old-fashioned desk diary. Peer's teaching slots had stopped several weeks back in the run-up to exams, but Theo found Dr Shrimpton's seminar noted (and underlined in red) plus the meeting Haswell last saw the professor at. For the current and following weeks there were further meetings and a scattering of student supervisions booked in. No mention of the British Library trip his wife said he had planned. *It doesn't look like the diary of someone who had decided to leave. Unless he went on impulse? Was Harrison Peer impulsive?* It didn't fit with Theo's image of him. *But then there was what Haswell and Shrimpton had said, about his lack of regard for other people's feelings and the needs of the students.*

The estate manager's, 'Are you done here?' broke through his musings. The man obviously had other places to be as he ushered them out of the office and relocked it.

'At least we know he isn't in there bashed over the head by the complete works of Shakespeare,' said Shilling as they walked towards the reception. 'Or even his own opus magnum.'

He was glad to hear some levity in her tone.

After dropping Shilling back at the station, he parked his car at his house and walked the fifteen minutes to Sea View Lane, though it was just across the road from the university where he had spent the majority of the day. He needed the exercise. It was another balmy evening. The air was filled with the scents of gardens: privet and mown grass sweetened by honeysuckle and hyacinths. Turning the corner, he saw the end of Sea View Lane as a rounded shoulder against the darkening sea and sky. A lone gull drifted into view, a grey tattered ghost tossed up by a giant's hand.

The interview, *if you could call it that*, had to be conducted around Oli's evening meal. Theo happily kept the toddler entertained while Aurora chopped, cooked and pulped and then equally cheerfully spooned the resulting mush into Oliver's eager mouth.

'You're good at this,' Aurora said, busying herself with tidying and preparing a bottle of formula. 'He never takes it as easily from me.'

'Plenty of practice with my nephews and nieces. And babies are always more fussy with their mothers, testing the boundaries.' He had heard the slight edge of resentment in her voice and wondered whether he should make more of a mess of it. 'So, tell me about the premiere.'

She admitted, rather sheepishly, to having slept through most of it and to not having seen 'the face'. In response to further questions, she said she didn't know Professor Peer and had only met Dr Shrimpton and Felicity Pritchard that evening. 'Sorry, not much help am I? Has he finished? Here, you can give him a yoghurt if you like. And you've got some carrot on your tie.' She was distracted, in a rush, the only brief pause in her movement came when he'd asked about Professor Haswell. Then she said, 'I'm doing a course with him. I'm enjoying it. He's good at what he does.'

At which point Max crashed in and, delighted to find Theo there, offered him a beer, saying he fancied one himself.

'Theo's on duty,' Aurora said sharply. 'And you can take your son upstairs, bath him and get him ready for bed.'

Max seemed about to protest, then with a lift of his shoulders and a smile he whisked Oli away.

The kitchen was getting hotter; the dishwasher whirred. Potatoes, oiled and speared, were now baking in the oven, while Aurora sorted through a pile of washing to go in the machine. There was an element to her which reminded Theo of his mother. Perhaps it was her skin, the colour of a ripe acorn; or her long dark hair twisted up off her neck; or the way she stooped and separated out the clothing. *You're doing fine,* he wanted to say. Instead he ensured his parting hug was extra firm.

'Is that how you end all your interviews Detective Sergeant Akande?' she said with a laugh, pecking him on the cheek.

It is a relief, therefore, to now be ensconced in the sitting room of the house next door. The walls are still a bright yellow, but the cabbage-green sofa and chairs have been temporarily upholstered with wheat-coloured throws and pastel-lemon cushions. The dark-brown rococo-style occasional tables have been banished, replaced by an oval pine coffee table. A couple of Kandinsky posters have supplanted the old-masters reproductions in heavy frames. Ben had brought in drinks before returning to cooking something tomato-ey and herby in the kitchen. The Dixie Chicks were playing when he arrived. They have just finished singing *Not Ready to Make Nice* and Hannah turns the player off. For a moment there is hush. Theo feels the tension in his neck ease. He sips his wine, it slips down easily. He could dismiss all thoughts of the day and the questions it has raised, sink into a welcome doze. *Only I'm not quite finished.* He opens his eyes.

Hannah, curled up in one of the armchairs, is regarding him, her hazel eyes intense. 'Should we leave it for another day? You look bushed.'

He shakes his head, 'It would help me to get your perspective on things.'

She's surprised, 'It would? I'm not sure I have anything useful to say.' As she obliges, she describes the atmosphere of the premiere so he can taste it. He can hear her slight indecision when she talks about the dynamic between Dr Shrimpton, Felicity and Professor Haswell, as she names them. 'I would say there was a jostling for attention, I can't be certain who wanted whose, a strange threesome.' She leaves a space, as if again weighing up whether to add anything, before explaining how she'd been drawn into the film, so much so she was initially certain it was Professor Peer at the window. 'But it can't have been, can it?'

'You know him?'

'Seen him, once, at a seminar given by Dr Shrimpton.' She goes on to talk about the verbal sparring which occurred there.

'Academic debate?'

She shrugs, 'Maybe. Only Clare ...' She scrapes at her lower lip with her teeth, 'Well, it did seem more ... more personal.' She sits forwards, searching his face, 'It couldn't have happened, though, could it? I mean Professor Peer going over with the house. It's not possible.'

'I don't know.'

'If you know how, you'll know who – DL Sayers. The crime writer? The house was apparently on its way over, but how could you be sure it would go over when? And how could you lure Professor Peer inside at just the right moment?' She shakes her head, 'No, he must have gone off somewhere, that's the rumour, over at the uni.' She smiles, 'Ben brings me the gossip.' Another pause. She offers him a drink, ready to bounce up and get the bottle from the kitchen. He refuses, she's got a glass of juice, he doesn't want to make it harder for her. Finally she sits up, her feet planted on the floor. 'Have you heard, I mean is there anything from, news, I mean, from DI Wiltshire.' Her voice is none too steady.

'Sorry, no.' His precarious mood takes a dip, the words of the song they'd just been listening to come to mind.

'What did she want from me?'

'I really wish I could tell you,' he has the disconcerting feeling that he is looking into a child's eyes, a hurt child's eyes. It punches into his chest. He looks away.

'Is it because you don't know or you can't tell me?' Receiving no definitive answer, she continues, 'If she's making connections, between Dad and those others, then maybe, you know, someone will go to court. I'd like that. I fantasise about it, you know, them being in court, hearing the word guilty. Stupid.'

He puts his glass down and gets up swiftly, goes over to her and puts an arm around her narrow shoulders. 'Not stupid. Not stupid at all.'

This time the quiet is punctuated by Ben singing tunelessly with the radio and the clatter of crockery being put down on a counter. Theo can feel Hannah breathe deeply under the palm of his hand. She stands up. 'Sounds like dinner is nearly ready. Go and see if Ben needs any help will you? I'll be with you shortly.' And she is gone, leaving the fragile feel of her on his skin.

Ben greets him warmly and they both set the table by the French windows into the garden. Hannah returns, more composed. She's brushed her bronzed curls into a large green enamelled grip at the back of her head and made up her eyes with some gold-dusted shadow, added some red to her lips. She relaxes during the dinner as the chat moves easily from music to books to films. With Ben by her side, paying her affectionate but discreet attentions, she becomes bubbly. *Happy, even?*

As she makes coffee at the end of the meal, Ben's mobile rings. He checks it, then answers. The conversation is curt: 'Hello Maya.' 'No, I'm busy.' 'No.' 'Alright I'll ask her.' When he finishes, Hannah says, 'What was that all about? She wants money?' The indulgent smile on her lips doesn't quite reach her voice.

'She wants to have her anorak back.'

Hannah picks up the tray and leads them back into the sitting room. 'Anorak? What anorak?'

This question goes unanswered and their pleasant after-dinner coffee and conversation is truncated. It is interrupted by the noise of the front door being shoved open and banging against the hall wall.

Hannah is on her feet, startled, 'What the ...?' She rushes out of the room, Ben and Theo quickly following her.

Theo recognises Hannah's brother, Stephen, immediately, it takes him a minute longer to fit the apparition in the hall with his picture of Hannah's mother. Short and stout, the woman is the right shape, only the rolls of fat are too obvious. The hair which clutches at the edges of the crown of her head is too thin and the blonde dye too cheap. The make-up — bright green around the eyes, scarlet across the cheeks and mouth — has been applied by a five-year-old. And the clothes are a mismatch of baggy slacks and a washed-out sweatshirt which is tight across the chest.

Val Poole is immobile, barely over the threshold of her home, only her eyes skitter back and forth and the folds of flesh around her chin wobble. The person dominating the scene is Stephen. Solid, tall, his square scalp brushed over by a beige gauze, his pupils diminished to hard nail heads by the lenses of his glasses, he is fleetingly nonplussed by having an audience. He drops a holdall and a black plastic rubbish sack on the floor, announcing to the spider who lives in the coving above the staircase that his mother is returning home and this is her luggage, adding it has all been laundered by his wife. He gives his mother a tentative shove on the shoulder. She lurches a little way further into the hall.

He's holding out a letter, he says it is from their father's solicitor. 'I'm contesting it, of course, it is all nonsense.' He looks as if he might fling the slim white envelope onto the floor, then he yells, 'Take it, take the bloody thing.'

Hannah goes towards him and he thrusts it into her hand when she is an arm's length away. She comes to a halt, for an instant they are caught in each other's stares. Theo can smell the anger emanating from Stephen, it radiates into air already made dense by Val Poole's perfume.

Now Stephen turns abruptly and strides out. The front door is slammed. After a moment they hear a car door getting similar treatment and the throaty roar of a large engine being brought to life and revved before Stephen drives away. Then there is silence. Or it feels for a moment as if there is silence, such is the chasm left behind. Slowly Theo attunes to other softer traffic noise, and the guttural laugh of a seagull from the outside, and inside to the wheezing of Val Poole.

Finally she shuffles, her arms out, taking her daughter into a sagging embrace. 'It's good to be home,' she mutters.

Hannah remains stiff and then steps back. 'I didn't know you were coming.'

Finding herself unheld, Val droops, she says sulkily, 'I didn't know I had to ask permission to come back to my house.'

'I, I didn't mean that,' Hannah says peaceably. 'I just meant I would have got things ready for you, if I'd known.'

'So what,' her mother says sharply, looking from Ben to Theo. 'You've got lodgers in?'

Hannah half-laughs, 'You know Ben and Theo, Mum, they're only here for the evening.'

'Then they might as well leave. I didn't invite them. This is still my house.'

'I didn't say it wasn't.'

'And Stephen says you won't be able to do anything about it.'

'I don't know what—'

But Val is on a roll, she steps up to her daughter, bringing her portly body and her flabby face in close, says sharply, 'And another thing, I know you've a lot to say about your father, but I don't want to hear it, you understand me, Hannah? I don't want to hear it. Stan was my husband, he was my life, I loved him. And he loved me. Don't think he needed anyone else but me, because he didn't. Are you listening? No one's going to take any notice of your lies, not once dear Lawrence writes Stan's biography and puts it all to rights.'

Theo can see the emotions of defeat and anger meshing and tangling in Hannah's face and through her body. *She's going to hit her.* He readies himself to intervene.

But it is Ben who walks over and says firmly, 'You mustn't talk to your daughter like that, Mrs Poole. Come away, let me take you and your luggage up to your room.'

She appears about to protest. *But she doesn't know how to defy a man.* Her posture slackens, her voice is a whine, 'I am tired, and I could do with a sip of tea, perhaps a little sherry.' She allows herself to be manoeuvred towards the stairs, Ben's hand on her back.

He tells her, 'I am going to take you upstairs where you can lie down and then I am going to phone Rose to come and help you unpack and get settled.' He now has to assist her up, step by step, to the next landing.

Theo sees the scowl on Ben's face as he turns the corner in the stair.

'Well that fucked up our evening,' Hannah says, hitting out towards the wall but not making contact.

'Do you want me to stay?' The sense of well-being the dinner had brought has been shattered, he is more than exhausted.

She manages a grin as she shakes her head. 'Best not, you might have to arrest me for matricide.'

He reaches out and touches her cheek, it is taut, teeth clenched. 'Call me if there's anything I can do.'

Her fingers which briefly grip his are cold. She nods. 'I'll be alright with Ben and Rose. Don't you worry.'

As he collects his coat and lets himself out, he hears the Dixie Chicks' *Not Ready to Make Nice* on again and cranked up loud.

CHAPTER 18

Friday 21 May

It starts with an argument over the ironing. Though, of course, it is not about the ironing, at all. Aurora can hear her voice become querulous. She can hear her mother's voice coming through. She is reminded of teenage arguments over untidy bedrooms, over lack of application to schoolwork, over lack of attention to various aging family members. Still she cannot temper the voice, it keeps on clanging forth. Her words are reasonable. *How can Max think it's OK to do his own shirts and leave everything else to me?* If only she could say them in another tone. At first he ignores her, which only encourages the voice. Then he grumphs a bit, he's been busy, he's been chasing jobs, he's doing it for her, and their son.

Oliver is sleeping upstairs. They're in the kitchen. The French doors are open, letting in the slight breeze from the verdant garden. Thank goodness they still have Rose to keep it in trim as well as do the basic cleaning. *Thank goodness we have Rose full stop. She was there for me during those awful months, after Oli came along.* Even over a year later, Aurora doesn't quite know how to explain or describe those months. The warping of reality, the strangeness of it all, it still catches her by surprise and makes her want to dig herself a hole to hide herself in. *I'd have not got through without Rose, without Hannah.* And yet, knowing all this, Max has recently begun saying they could save money by letting Rose go.

This Friday, she has taken the day off and he has been prevailed upon to do the same, to get the house straightened out. He has been emptying the dishwasher, tidying away and wiping surfaces; but only since Aurora put up the ironing board and suggested he got off his backside and did something useful. He's having difficulty finding a place for all of the plastic dishes and utensils needed for preparing and serving his son's meals. Max is shoving them in the cupboards where they aren't kept, hoping his wife won't notice. She does. She snaps at him. He pushes the last of the fluorescent bowls on top of their best china and slams the cupboard door shut. Unbending, he finally comes out with it. 'If you weren't so obsessive about Oliver, you'd have more time.'

The words lash at her. *You're a fucking awful mother, Aurora.* He'd said it to her once. He'd been overwhelmed. She'd been ill. She's come to accept this definition given by her GP, her parents and her network on Facebook. However, Max's words are never far away, they sit in the ether between them, and sometimes they become solid again. At times like these. They'd always argued, but those words have added poison. Her hand wobbles as she puts the iron down. *How dare you? How dare you say that?* Her arm winds round her abdomen. She recalls making a similar movement, protecting her unborn child, or so she thought. She'd cried then, dry heaves. She won't cry now. She becomes still.

Max eventually notices. He leans back against the pine kitchen units, crosses his arms, looks at the tiles on the floor between them. Aurora can hear the fluty peeps of the birds in the garden. Oliver's snores come through on the baby monitor. She can smell the bin which needs emptying. A job she'd asked Max to do last night.

'What do you mean?' Her voice is now dangerously level and quiet.

He takes a moment to respond, perhaps weighing up his options. 'I just think you don't have to fuss about him quite so much. He's old enough now, he doesn't have to get everything immediately he wants it. He can learn to wait.' He appears to gather some strength from this last thought, he looks up. 'It would be good for him to learn to wait.'

'This is about the other night, isn't it?'

His gaze drops, 'I think we don't need the baby monitor with us all the time, not anymore. He's got a good set of lungs on him, we'd hear if there was a problem.'

Coitus interruptus, a baby monitor, one of the best kinds of contraception there are. She'd be laughing if the anger hadn't invaded her. 'Anything could happen to him. Toddlers hang themselves with their bed clothes. They can't scream out then.' *I've been through so much to get him safely thus far, I'm not taking any risks.*

'And what about us, Aurora? When are we going to get any time together, just the two of us?'

'You're so desperate for it, you'd jeopardise our son's safety?' Her tone is as hard as her ossified insides.

'Don't be ridiculous Aurora.'

'Me being ridiculous?' The shriek of a lioness at a predatory incomer.

Max thumps the counter top, 'You're impossible.'

His complexion, always florid, has reddened. Aurora can see the flabbiness around the chin, under the eyes, the blonde thatch is no longer as full, as rakish, as it used to be. She registers her aversion.

They might have stayed like that, two statues caught in a petrified tussle, if the baby monitor hadn't come to life with a lustful 'Mama, Dada' from Oliver. Both his parents look at the plastic contraption as if it has landed there from some other world. Neither moves. Their glares meet each other. Aurora is pulled one way by the sound of her son's voice which is becoming more plaintive and in the other direction by her desire to prove something — her sanity perhaps — to the man across the room from her. The tugging is cementing the knot under her sternum. *What now? What now? Who blinks first?*

Max does. He stalks out of the kitchen and hurries up the stairs; it's not long before she can hear him comforting 'my big boy' and their son's grizzle turns to giggles. She listens to them both moving about above her and tries to finish ironing her blouse, only she puts in more creases than she takes out. She's turned off the iron and has begun to investigate cupboards and fridge to make them all lunch when Max returns carrying Oliver on his hip, their son's chubby arms locked around his neck. Aurora feels a stab of jealousy. They're both dressed for the outdoors and Max tells her he is taking Oliver out to his sister's where he can have a run around with his cousins. 'Why? He gets to see them most days when he's with your mum.' *And what about me? What about what I want?*

'And he loves it. Don't you old chap? We should think about getting him into a nursery, he thrives on company. We'll be back later.'

'Nurseries cost money,' Aurora yells at the closing front door. Then she wails, uselessly, at the partially ordered, empty kitchen and at the half-finished ironing. She feels limp, tired, wants to curl up in the bed until their return. *That'd teach him. Spoiling my day off like this. Let him see how hurt I am. Let him feel guilty. For a change.*

By the time she's eaten some hastily put together salad, bread and cheese, followed by a cup of real coffee, Aurora has changed her tactics. *I'll show him I can get on fine whether they're here or not. He won't ruin my day.* She'll go out. She doesn't like the feel of the house now Oli's gone – an aching abandonment – besides, everywhere she looks there's some task half-done, or hardly started, which needs finishing. Doing the chores won't prove Max wrong, quite the reverse. She has a shower and dresses carefully, her favourite turquoise skirt now fits and she matches it with a loose fawn T-shirt and flat sandals. *I don't want to appear as if I'm trying too hard.* She twists her black hair into a coil. She puts her folder and books into a flowery 'bag for life' and checks the time. *I may be too late anyway. And that's fine. I can spend time in the library.* She sets out.

Professor Haswell had designated this Friday between 11 am and 3 pm for his students to have a tutorial about their first assignment if they wanted one. He'd asked everyone interested to make an appointment. Aurora had thought she might until the night of the preview and then she'd decided she could manage without one. Now she hurries despite her warnings to herself and arrives overly warm in reception as Aiden is coming down the stairs. He expresses surprise and looks relieved when she assures him they'd not been due to meet. She adds there's no problem, her questions can wait. She hopes she sounds convincing.

His gaze rests on her, takes her all in. She feels even warmer. He smiles broadly. 'Listen, I've got to get out of here, it's too stuffy on a day like this, and I need to drink a cold beer. I was intending to do this on my balcony. Want to come? It's not far and it's got a good view.'

She appreciates the neatness of him, his unlined skin, his white teeth in his tanned face. She's reminded of the first boy she ever fell for, a friend of her cousin, the summer in Mumbai when she was fifteen. *Why not? Why bloody not?* She agrees.

Haswell's apartment is on the top floor of one of the Edwardian blocks which grace the Esplanade, and his balcony does indeed have a wonderful view across the South Bay to the castle. To get to it, they pass through the sitting room furnished with a well-used chaise longue and a couple of armchairs. Shelves hold books, there is a modern sound system, a wind-up gramophone with a large horn and an acoustic guitar on a stand. On the wall above the small wood-burning stove, there's a large print of a woman dressed as Red Riding Hood glancing coquettishly over her shoulder. The balcony is a narrow space and the two wooden slatted loungers are drawn up close to each other.

Aiden brings out cushions for the loungers. He's decided to make them cocktails and Aurora is left to herself while he busies himself in the kitchen. Little figures populate the beach below the cliffs and a few hardy souls tackle the sea, its surface ruffled by the persistent breeze. Clouds blank the sun by moments. A donkey brays. It reminds her of Oli's enjoyment at being taken to the fields to pet them. As Aiden brings out their drinks and dishes of olives and nuts, she wipes the image of her son's excited face from her mind.

On the way over he'd asked her, 'What's your story?' And she'd told him she'd been born in Scarborough. She'd talked about her parents, GPs, now retired to Cornwall. He'd remembered they'd met at medical school, and she added that her father had come from India to train and stayed for the love of Aurora's mother. She'd explained how they'd settled in Scarborough, overcoming the prejudice such a mixed couple would invoke, becoming well respected by their patients and colleagues. How she couldn't wait to leave, went to Leeds to become a solicitor, only to return, drawn back by the sea. *And the love of my man*, though she keeps this to herself. And yes, downplaying it as much as she can, she admitted to being married with one son.

Now she asks him about himself. He talks freely about his work. He'd briefly been a barrister, but it had always been the academic world which had interested him. 'I like to listen to people's stories, but I don't necessarily want to have to act on them, find the legal device which will solve their problem. I'd prefer to hear about an individual's sense of justice, which isn't always delivered by our courts.'

'Didn't you say your dad was a miner? What got you to decide to be a barrister?'

He smiles a little tightly. 'He did, Dad. After the strike, he didn't want me down the pit, there wasn't much chance of it anyway, the jobs were all going.'

'The strike?'

What had been scenes in a serial on the TV for the nine-year-old Aurora, had been actuality for the fourteen-year-old Aiden. Men – his father, brother, uncles, cousins, neighbours, joined by strangers from other pits – talking about wars and battles and 'not letting the fuckers win'. Everyone was out on the streets, in front of the work gates, all that long hot summer. For the kids like Aiden it was exciting; it was only a small village, a relatively insignificant pit, it was as if the whole world had come to stay. He was forever being sent on errands, to get food or drink, to pass on this message or deliver these leaflets, given coins, which began to add up, for his trouble. 'Me da was short, like me, wiry, not a burly miner like the others, but he was one of the NUM organisers. People treated him with respect.' And young Aiden basked in the reflected glory. 'Then the police turned up one day, just for that one day, it didn't take them long ...' Haswell's voice tails off into silence. The ambient noise fills the space, a pigeon woo-wooing, someone laughing, a motorbike roaring away in the road below.

'To do what?' asks Aurora quietly, her breath held.

His face is as tense as his voice, 'Break it all up. They stormed in. I remember some were on horseback, you had to get out the way quick to miss being struck by the hooves, or the truncheons. No one was really prepared for it, everyone scattered, people got injured, they got arrested. My brother spent the night in a cell. After that day it wasn't the same, the pickets from other places went back to them, some of the men decided to return to work. It was chaotic, messy, everyone argued about what to do, whose fault it was. Me da was injured, a blow to the kidneys, spent a while in hospital. He, he took it all very hard. Stokes he was called, the officer in charge, DS William Stokes. Dad never forgot his name and I won't either. It wasn't as if Stokes was one of those trucked in, he was one of us. Dad spent the rest of his life on the sick. He died recently, eight months ago.'

'I'm sorry.' She wants to reach over and stroke that rigid skin over his cheekbones. She senses that if she did, tears might escape his blue eyes.

He looks into her face at last and grins stiffly. 'It hasn't been easy being his son since the day the police came.'

'He must have been proud of you though, all you achieved?'

He shrugs, 'I'm not sure pride was something he could feel anymore.' He swiftly fills up her glass again without asking whether she wants any more. 'Scarborough was always a bit of an escape from him, to tell you the truth. Dad couldn't be doing with holidays since that summer and, anyway, we didn't have much money. We had some neighbours who came here every year and I'd tag along. It was a bright spot in a pretty bleak time. Maybe it's why I took the job here when it came up. I had better offers, obviously.'

By now the cocktail is beginning to take effect and she's happy for him to lead the conversation away from what is obviously making him uncomfortable. He becomes more verbose, more entertaining, as they talk about his time in chambers and the characters he met there. The shadows come round. Aiden fetches her a pullover which holds his scent, some aromatic and expensive aftershave. Her head is far from clear. When she makes a trip to the bathroom, she glances at her phone in her bag. There are five texts, all from Max. Over the previous couple of hours they have moved from: 'sorry', to 'Oli is having a great time but wishes you were here', to 'I love you', to 'when are you coming home?', to 'the dinner's cold and I've put Oliver to bed'. She reads the last one and her mood deflates. She's always made every effort to be there for her son's bedtime. There's a soreness as she thinks about him tucked in, how he could have been listening to a story she'd made up for him, his long dark lashes brushing his cheeks even as he tries to stay awake to hear the end. She catches sight of herself in the mirror. *Who am I trying to fool? I'm a wife and a mother and boy doesn't it show?* She sees the lines, *no, wrinkles*, collected around her eyes that never get enough sleep and her mouth which is beginning to frown too often. *Come on Mrs Harris, get you home.*

When she goes back out, he offers her more drink, 'I have a fine brandy, a Courvoisier Connoisseur.' She steadfastly refuses. She feels somewhat lightheaded as she leads the way to the front door; in the narrow entranceway she struggles with the Yale. He comes up and twists it the other way. The catch releases. He doesn't immediately let the door swing open. They stand close together. *If I leaned towards him he would kiss me.* It's an effort for her not to test out her theory. She imagines what it would be like to be held against his compact body, there'd be hard edges against her softness. His mouth would taste of cranberry and alcohol. *What would it be like to have sex with someone other than Max? It's been a long time.* Temptation flutters through her. Aiden is on the way to reaching out to her, she is convinced of it, she closes her eyes in anticipation, then she hears, hot breath against her neck, 'What was it you wanted to ask me about your assignment?'

This shakes her out of her reverie. She finds she's leant against the wall. She sets herself upright and grabbing hold of the door, pulls it open. Their hands touch fleetingly, sparking a lurch inside her. *Be sensible, Aurora.* 'Nothing much, it'll wait,' she tries to sound nonchalant, then is ungainly as she leaves. 'Thank you and goodbye.' She walks quickly away, down the stairs and out onto the Esplanade, where the cool air douses the heat in her body. She continues on rapidly, glancing back to see him watching her from the balcony. He raises a hand. She does not, only turns and resolutely forces herself homeward.

Her welcome at home quenches any residual warmth in her mood. Max is sitting watching footie on the TV, a six pack already well on the way to being consumed. He grumphs at her entrance, says her dinner is in the kitchen. She investigates and finds some pasta in congealed sauce in a kitchen which has forgotten it could ever have been ordered. She loses her appetite and returns to her husband. She manages to insinuate herself onto the sofa beside him.

    He draws himself away from her, 'Where have you been?'

    'I'm sorry love, I got carried away researching my assignment, in the library.' *Lying, Mrs Harris? So easily?* Then she remembers how he'd lied to her once, how much it had hurt. Hers is a fib to avoid hurt.

    'Didn't you get my texts?'

    'You can't have your phone on in the library.' She rubs herself up against his rigid arm and side. 'I really am sorry. And thank you for looking after Oliver. You were right, I did need some time to myself. Thank you for dinner, it looks delicious. I'll enjoy it tomorrow.' She kisses him on the cheek.

    'You smell of alcohol.'

    'Don't be silly, where would I get a drink from the library? It's you who's drinking.'

    He grumphs and takes another swig.

She puts his arm around her shoulder and finds his body beginning to loosen against hers. 'I am sorry, Max.' She feels him yield further, she curls up against the softness of his chest and starts to drift into sleep. Guilt comes with the headache in the early hours of the morning.

Chapter 19

Monday 24 May
The station is like the *Marie Celeste*. A number of officers have been called to an incident up the coast on Teesside. A man had been holed up with his ex and two of her children, threatening them all harm. From the police radio reports coming in, Theo is getting the impression of a rapidly deteriorating situation where the harm has been done and a manhunt is in play. DI Hoyle had gone. Theo had rarely seen him so energetic. Ignoring Theo's domestic siege training and experience, Hoyle had taken Chesters, his eager features reminding Theo of a whippet out of the traps, plus one of the other DSs. If the snub hadn't been obvious enough, Hoyle had given one of his little homilies about the force needing a better clear-up rate. 'Go for the bleeding obvious,' he had said on leaving. 'If it smells of pork then it's from the bacon factory.'

And for Hoyle, Jayson Smith's the piece of tenderloin, who'd give it up with a bit of pounding. After a pleasurable weekend not doing much, this Monday morning had been dispiriting enough without Hoyle's sermon. It had started with an encounter with Mrs White. She'd obviously been watching for him, as she was out quick enough when he went to his car. 'I haven't had a chance to thank you properly, for the other night,' she said. She was dressed smartly, her grey hair carefully combed.

There was something about her primness which irritated Theo, even as he smiled and said it was nothing.

'And the other stuff I told you, it was all nonsense, I hope you've forgotten about it.' She patted her set hair nervously.

He paused. 'You mean you didn't buy fake brandy for your son?'

'For my son? No you're mistaken sergeant, I didn't buy it for my son.'

'But you did buy it?'

She shook her head, taking a step in retreat towards her front door. 'My daughter mustn't know, it would be too embarrassing,' she said in a lowered voice.

He pulled the car door open. 'It's part of an ongoing investigation Mrs White, there's others been scammed like you, we can't just drop it. I'll send a PC round, PC Trevor Trench, to get your statement.'

She moved onto her freshly cleaned doorstep, shaking her head.

Her dejection raised a mote of compassion. 'He's very nice, Mrs White, and the likelihood is we'll only use it for background. He'll want contact details for the person you did buy it for, in case he noticed anything useful about the bottle.'

Her response was lost in her flounce into her house and the slam of her door, but Theo was certain she said a name, *'Ade'? 'Ade wouldn't like it'? Trench'll get it out of her.* However, with the mass exodus, Trench couldn't be spared from the station. He had promised to go round as soon as he could. *It can wait.*

As his parting shot, Hoyle had told, *ordered*, Theo to go and talk to Stokes. There had been another letter. Theo would have liked to have taken Shilling, *make it more official*, only she is nowhere to be seen.

Stokes is on his own. 'Some nutter gunning people down, they can't get near him,' he says as he leads Theo through to the conservatory. There is something less smooth about his exterior. His lips are dry. An almost imperceptible twitch draws one corner down then releases it into its grim set line. 'They've kept you at home, then,' he continues, as if talking about a youngster kept back from a school trip because of a sniffle. 'Or aren't you allowed a gun, DS Akande?'

Not the best strategy to get someone to help you: insult them. Theo eases his shoulders into the cushions padding the generous wicker armchair. The sky is grey and a chill breezes in through an open louvre. He hadn't been offered anything to drink. Stokes shoves a plastic pouch into Theo's hands. He notices the tug on the edge of those parched lips and a slight contraction of those flinty eyes, *you're afraid. Afraid some nutter's going to come after you with a shotgun.* A quick skim of the letter tells him it is no different from the others.

'Nothing from the forensics.' Stokes states glumly, he apparently doesn't need Theo to tell him.

'This one's from Carlisle.' *Phil Rattenbury?* He tries the name out on Stokes.

'Bert Rattenbury's son? I know old Bert. He'd always be at the force's Christmas do, come along with his lass, Eunice, quite the looker she was in them days. And he'd contribute generously to the party, back when a grateful public could show their appreciation.'

Bribes?

'Always had bottles of a fine whisky or brandy for after dinner.'

Smuggling?

'If you're thinking of him for this, you're mistaken, we allus got on well.'

Even with the air coming in from the fields around, the atmosphere is leaden. He thinks about what Suze said, and asks, 'What brought you to Scarborough?'

'What do you think? The job, promotion.'

'You didn't get the DI until after you transferred here, you switched for a job of the same rank.' He has an image of waves of police officers confronted by hordes of burly men one long hot summer. Stokes had moved on, or been moved on, shortly after. 'What were you doing in 1984?'

Stokes shrugs wearily, 'I was a DS in the Durham constabulary, what do you think I was doing? We were all drafted in, leave cancelled, to bring some semblance of order. But I was on the fringes, no Orgreave for me, none of the big ones. You're right, I was glad to get away after it all, I have – had – friends and family who were miners, so did our lass. It wasn't easy to be up against them and it was very nasty afterwards. We had young kids, we wanted out, to get away from the unpleasantness.'

'And maybe it's followed you here after all?'

'Twenty-six years on? Why now?'

Theo doesn't have an answer. 'Nothing on social media, Twitter, Facebook?'

'I don't look.'

'And your daughter, her husband, your grandchildren?'

Uncertainty slips into Stokes's tone, 'I haven't asked. I didn't want to worry them, so I've not told them anything.'

'Maybe you should.' His pleasure at knowing he's come up with something Stokes hasn't thought of is tempered by the anxious expression which momentarily flits across the older man's tautened face. 'Why now?' Theo continues quietly. 'It's a good question. Is there any reason you can think of? An anniversary? Somebody out of prison? A reopening of a case?' *Not that Chesters had unearthed anything.*

Stokes shakes his head. 'Don't you think I've been over and over everything, asking myself those things?' he snaps.

'I don't know what else to suggest, we don't have much to go on, or rather we have too much to go on.'

'I hope you don't use that line with your other victims, I don't think it's what you might call best practice.'

'I'm being honest. If you'd prefer me to flannel, I can do that too, Bill. I thought you'd want the truth,' Theo responds firmly.

'What I want is for this to stop.'

'I want that too.'

After a protracted moment, amusement flickers into Stokes's eyes, 'At least we're batting for the same team, Theo.'

Theo holds the other man's gaze, he is not going to flinch, nor is he going to join in the joke. He has that sense again of a bridle in the corner of his mouth being yanked. As Stokes accompanies him to the door, he slaps Theo on the back, asks where the lovely DC Shilling might be that day, adding, 'Now she's someone who should be watching what she's doing on Facebook.'

Suze comes to find him as he is tucking into an over-filled cob at the desk used by the DSs. She smiles at the mess he is making and finds him some paper napkins. She looks round, 'It's the *Jessie May* today.' He gives her a questioning glance and she clarifies, 'The ghost ship which runs up and down this coast, no hands on board. Supposedly. It's seen when a storm's a-brewing, or, mostly, after there's been too much beer swilled in the harbour pubs.' She hands over a message she's taken that morning. She could have emailed it to him, he's glad she dropped by instead.

It's from a jeweller in Birmingham. After throwing away the last of his lunch, Theo gives him a ring, slipping into his childhood accent as the conversation continues. His quest for the Peer diamonds had found its way to the jeweller. He'd been offered them about a year back, by the owner, a Mrs Caroline Peer. 'I remember her name, that's how she was, im-peer-ious. I didn't take them, she wanted too much money, I'm only a small outfit, but they were beautiful necklaces, I was tempted. I would have had them reset, the jewels were first-class. I did wonder why she'd not gone to one of the big boys, in London, that's what I told her to do. She seemed …' A hesitation. 'Seemed pretty desperate.' And there is more. He is convinced he'd seen them since, online, on another jeweller's website. He'd tried to track them down before calling, but hadn't been able to.

'You saw them online recently?'

'No mate, musta been six months ago, a bit more.'

Without Hoyle there to tell him to do 'summit more useful', the phone call gives Theo the impetus to check over what's been gathered around Harrison Peer's disappearance. Dr Denver had sent in all the outtakes from his film and Chesters, not without complaints, had reviewed some of it. He'd been working backwards from the moment the house collapsed and had realised the times embedded in the film were not continuous. There were hours missing which were not covered by the sections edited out.

He had not had the time to properly catalogue all of them nor to talk to Denver about it. Theo starts a list of questions to put to the lecturer.

Dr Denver had brought in the objects he and his students had salvaged and Harry had listed them: various light fittings, a metal bolt, a Formica shelf, a broken ceramic pot painted with an Alpine scene, a (miraculously unscathed) snow-globe of Scarborough castle. It's not clear they all came from the house, some may have been washed up onto the beach from elsewhere.

Trench had interviewed some of the residents at Knipe Point. Nobody had seen anything on the sixteenth of May, though someone did say they thought they'd seen a gardener working around the house the day before. The description is familiar to Theo; a white man in his mid-thirties, around five foot seven, short mousy hair, sturdy, 'built like a builder'. And he used a white van. Trench also talked to council workers who had been the first on the scene, though after a tide had already been in. They talked about splintered wood and bags of concrete which had split and solidified. Theo adds to his notes.

Then there is the work DC Shilling did when Marta, on Mrs Peer's instructions, telephoned over Professor Peer's travel plans. He had taken a taxi to the station Sunday afternoon, that much had been verified, and his ticket on the 4.47 train to London had been used. Harrison's photo had been circulated to the station staff and the British Transport Police, but no one had come back with a sighting and Theo wonders whether much attention has been paid to the request, *it's hardly high priority.* Whatever else he may have done, Professor Peer did not go to the hotel. Nor has he been in touch, despite the request from his wife, *if she did text him as she said she would.*

If you know how, you'll know who. Theo isn't in the habit of taking advice from long-dead crime writers, *but why not?* He reaches for the phone and finally tracks down a civil engineer at the council. She tells him: 'Those houses are essentially wooden boxes, they have no foundations to speak of, once enough of the box is out over the cliff, very little would encourage it to fall, a couple of sacks of concrete would do it.' After a short pause she carries on in a more musing tone, 'The cliff face had stopped moving back though. Dr Denver rang the other day to check and I told him, he seemed a little annoyed by the news. But the cliff had definitely stabilised. The house had not reached its tipping point. It would have needed a nudge of some sort.'

'A push from behind?' asks Theo.

'Maybe, though the force needed would have been more likely to flatten it. No, destabilising the cliff face would have worked better, it would have been more dangerous as the result would have been more unpredictable, but that's what I would have done. You wouldn't need much, one of those small rotavators would do it, you can hire them very easily, you know, they can be used for heavy gardening and such.'

Theo now has his questions for Denver. He decides another phone call will suffice. He regrets it, the artist is distracted, there's a lot of noise – music, shouting – in the background. When Theo asks if the volume can be turned down, Hal says it's his students working. Plus Theo can't see Denver's facial expressions, he can only hear where the pauses come. Hal is quick to say the bags of concrete are nothing to do with him. The first pause comes when Theo asks about the breaks in the timeline on the film. 'I don't know anything about it, I didn't take much notice.'

I thought that's what artists do, notice?

'Maybe it had something to do with those cameras being nicked? Once someone knew the system they could hack in, I suppose.'

'Why?'

Another pause. 'A joke?'

Denver takes even longer before denying any knowledge about the gardener. When Theo asks him if he's ever hired a rotavator, his tone turns sharp. 'My purpose was to explore randomness, what happens when nature takes over. I was hardly going to undermine that, was I? Now have you finished, sergeant? I have to get back to my students, we're preparing something for the festival, in Edinburgh.'

Theo lets him go. Assuming her return to work won't be too far distant, he shoots off an email to DC Shilling asking her to track down the boys who stole the cameras and quiz them what they did with them. He adds a reminder for her to tell him what she's found out about the link between Felicity Pritchard and Jayson Smith. Then he asks Trench to check who hired a rotavator locally the couple of days before 16 May.

He's about to turn to his notes on bootleg brandy, when a call from the front desk tells him there's someone here to talk to him about a wedding ring he'd found metal detecting at Knipe Point.

CHAPTER 20

Tuesday 25 May

'She needs to learn to put a stopper in the waterworks.'

'Suze, it's not like you to be unkind. No one asks to be bullied.'

'If you don't want to be fried, don't wear batter,' Suze's tone takes on the heavy vowel sounds of the local accent. Then her navy eyes soften. 'You be careful, Theo, which boat you hitch your lobster pots to right now. Hoyle'll be gone soon and everyone says you've a good chance of taking over, that'll be your opportunity to make change, don't scupper it for the sakes of Ms Shilling.' Despite this warning, Suze has nevertheless alerted Theo to Harry's predicament. She delivers the red-eyed DC from the ladies toilets into Theo's care, ushering them both towards a local café.

Here Theo learns how Hoyle (positively bumptious on his return after the bloody end to the manhunt on Teesside) carpeted Shilling that morning for bringing the force into disrepute. A photo of the young woman had been posted on Facebook early that morning; it's a close-up of her dressed in a low-cut top holding a sheet of paper on which is written, 'Hoyle wipe my arse'. In it Harry is laughing, she looks drunk. She admits she was. The photo is tagged 'DS Shilling out on the town'. She disputes this. She'd been at the house of a WPC who she is friendly with, there'd been the WPC's brother, his girlfriend (neither of them police officers) and Chesters. A group of young people who'd drunk too much and who'd begun to mouth off about their bosses in their various lines of work. It was the WPC who had written on the paper, Harry had merely held it, for a moment. She does not remember a photo being taken.

'Who could have done it? And who would have posted it? We're all friends,' her voice wails and she hiccups back a sob.

And how did Stokes know about it, apparently before it had been posted?

The others are avoiding her, she's tainted and it could be catching. Chesters, in any case, has been subdued since his trip north with his DI. Hoyle is still deciding what action to take. Theo provides tissues and doesn't tell Shilling what an utter plank she's been. *Watch your back, you always have to watch your back.*

She wants to take the rest of the day off sick, but he won't let her. Being told he needs her for his visit to Mrs Peer brings some resolution back into her stance, into her face. Even so, her brief return to her desk to collect her things is done at a scamper, eyes not meeting anyone else's, a nervous rabbit determined not to see the gun barrels pointing her way.

* * *

It's like a layer of skin is missing, her nerves are revealed. The tinny music from the amusements is too loud, the sugary smell from the doughnut stall too cloying, the pink T-shirt emblazoned with 'I'm his bitch' on the ample bosom too vibrant. Then the baby's cry cuts through it all and saws into her gut. She wants it to stop. She knows if she looks round she will put the evil eye on the child. Knows she will put her hand across the bloody scar of its mouth and smother it. *Bad girl. Your fault.* She is sitting on his lap. Screwed there. Cannot get away. Evil in her veins. Evil in her DNA.

'Can you tell me something of what is going on for you right now, Hannah?' Izzie's voice reaches her, it is not raised, not strident, yet it is firm.

Hannah looks up into her therapist's face, the freckles rampant across the fulsome nose, the amethyst earrings dropping below the silver and wheat hair. Hannah does a survey of the features carefully, rooting out any sign of disgust to latch on to. It's a difficult task, but Hannah is an expert at it and is rarely defeated. *It's not true, Izzie doesn't hate you*, she tells herself. She tells Izzie about how she is affected by a baby's cry and the rage it engenders. Rage against the child: for crying, for being hurt, for being comforted. Rage against the perpetrators of the hurt. Rage against a world where a baby cries. Rage that would split open the blue dome of the sky, allowing the seas to drain into the cosmos.

She expresses it. Izzie makes some sense of it. Again. And still Hannah fails. She fails to hold on to the rational explanation for very long. She falls back on the scripts she absorbed long ago. 'You must get immensely frustrated with me,' she says. 'I do.'

Izzie grins. Hannah knows what she is going to say, 'Be kinder to yourself, you're dealing with a lot at the moment.' Hannah remembers saying similar things to clients she'd had when she was training. *I could say it to them, and I meant it, but I find it so hard to say it to myself and mean it.* She's been thinking of seeing clients again, has set up a meeting with her supervisor, to discuss it. *Am I ready? Am I really ready?*

She talks some about having her mother at home. How they manoeuvre uneasily around each other. How they squabble about what's unimportant. How Val is beginning to do odd things, like putting her keys in the fridge and the milk in the under-stairs cupboard. How she has frightened off with inappropriate comments the couple of Women's Royal Voluntary Service colleagues who had ventured over to see her. Rose has finally stepped in, persuading Val to get an appointment with her GP. And underlying all this is Hannah's desperate need to be sure how much her mother knew, how much she sanctioned, how much she ignored. That discussion is off-limits. *And soon it may be impossible.*

She mentions Aurora's obsession with Aiden Haswell, maybe she's having an affair? Hannah can't say why she brings it up, except she's used to not censoring her words with Izzie.

The other woman's expression is quizzical. 'What's the significance of this for you?'

Hannah shrugs. 'I don't trust him.'

'What is it about him you don't trust?'

'He's full of himself, controlling.' She surprises herself with this assessment and adds, 'But then I only met him a couple of times, so what do I know?' After a pause she says quietly, 'I just don't want her hurt.'

Hannah glances at the clock. Only ten minutes to go. There'd been a time when the therapy hour had appeared interminable. *I can't imagine it now.* She's been talking about Lawrence and she feels sad. There's been some warming of relations, though, irritatingly, Lawrence has urged her to be more patient with her mother. *It's not how it was. Does everything and everyone have to change?* 'It's like this thing, this terrible thing that happened to me, that my father did, to me, keeps on leaching out, corrupting it all, sullying everything. And I opened the gates. I let it escape.' *My fault.* 'Does it ever end? Does it ever stop?' She glances up from her grappling hands. Her vision is hazy. Izzie hands her a tissue. Hannah mops her face, grasping at breath, 'I want to make it right. Return things to how they were.'

'This is not your responsibility. Give the responsibility back, to your dad, to his so-called friends. Don't hold on to it. How is it benefiting you to hold on to it?'

'I don't know.' She pauses in her ministrations, suddenly confused, *another thing I've got wrong?* Through the window, clouds the colour of bruises are slipping into view. The green-clothed arms of the trees are moving oddly, trembling, as if being groomed by chilled fingers. Hannah stares at the still misty view of her therapist's face. *Tell me, tell me the secret of how, how to keep breathing.*

* * *

I only want to make sure he gets it. Aurora is aware she is selling herself a line, has been selling herself a line since sneaking from work early. Leaving her assignment at the university reception would be quite sufficient and, indeed, there are dire warnings in the course handbook about not following procedure when handing in work. She's always been one for procedure (even her teenage rebellions were slight) but something more weighty has superseded her habit of following the rules and kept her feet carrying her in the direction of Haswell's flat.

The Esplanade gardens are ablaze with colour – delphiniums, lupins, irises and a remaining few slack-lipped scarlet tulips cluster around the stunted palm trees. The purple buddleia droops languidly into Aurora's path, its flocks of butterflies briefly rising as she passes and then settling back into its scented tips. But the late afternoon shadows stretch themselves out, bringing a stilling coolness after days of warmth. There's the taste of rain in the air.

Aurora doesn't have to get herself buzzed into Aiden's apartment building as there are some residents sitting enjoying a drink on the lawn in front; when she says who she is here to see, they let her in. She is, of course, imagining their meaningful glances. She takes a moment to smooth her appearance in a large ornate mirror in the entrance hall. Then she forces herself to go slowly up the carpeted stairs and arrive at the third floor unhurriedly.

There is a delay between her ringing the bell and the door being opened. *Maybe he isn't in after all and his neighbours were wrong.* As she is about to push the bell button again, the door is pulled back a margin. When he sees who it is, Aiden doesn't (as Aurora had imagined he would) grin and invite her in, instead he blocks the gap with his body and smiles cautiously. He is wearing cut-off jeans and a cotton shirt. No shoes. There is an unironed quality to him. His dark curly hair is more unruly than usual and he has the air of someone awoken from sleep.

She begins her explanation, continuing to hope he will take her to sit on his balcony, give her a drink, talk with her in that intimate way once more. On the contrary, he says she needs to take her assignment to the university, follow the guidelines in the handbook. His tone is blank. His face is blank. Then she notices a figure behind him, a tall woman. She catches sight of a square-ish face, of dull blonde hair. It is the voice asking who it is which clinches it for her. The woman is the one who had been with Haswell at the film preview. Not the dusky beauty, the other. Aurora can't remember her name. She can, however, recognise when a man is attempting to shield one woman from another.

Plus, she's aware that Aiden's house guest has emerged (dishevelled) from his bedroom. Aurora is being described as 'one of my students'. Her skin burns.

She flings a perfunctory goodbye over her shoulder and stalks back the way she has come, rushing as fast as she can past Aiden's neighbours. They watch her go as they decamp inside, the breeze becoming more of a bluster. She can feel their gaze on her spine, she straightens it and juts her chin out, keeping herself moving fast. Thunder cloud claws its way across the brow of Oliver's Mount, a thick dark cloak spreading out from its shoulders. Various derogatory terms flash through her mind. *I'm no idiot, I read the signs correctly, he's a low-down, two-faced rat. He'll regret making a fool out of me.*

* * *

Caroline Peer is looking frailer and older. She slips the ring onto the finger where its twin sits, staring down at it. 'You say it was found on the beach at Knipe Point, where the house went over the cliff?'

Theo nods.

'And you think this means my husband is dead?' She jams the ring across her knuckle. 'You're wrong, detective sergeant.' She raises her gaze. 'Harrison isn't dead, I'd know if he was.'

'You've heard from him recently?' asks Shilling.

'I told you, I heard from him on the seventeenth, which is, I believe from the papers, the morning after the house collapsed.'

'And not since?'

She shakes her head.

'We haven't heard from him either,' says Theo. 'You did ask him to contact us?'

She nods. For a moment she is lost, she is bereft.

Briefly, Theo feels sympathy for her. He says gently, 'Tell me about the diamonds, Mrs Peer.'

'He took them,' her voice is flat, as if she is saying something learnt by rote.

'You tried to sell them a year ago to a jeweller in Birmingham and he saw them several months later through another jeweller's site on the internet. You'd already sold your diamonds before the burglary, which you now say your husband staged. What were you doing? Hoping to hide the fact you'd already got rid of them or claim the insurance on them in addition to having sold them?'

'Harrison took them,' she repeats in the same tone, but she cannot hold Theo's gaze and she twists and twists the rings. 'I'd really rather you went now,' she mutters.

'Were the insurers making a fuss because the diamonds weren't in the safe-deposit box?' asks Shilling. 'Is that why Professor Peer had to go off with them? But then how were you going to get any money?'

Then Theo remembers Hannah and the local history book she'd been copyediting, 'Misused and forsaken. You can claim the money your ancestor left to women in your family who are "misused and forsaken".'

Caroline glances sharply up at him and he knows he is right. *At last, at last something gives.* He ploughs on despite the scare he clearly sees in her watery pale eyes, 'So it's all been a set-up, Mrs Peer. The burglary, the disappearing diamonds, your husband leaving you? All for the money?' He takes in the sumptuousness of the room again, *some people can't get enough of the stuff.* 'Where is he? Your husband? You don't know, do you? You can't be sure.'

'You can go now.' Though her voice is growing in stridency, Theo hardly hears her.

'But you didn't organise all this yourselves, did you Mrs Peer, you and Harrison? Money can buy lots of things. Who did you pay to help you?'

'I said will you please leave.'

'Let me guess, the name Rattenbury mean anything to you? Robbie, Felicity, or Phil?'

Caroline is on her feet, her fists clenched, arms across her chest, her face the colour of dusty chalk. 'I said go.'

Theo is abruptly aware that Shilling has shifted towards him, a frown deepening, 'Perhaps we'd better, you know, leave it for now, sarge? Mrs Peer has asked us to go.'

The heave of energy which had brought him thus far dissipates and it is an effort not to sink into the armchair. The room is cold. The tall woman in front of him is rigid with fear. *What am I doing?* He stands, 'Mrs Peer, please think again about what you are telling us and if there is anything more you can add, then please do so.'

Caroline's head twitches sideways.

'We need the ring back, Mrs Peer, it's evidence.'

'Evidence of what? Evidence my husband has left me?'

Shilling gets to her feet, she touches Theo's arm, 'I'll sort this, sarge. You see if Marta is around to come in with some tea or to get the fire going or something.'

Feeling slightly chastised, but pleased to be away from the unyielding Mrs Peer, he goes in search of Marta through the door at the back of the tiled hall. It leads him down a short corridor to a kitchen. The warmth, the rustic colours and the smell of bread baking assault him, lifting his spirits. Marta is there washing and chopping vegetables. When he says her mistress is in need of some support, she immediately wipes her hands and is about to follow him out, when she stops. 'You are police?' she asks, her accent rounding out the vowels.

He nods.

'There are big problems here, I don't know what to do,' she fiddles with the end of the long dark plait which curls onto her shoulder. Her eyes are dark above sharp Slavic cheekbones. 'My husband tells me to say nothing, otherwise there will be trouble for us.'

Theo wonders whether he can offer any guarantees, he hopes the couple are here legally. Finally he says, 'If there are problems, it's best to tell the police, in this country.' *Best for whom?*

There is relief in Marta's voice as she explains, 'My husband and I, we like it here, Mrs and Professor Peer, they are kind, a bit strict, but kind, and fair. And they love each other.' This is said with a passion which catches Theo off guard. Marta continues, 'Only Mrs Peer, she can't stop herself, on the internet, all the time, gambling, all the time, all the time. She promises she will stop and then she doesn't. She borrows money, more money. At first she tries to hide it from the professor, but she cannot, she cannot keep anything from him. So they make a plan, only it doesn't work so well, the insurers aren't going to pay anything. And they make another plan. Only I don't think that works either. The money-man is back. Mrs Peer is very afraid.'

'She is, Marta. Do you know who the money-man is?'

She shakes her head, then when prompted, gives a description of a man in a white van which is becoming all too familiar to Theo.

'You'd better go into Mrs Peer, Marta, she needs you. Here's my card, if you hear about the money-man coming again, please phone me.'

She nods and brushes past him. Shilling is already in the hall and they let themselves out. Harry's frown has not completely disappeared. Once they are sat in the car, Theo says, 'OK, DC Shilling, what is it?'

After a pause, she says slowly, 'I thought you went in a bit hard on her, sarge.'

The clouds have darkened. They are chafing against the rounded hill tops, then they are sliced through by a narrow white line and they growl in protest. There's an instant, a suspension, before large drops of rain begin to splatter on the windscreen. Theo clips on his seatbelt, 'I was right though. The Rattenburys are somewhere in the mix.'

They don't speak as Theo drives towards town. He uses the time to turn over what he knows, the connections he can be sure of and what to do next. He assumes Shilling is doing the same until she says, her voice stretched tight, 'Can you drop me in town? I'm going home. I have a headache.'

Oh yeah? Don't do this, Harry, don't run and hide. Though he has to admit to himself he's done the same. A mysterious stomach bug when he started as a DC at Manchester after some drubbing or other. *I can't even remember what that one was about.* But he does recall the fear of failing, the yearning to disappear. He'd told his mum he was rethinking a career in the police and she'd kindly and firmly told him he would do no such thing. He glances over at the DC making herself small in the seat beside him. He wants to do for her what his mum did for him, only realises he has neither the skill nor the relationship. Finally he chooses to say decisively, 'OK, but first you can tell me whether you got anywhere with the link between Felicity and Jayson or with finding those boys who stole the cameras.'

She mumbles, 'Sorry, should have typed it up by now.'

And what she tells him has him returning to the police station with a renewed gusto. On his desk he also finds a report from Trench on rotavators hired locally on 15 May.

CHAPTER 21

Tuesday 25 May

The arriving summer has been buried in a soggy shroud of grey. Despite the vigorous wind blowing up from the deserts, the fossil-coloured sea lies unruffled at the base of the cliffs, its only movement is a placid sway. It is untroubled by the meteorological turbulence above. Hannah arrives home as the intermittent drops of rain begin to organise themselves into a bead-curtain.

She'd spent the last hour with Clare Shrimpton, in the lecturer's office. Clare had asked her, *summoned me*, to … what? Ostensibly it had been to discuss something about her chapter, a minor rewrite the editor had requested, but that had been a mere transmission of information which Hannah didn't need and could have been accomplished via email. However, then Clare quickly began to talk about Harrison Peer. 'Aiden says Peer's gone, left his wife. It's what she says, isn't it? It's what the police think, isn't it?' They were sitting on the comfy chairs, their knees almost touching. It was warm. Clare was agitated. Hannah was taken back to when she was counselling, the sense of intimacy, of shared confidences. *But I'm not Clare's therapist. I don't have to listen.* She was caught between wanting to, *to prove I can*, and being nervous, *what if it's too much for me?*

The other woman was waiting for an answer. When Hannah said she didn't know what the police believed, Clare looked down at her clasped hands. 'It's the only explanation they can possibly accept. Aiden says it is.'

You don't seem so certain. The words formed themselves in her mind. She holds them back. *I should leave.*

Clare suddenly expelled a breath, 'You know about these things, Hannah, with your training, what humans are capable of, below our civilised coating.' She gave a short laugh, 'It's what obsesses writers too, especially crime writers, I shouldn't be surprised about what we can do when pushed. And Harrison, lord, he knew how to push.'

This time Hannah did not check herself, though she was unnerved by the compulsion to ask, 'What did he push you to do?'

'Me?' Clare glanced up. 'He stopped me, stood in my way.'

For a moment, Hannah was entranced by Dr Shrimpton's dark eyes. Then she noticed the faint worry lines which contracted at their edges, and there was a spot scraped to a scab on the side of the otherwise flawless face. 'What's troubling you?'

The laugh was more prolonged though no less mirthless. 'Nothing, nothing is troubling me, except a colleague has mysteriously disappeared, and it's, it's getting to me, not knowing.' She stood up in one fluid movement and walked to the window, a frame for the clouds skidding past. 'I thought it could have been to do with me, him going. I even thought he'd maybe, you know, staged the whole thing, to get back at me, make me feel bad. Or maybe he really had gone over. Suicide. I told the police that. Aiden made me see I was letting my imagination get the better of me.' The wind rattled the pane of glass. She turned back, with an almost convincing curving of her lips, 'Did I say his publishers have been in touch, want to talk about a possible project? Good news, huh?'

Hannah nodded uncomfortably. She got to her feet and started to put on her coat and hat. She debated with herself before finally saying, 'If you know anything, about Professor Peer's disappearance, you should talk to the police.'

The nascent smile was stillborn. 'I don't know anything, Hannah, it's why I'm so upset. I want to know what has happened, we all do,' there was a metallic timbre to her tone.

Hannah had been glad to get out of there, to escape the cramped, febrile atmosphere and breathe the chilled air outside.

On her way home, she considered telling Theo about what Clare had said. *Is it relevant?* But then her mother consumes all her attention. She finds Val Poole, agitated, in the middle of trying to bake a cake, under the misapprehension that Stephen and Veronica are coming for dinner. Cleaning up the kitchen and her mother, Hannah does her best to calm her down and feed her something nutritious, before (guiltily) supplying her with sherry and sleeping tablets and persuading her to go to bed to watch TV. *Can I not leave her alone in the house for even a few hours?* The urge to sob – perhaps for herself, perhaps for her mother – collides with the urge to scream and kick the hall wall. In the end she does neither, her phone rings. A commanding voice announces it is Caroline Peer wanting Hannah's help in preparing her husband's opus magnum for publication.

Chapter 22

Tuesday 25 May

Lawrence had been dubious about his plan, 'Can't it wait until daylight? Mightn't this suspect be dangerous?' Theo isn't in the mood for caution. There's something about a gale blowing in from the sea which invigorates him. The 'crazy-making wind' as Suze calls it, fills the cells at the station. The hefty rain plummeting on the windscreen gives him a sense of being in a small boat braving the elements.

The Rattenbury's yard is lit by a sole bulb on the outside of the warehouse. From the warm cocoon of his car, Theo can see the office is in darkness, but the large storehouse door is ajar and there is a yellowy glimmer to the interior. *I could just drive away, leave it, for now. Take Lawrence's advice. For once.* It's not fear which gives him pause, but uncertainty whether this will produce the results he desires. Then the wind buffets the vehicle, as if intending to throw him out into its clutches. His resolution solidifies, *this way I'll catch him off guard, get him before he's prepared his story.*

In the sprint from car to the warehouse door, Theo's clover-coloured linen jacket becomes soaked through, and his determination is strengthened by annoyance he'd let the earlier summery weather trick him. Inside the threshold he stops to wipe the lenses of his green-framed glasses. The clatter of rain on the metal surrounding him confuses the direction of any noise; even so, he thinks he can hear someone moving about at the far end of the cavernous building. Bert, Robbie or, his quarry, Phil?

He begins to move forward, quietly. On either side of him is tall shelving holding a variety of building materials, including, he notices, bags of concrete, the same make that were found on the beach below Knipe Point. *Significant or standard fare?* His sight lines are limited. He thinks he is going towards the sounds of human activity, then the whole structure around him shudders, slammed by a blast and a ricochet of icy rain which echoes around, until he can't be certain again. He stops. Tries to orientate himself.

'You lost mate?' the tone is unfriendly. And behind him.

He turns round quickly, his oxygen intake abruptly accelerated, he touches a cold metal shelf to steady himself. For a moment, it's as if they are both held in stasis, weighing up the potential dangers of the other. Then Theo, his respiration once again under control, introduces himself.

After a beat, the other man reciprocates, his tone flat. *Wary?* Of the twins, it is Phil who has inherited the most feminine features. His face is narrower than his sister's, his mousy hair finer. He is tall like her. He has the muscles built up by his kind of work, however he's not got the spherical stockiness of his father or elder brother, and his pale skin, already reddened by sun, is clean of tattoos. He takes Theo's proffered warrant card. Most people barely glance at it; Phil inspects it before handing it back. 'You've been talking to Dad and Fliss,' his voice remains measured.

'And now I'd like to talk to you, Mr Rattenbury, if you've got a moment?'

He shrugs, crosses his arms.

The lack of heating in the building, combined with his wet clothing, is beginning to chill Theo. He'd like to sit down. He realises he is less in shadow than Phil. He wonders if they are alone or whether there are others, perhaps halted in their work, listening. And which scenario would be preferable. 'I didn't realise the Rattenbury empire included gardening?'

Phil doesn't move, doesn't respond, it's impossible to tell how this question is greeted.

'What were you doing on the fifteenth and sixteenth of May, Mr Rattenbury?'

The reply is slow to come, the tone unflustered, 'The fifteenth was a Saturday, I believe I was doing a spot of work for Dr Denver around his house at Knipe Point.'

'With a rotavator you hired? And the purpose of the work?'

The nod and shrug come together. 'That's for Dr Denver to explain, he told me what to do and I did it. It's a bit of business I do for meself. Fliss got me the contact. It's all legit, I pay me taxes.'

'And the Sunday?'

'I went up to Darlington, to prepare a job, with Robbie's boy, my nephew. We were together all day.' A slight hesitation. 'Except he took the van off late afternoon to see a football match. I stayed at our B&B, we met up for one drink when he got back. Exciting life, eh?'

'Do you know the Peers, Mr Rattenbury? Caroline and Professor Harrison Peer?' The wind moans through the shelving. Theo feels as if his spine is being splintered with icicles.

Phil shifts further back into the gloom. 'Professor Peer? Fliss was talking about him. He's disappeared hasn't he? Gone off, left his wife. Terrible.'

Just answer the question. Theo is beginning to think maybe none of this is a good idea. 'Have you met either Caroline or Professor Harrison Peer?'

Phil shakes his head. Theo can no longer see his features clearly. He tries asking him about the dates the bootleg brandy was sold in the pub and to Mrs White.

'You asked Dad about them dates, didn't you? Wusn't he going to get back to you?'

'Can't you remember then?'

Again the delay before replying, 'I was away, most likely. The first date was a job in Leeds, I'm pretty sure. The second one, Carlisle maybe?'

In other words *Cumbria.* 'Do you know a retired DCI William Stokes?'

He obviously doesn't have to think about this one, 'Dad does, or he did, likes to tell stories about the "good old days". Mates of a sort, I reckon.' He takes a step forward. 'Now detective sergeant, are we done? I've got to finish loading up.'

'Do you own a white van?'

'No.'

'Does anyone in your family?'

'No.' No alteration in tone. Phil moves in closer. He is dressed in clean grey builder's trousers with sewn-in knee pads, multiple pockets and a belt ready to receive a variety of tools. A toned physique is visible under his black long-sleeve polo shirt and quilted gilet.

Theo both appreciates it and recognises it as being worked on. *Those fists could do some damage.*

'I think we're done, don't you?'

Phil's warm breath mists in front of Theo's face. He dislikes the attempt to push him around. However, he doesn't think he will gain anything further and would prefer a dignified retreat. 'I'll send PC Trench down to check those dates, so we're all clear.'

'Old Trev? Sure why not, just make sure Robbie's not around.' He laughs as he strides off, calling over his shoulder that Theo should see himself out.

Theo sits for a while in his car in front of the warehouse, the heater on full blast. *Did I learn anything new? Did I make a mistake? In talking to him at all? In what I said?* The questions unsettle him, for a while. Then, as his body thaws, he becomes more sanguine, *I did right to rattle him. Who knows what will fall out.* And Phil lied, at least once, *the problem is, I wouldn't have known when he did, if it hadn't been for Shilling.*

He's about to drive off when his phone rings. It's Pippa Wiltshire. He gathers she's been put on sick leave against her will. 'I was getting too close, too close to what they've been covering up, for years, what they don't want us to know. Men are all abusers.' Her words slur into each other. 'You watch your back, Theo. You and your lover,' she sneers. 'I've heard you didn't investigate Dr Greene's murder enough, didn't accept Hannah as a suspect, because you got involved with 'im. They'll use it to bring you down if you get too uppity, push 'em too hard.'

'It was Hoyle ...' But he knows it's as if he's shouting into a raging tempest. Pippa cuts the connection.

Chapter 23

Wednesday 26 May

By the morning, the storm has blown a sky of glass, stained with diluted cobalt; a high-domed cover for the leisurely sun and the languid waves. Only the sand and seaweed tossed onto the pavement at the top of the beach is testament to the sea's vigour during the night before. The kittiwakes screech and squabble as Hannah hurries under the Spa footbridge. She glances at their nests, clinging precariously seventy-five feet up where stone pillar meets metal strut. One has not survived the gale, the tangle of grass and broken eggshell tipped indecorously onto the ground.

Hannah is eager to see Ben. Their weekend plans had been disrupted by the return of her mother. He had phoned her earlier to say he had a couple of hours spare at lunchtime, and she feels the need for his comfort and for a conversation which isn't fraught by what is being left unsaid. She walks quickly along South Bay beach. A few hardy souls are making camp on the sand, while keeping warm in layers of pullovers and scarves and coats done up to the neck. An extended family have pitched a plot with blankets, towels and bags of food. Some are playing a disorganised game of rounders. Three women, two in jeans and jackets, one in a black niqab, stand at the water's edge, shrieking at the waves.

Hannah passes the stalls selling dressed crab and whelks in little polystyrene pots on her way to the harbour. Here the trawlers, pulled in from their deep-sea hunting grounds, smell of oil and rotting fish. Two seagulls do a flat-footed paso doble, their wings grey capes, screeching at each other to lay off the scraps from the boats and from the Styrofoam boxes discarded by people. The breeze plays with the cleats on the tied-up yachts, tapping out a metallic castanet rhythm.

Ben's house is on one of the small streets that rise steeply from Sandside. Once the dwelling of a fishing family, it is narrow, no floor or wall is straight or at right angles to any other. Hannah lets herself in. The front door opens straight into one elongated space which incorporates a living room, with crammed-full ceiling-high bookshelves, at the front and a kitchen at the back. In the middle, spiral iron steps lead to the floors above. The ceilings are low enough for even Hannah to consider ducking. She pauses, adjusting to the more subdued light. A clatter of crockery tells her Ben is in the kitchen. A movement from one of the armchairs by the metal wood-burner tells her they are not alone. *Maya? What is she doing here?*

Ben interrupts Maya's greeting by coming up to Hannah, kissing her briefly on the cheek and saying, 'She's just going.'

What was she doing here in the first place? Don't tell me she still has a key.

'My neighbour let her in.'

'I haven't finished my tea,' Maya says sulkily. She has curled her legs under her, is wearing tight jeans and a bulky jumper, her dark hair, streaked with scarlet, is pulled away from her elfin face, which is clean of make-up. 'Anyway, Hannah will be interested in my news.'

Will I? Ben takes her coat to hang it up, returning with a denim jacket. He tries to give it to Maya and she lets it drop to the floor.

'Five minutes, Maya,' Ben mutters, resuming his preparations in the kitchen.

'You'd be proud of me, Hannah,' Maya sits up a little straighter. 'I've been working so hard, you wouldn't believe, I've almost got enough to join Dad in France, for six months. I need to get fucking outta this shithole, get somewhere with a bit of fucking life.'

Hannah perches on the edge of the sofa, *why do you think I would be bothered? I came here to be with Ben.* She directs a portion of her crossness towards him, *why don't you do something?* Yet despite herself her attention is captured by the younger woman's chatter, because of one name: Aiden Haswell. He visits the miners' convalescent home, especially, according to

Maya, when she's on shift. 'Thinks he's a bit of a dude,' she laughs. 'Says he'll come and see me in Nice when I'm there.'

Against her better judgement, Hannah asks, 'What's he visiting for?'

'Says he's collecting stories. Got this thing about some bloke called Stokes, always asking about him. Pretends he's all intellectual, but I don't think so,' Maya giggles and arches her back. 'Hey, I hear you're an heiress, Daddy left you the house. Jammy dodger.'

'It's not settled.' She doesn't want to talk about it. The letter from the solicitor Stephen had flung at her when delivering their mother had explained their father's will gave her the house, while her mother retains a right of residence. Stephen has been threatening all kinds of legal action, saying he should have half the value of the house. She had been about to acquiesce to him when Lawrence had stepped in the previous weekend, promising to try to broker a solution.

'Maya, you still here? We're about to eat,' says Ben. He gives Hannah a glass of fruit juice.

'OK, OK,' Maya stands and pulls on her jacket.

'Is that all you have? You'll freeze.'

Oh don't get her anything. It's an automatic reflex with him. She feels the tenseness in her jaw seep into her neck.

'Here.'

Hannah is only slightly mollified to see it is not the woollen hat and scarf she'd given him as a gift and then has to grit her teeth again as Maya plants a smacker of a kiss on Ben's lips. 'I'm outta here, leave you two love birds to coo at each other.' Then she turns to Hannah, 'I'll be over to pick up my jacket.' She pecks her on the side of her face with warm soft lips.

'What jacket?'

'The one I left at yours, the other night. I need it.' She grips Hannah's wrist. For a second, an alteration passes across her features.

Could it be fear? If it is, it's gone as quickly, and Maya strides out of the door.

Hannah had hoped the younger woman's exit would change the atmosphere in the house, but Ben sounds testy when he suggests they sit and eat at the table in the kitchen area. He's distant, asking inane questions about her mother, about Aurora. *What about me?* His face is pale, jowly around the chin. She can see how tired he is, but there is something else, a crossness, perhaps. *Cross with me?* She touches his unyielding hand. 'Ben, what's up?'

He snaps, 'Nothing. Thought we were having a nice relaxing lunch, that's all.'

She takes another mouthful of goat's cheese and bulgar wheat salad. The dressing is zesty and peppery, 'It's lovely.' She watches him for a moment, *Do I let it go?* It isn't as she had imagined it would be, the easy back and forth, the reassuring hugs. Less than a month ago, at the Beltane celebrations at Rose's, they'd jumped the broomstick together and he'd pressed her tenderly against his lithe body. His treacle-hued eyes had been on her then, not like now. *Eyes I could sink into.* Disappointment wraps itself around her chest cavity. 'Did something happen this morning?'

He shrugs. 'You know I can't tell you anything.'

Do you want me to go? Without a great deal of effort, she would have been out the door. Instead she says slowly, 'I'm sorry you've had a shit day.'

He shrugs again.

His shrugging is beginning to irritate her. *Don't be so fucking petulant. Leaving Mum wasn't easy for me. Don't I get some credit for that?* However, she pulls back from her immediate response. *If I fire off, I'll be the unreasonable one. And I don't want to always be the unreasonable one. The one with 'handle with care' branded on her forehead.* 'Is there anything I can do?' She thinks briefly of Ben's bedroom, two flights of stairs up, in the eaves, with views of

the harbour one way and Flamborough Head the other. *Should I take the initiative?*
Another non-committal lift and fall of the shoulders.
She gazes at him, trying to divine, *Do you want me to stay?* He gives nothing away. *The skills of a therapist*, she thinks overly sourly. She knows he's sat with and listened to and consoled his clients all morning, *yet he can't do it for me. He's got nothing left for me … Enough.* She puts down her cutlery. She glances towards the exit. *Are you going to walk away? When people don't want you, you run after them. When they do, you walk away.* She and Izzie had identified that habit a while back. *Not sensible Hannah.* She goes over to him, pulls him up into her arms, feels the weight of his head against her shoulder. His long chestnut hair is silky against her skin. 'Go and sit on the sofa,' she says. 'I'll make the coffee. I bought cake.'
'Don't move,' he mutters into her ear. 'Not yet.'

Chapter 24

Wednesday 26 May

The storm has left the cells at the station full and DS Theo Akande more disgruntled than is usual. He'd been wrong about Phil Rattenbury. *He's clever.* Rattling his cage may not have been such a good idea. *He'll cover his tracks better, which makes him more dangerous.* Theo realises he's got to equip himself with additional, and more meticulous, intelligence before he makes any decisive move.

He's asked Shilling to gather Trench and Chesters together. They are waiting around a desk near the door of the CID incident room discussing the new interactive board which now hangs on the wall. It had been installed the previous evening, Theo can see the tiny mounds of sawdust on the carpet under the four corner fixings. Chesters is holding court. He has worked out how the panel can be illuminated and how pictures can be uploaded to it and then smoothly moved around. He has photos of Professor Harrison Peer, the Rattenburys, Dr Clare Shrimpton, Dr Hal Denver, even Dr Aiden Haswell, up there and is adding a network of coloured arrows with the light pens. His gelled hair-spikes are perky, he's the most animated he's been since his return from Teesside. As he talks, he flattens his vowels to a vague approximation of Theo's soft Birmingham accent. Shilling notices Theo first and quickly conceals her grin. She pokes the chuckling Trench in the ribs. It is only when those two have turned their gaze to just to the left of his shoulder that Chesters stops and looks round. He drops the pen he's been using and does an awkward bow of his head.

He's scared of me? This is a new phenomenon for Theo. *Crims being nervous at my entrance, yes, but colleagues? Even if they are junior ones.* He makes his smile extra warm. 'You've got it all worked out then?' His voice mocks gently Chesters' broad local accent.

A blush rises through the young man's prominent ears. However, he joins the others in genuine, if sheepish, laughter.

With a touch of a button he clears from the screen the marks he's made and is about to delete the photos.

'Leave them, for now, our rogues' gallery.' Theo sits in a spare chair and puts the files and notepad he has brought with him on the table in front of him. In the next hour they go through everything in pernickety detail. 'Firstly the bootleg liquor. Information from coastguard and customs suggest it could have been brought in with a drug shipment, cocaine from Venezuela, on a yacht. Could have been anywhere up or down the coast. Imitation alcohol is made by and used to fund criminal gangs, particularly in parts of Eastern Europe – Macedonia, Russia. It could have been brought on board the yacht in the Channel. It was probably used to pay off whoever it was who initially landed the shipment. They would have been responsible for passing it onto those who would take it to the cities and the dealers there. At this point this is all supposition.'

'The descriptions of the seller in Scarborough fit Phil Rattenbury,' says Chesters.

'And the Rattenburys have been smuggling for centuries,' says Trench with relish.

Theo reminds himself of the bust-up between Trev and Robbie Rattenbury. He knows in this town, family rivalries run deep.

'And you checked,' Shilling points out, 'Phil Rattenbury was working away on both occasions.'

'He could have come back, in his van,' says Trench stubbornly.

'His nephew was using it and there are witnesses to that. Anyway, the works van is blue.' She pauses before saying rather dramatically, 'But his twin sister's van isn't. It's white.'

'And he lied about that,' says Theo. *One thing which did come from last night's 'chat'.*

'Trev confirmed it, Phil went to those jobs in the works van,' says Shilling.

'Could he have got back to Scarborough any other way?' asks Theo.

'Train,' says Shilling. Then adds, through Chesters' derisive laughter about public transport, 'I checked, it was just possible.'
'Nothing conclusive on CCTV I suppose?'
'I've asked, nothing yet.'
After ascertaining that Trench has not got a statement from Mrs White and reminding him to do so, Theo moves on. 'OK. We have a plausible scenario.' He hears Chesters mutter, 'hardly'. He turns to him, 'DCI Stokes, what do we know?'
Chesters straightens and gives a good review of what he has found out. Which is not much. The suspects are legion, however none can be particularly implicated. 'There are a few who might want, and be in a position to, exact some revenge, but literacy is hardly their strong point. They're more likely to be using their fists or an iron bar. And none of them live in North Yorkshire or Cumbria or appear to have close family there.'
'A dead end,' says Theo.
'Maybe it'll stop with a few nasty letters,' Harry says hopefully.
'We can't pin this one on the Rattenburys in any case,' says Chesters. 'By all accounts, old man Rattenbury was a bit of a mate to Stokes.'
'Too much of a mate, if you ask me,' says Trench quietly.
Chesters looks at him sharply, 'What are you saying?'
'It's not for me to say nothing,' Trev responds gloomily. 'Thems that speak out get it in the neck, so I hear.'
'If Wiltshire's being investigated, it's for good reason,' says Chesters.
'DI Wiltshire,' corrects Theo, surprised by a reverberation through his nerves. He jumps up and pulls the photo of Professor Peer to the centre of the interactive board. 'Shilling?'
'We have Jayson Smith for handling after the burglaries on the seventh of May. We have Felicity Pritchard, twin to Phil, as landlord for the house where Smith resides. We have Felicity owning a white van fitting the description of one seen near to one of the burgled properties. Though, I understand from her niece,

Felicity was conveniently out with pals on the seventh and stayed over with one of them. Her niece was pissed – upset at being left with her grandmother to care for, while her granddad and father were down the pub.

Trev butts in, 'Do we know where Phil was?'

'We don't,' says Theo. He imagines asking, receiving an unruffled response, *and I wouldn't know if it was the truth or a pack of lies.*

Harry continues, 'We have some missing electronic goods, most of which have not been retrieved, and some diamonds which remain missing also.'

'Or were taken by the owner's husband, as she claims,' interrupts Chesters.

'Who may or may not have gone over with the house at Knipe Point,' says Shilling.

'But probably didn't because he took a train to London before it happened and sent a text after.'

'Or someone did,' says Harry, her colour rising.

Theo has the impression they are squabbling pupils fighting over the attention of the teacher. *Me?*

Trench joins in, 'There's eye witnesses put Phil Rattenbury around the house at Knipe Point on the day before the house went over ...'

'He admits he was there with a rotavator,' Theo says. 'It's Denver who denied it.'

Trench continues: '... No one saw anything on the night of the sixteenth, when the cliff collapsed, but then there weren't many around to see much.'

'The recording was mucked about with,' says Chesters. 'Several hours on the Saturday and Sunday certainly missing. Denver says he knows nothing about it, claims it would have undermined "the aesthetic of randomness" he was going for.' The young man's tone takes on an exaggerated poshness which sounds to Theo more like Caroline Peer than Hal Denver.

Shilling is reporting on her discussion with one of the lads who stole some of the cameras from the Knipe Point house a couple of months ago. 'He showed them to Roy Rattenbury, Robbie's son, but he didn't take them once he gathered they were nicked.'

'Still should have gone to the police,' mutters Trench. 'Thick as thieves them …'

Theo interrupts, 'Roy's studying computer aided design at Sheff. With knowledge of the equipment could he have done something remotely?'

Chesters shrugs. 'What are you suggesting? Phil gets the house unstable …'

'On Denver's orders,' says Theo. 'He's not quite as committed to randomness as he would have us believe.'

'… then lures the professor there, in the hope it will go over?'

'He shoves bags of concrete in,' says Theo, 'To ensure it does.'

'But why?'

'To get the diamonds,' says Shilling.

'Which weren't real.'

The others stare at Theo, unspoken question marks on their lips. He explains about Caroline Peer's gambling and how, in her desperation, she got money by selling the diamonds and then through Phil.

'So the first plan,' says Shilling slowly, 'was to get the insurance, but, I'm guessing, having them in the house made that null and void. How did the professor going off with them help, he couldn't sell fake diamonds?'

'A clause in a trust fund created by one of Caroline Peer's ancestors would have given her some money once she'd been "forsaken" by her husband.'

'Phil was recruited …' Harry continues.

'Through Felicity,' adds in Theo.

'… to stage the burglary and then help Harrison Peer disappear. Only our Phil thought he'd get more if he took the diamonds instead. But …'

'… He's ended up with fake jewels …' *How angry is he now?*

'... and a dead professor,' Chesters finishes. Then he shakes himself, saying quietly, 'Crazy.'

'But possible?' asks Theo, genuinely wanting an answer. He gets a shake of the head from Chesters, a nod from Shilling and a shrug from Trench.

'He was working away on the sixteenth,' says Trench, looking back at his notes.

'Darlington has a station,' says Shilling.

'You are kidding,' says Chesters. 'And who went to London and texted Mrs Peer?'

'Felicity,' says Theo. *It's a theory. But is it enough?* He asks Shilling to send the British Transport Police a photo of Felicity and of Harrison Peer to check against CCTV on the late afternoon London train and at King's Cross on the sixteenth of May.

His gaze is drawn to the board. He pulls the images of Phil and Felicity centre and pushes daddy Rattenbury and Robbie to the right side. *Now for the others.* Professor and Mrs Peer come in and, under them, he writes a summary of what they have just concocted. He draws a red line between Felicity and Denver and back to Phil and notes 'destabilisation of cliff with rotavator'. Adding under Phil: 'bootleg brandy, Mrs White & pub'. *Now these others? Dr Clare Shrimpton?* He puts an arrow connecting her with Felicity. *Did Dr Shrimpton ask Felicity to organise a favour for her? Remove a troublesome professional rival? Another payment to Phil and another reason for him to decide to kill?* His finger touches the charming face of Dr Aiden Haswell, he recalls Hannah's words, 'A strange threesome.' Switching to a blue colour he puts in a dotted link between Aiden, Clare and Felicity. Now there's only Stokes, stranded in the left-hand corner. He hesitates. *Nothing, there's nothing.* He puts the pen down and turns back to his audience, almost expecting a round of applause. Instead he gets sceptic expressions, even from Shilling. *I can't act, not yet.* However, it's not in his nature to be able to walk away from something which is not sorted. He sends Shilling and Chesters off to track down and talk to the Rattenbury twins' niece, her of the low-slung jeans and black thong, and their nephew. His discontent is beginning to reassert himself. *I need more, I need more.*

Chapter 25

Wednesday 26 May

'Aiden Haswell.'

She had not thought to hear his name so casually tossed into the conversation, and by Ben. Aurora raises the last forkful of kaeng massaman to her mouth, decides she's not hungry and puts it down again. Things had been going so well, before the mention of Stokes.

Her parents had arrived for a fortnight stay and had immediately prescribed a night off for their daughter and son-in-law: 'Go out, have some fun, see some friends.' They'd even agreed to have Val Poole over. 'Your parents are so kind,' Hannah had said, relief softening her features. 'I can leave her, but ... Your parents are so kind.'

Max had been home early, bringing flowers for her mother and for her. As Aurora and Max showered and dressed, they tenderly touched and caressed each other in the guise of helping to arrange some clothing or fasten a necklace. Before leaving the bedroom, Max swept her up into a strong embrace, kissing her, saying gently, 'You look gorgeous. I'm a lucky, lucky man.'

'Yes you are,' she replied, laughing. *And I'm lucky too, what an idiot to have thought otherwise.*

So far the conversation has been light, amusing, the atmosphere in the Thai restaurant pleasant, the food delicious. Theo joined them thirty minutes ago, full of apologies. He'd been talked into a drink with some work colleagues, including DI Hoyle, *no love lost there,* and someone called Stokes, *where have I heard that name before?* She hadn't bothered to search her memory and it is Ben who supplies the answer, asking Hannah, 'Wasn't Maya going on about someone called Stokes? I know, she said someone was asking questions about him.'

Theo pauses in his eating, 'Who?'

'Aiden Haswell, Professor Aiden Haswell, works at the university I believe,' says Ben.

Max says, 'Isn't Aiden Haswell the bloke you've been on a course with?'

His question sounds innocent. Can he feel the heat coming off her face? Aurora dabs at her lips with the large starchy napkin. The last of her glossy lipstick stains it. She wants to bury her head in it. For a moment, she can't think whether to deny or confirm it.

Hannah breaks in, 'Reckons he's doing research. But here's the thing, did I tell you Aurora? Maya actually working for the first time in her life.'

Aurora knows what it has cost Hannah to mention Maya in such an off-hand way, *thank you, thank you.* There is a slight alleviation of the weight on her diaphragm, but she needs to get away, to collect herself. 'Let's go and freshen up,' she says to Hannah, leading the way.

Briefly Hannah looks surprised then follows Aurora to the toilets. She watches her (unnecessarily) re-pin her hair and then start to repaint her lips. 'What happened?'

'Nothing.'

'What happened?'

Aurora is about to repeat her denial, then she is arrested by Hannah's gaze reflected in the mirror. She has the most extraordinary eyes, a hazel colour, the green flecks more illuminated today. *It would be such a relief to tell her, tell somebody, and I can trust her.* 'Nothing, nothing happened, I was an idiot, imagined stuff, Aiden, he was being, merely being his charming self.'

'I bet. He feeds off people's adoration of him. He needed to prove he could make you adore him. Narcissist.' She grins. 'I can smell 'em a mile off. What you have to remember with a narcissist is the wound they've buried and are trying to find comfort for.'

Aurora stops fidgeting with her make-up, leans a hip against the sink, intrigued, 'What do you mean?'

'There'll be something in his past, left him hurt.'

'His father was badly injured during the miners' strike. Had to stop work. The family's life was never the same again.'

'There you go, he's still trying to find a healing balm for that.'

'And I was a convenient sticking plaster.'

Hannah laughs, 'A very beautiful one.' She gives Aurora a quick peck on the cheek, saying more seriously, 'I'm sorry he hurt you.'

Aurora feels a rush of warmth towards her friend, *thank you, thank you for not giving me the telling off I deserve.*

They begin to walk back to the table, 'I bet he led you on.'

Yes, he did, he bloody did.

'And,' she forces them both to pause, 'you do know there'll have been others?'

Aurora nods. 'Felicity,' she says quietly.

'Felicity? Felicity Pritchard? I thought you were going to say Clare.'

Probably her 'n' all, bloody bastard. Her cheeks are flushed again, this time with anger. *Do I let him get away with it?* They've reached the table, Hannah is asking where Theo has gone. Called away, she's told, to an emergency.

CHAPTER 26

Wednesday 26 May

The full moon is poised out over the sea, a barrage balloon balanced at his right shoulder on his drive out. Now it appears huge above the roofs of the bungalows and two-storey houses and the flat fields. It decants its glow onto the street, creating a silvery day, hours before dawn. Theo finds a PC he vaguely knows stationed by the front door. The crime scene investigators have arrived, so he lingers with the woman on the doorstep to be updated on what he'd already gathered from dispatch. Stokes's wife had called her husband: their home had been broken into and she'd been attacked. The services had been swiftly summoned into action and the ambulance had just left with Mrs Stokes, bruised and very shocked, with the retired DCI in attendance. She hadn't been able to give much information about the intruder; she'd been napping upstairs and she'd only woken when he was already in her room and he'd quickly covered her head with a pillow case. He had punched her. 'She'd gone limp like she was unconscious,' says the PC. 'Meant he left her alone, better 'n if she'd struggled.'

Smart woman. 'Any description?'

'Male. Tall, strong. Maybe mousy-coloured hair. Breath smelt of lager.'

'White?'

A moment of surprise passes over the PC's round face. She nods, though Theo doubts anyone had thought to ask. *At least the crims don't get routinely categorised as black.* When he is allowed into the house, he doesn't need the crime scene manager to tell him the destruction is methodical and comprehensive. 'Whoever it is has been careful,' says the CSM. 'And, despite what it looks like, clean. Our people might struggle to get anything useful once DCI and Mrs Stokes, their daughter, son-in-law, grandchildren and friends have been eliminated.'

Someone who knew what they were doing. Nothing to give themselves away. Access and egress had been through the conservatory and back door, the panes of glass carefully cut not smashed and the lock dismantled. If Mrs Stokes had employed the heavy bolts and chain installed on the door, she might have been saved from being attacked. *Might. And she might have been more likely to if Stokes had told her his real worries about the letters. Maybe.* He stands in the back garden. He can hear the horses in the nearby field moving restlessly in the stall in the corner, their snorts heavy and throaty.

It's getting close to midnight. Even so, Stokes's neighbours, mostly in a motley of nightclothes and outdoor-wear, have been roused by the activity in their street. Theo asks a couple of PCs to begin taking statements, while he investigates the way through the fields with the CSM. Theo has wellingtons in his car, along with the wax jacket, a new addition to his kit since coming to Scarborough. He discovers it would not be difficult to cross the field where the horses are safely penned for the night and reach a path leading to a close on the edge of the same development where Stokes lives. There he meets a member of the neighbourhood watch, summoned to the end of his drive by the flashing lights and the sirens. When he's given a summary of what has happened, the man says he saw a van, a white van, parked nearby, 'Doesn't belong around here.' And he has a registration number. Theo writes it down, he'll have to check, but it appears mighty familiar.

Back at his car, his phone rings. It's Hoyle, he's with Stokes at the hospital, he wants a report, but first he wants to vent. 'This would never have happened if you'd got your finger out, DS Akande. Instead of that poncy professor you should have been protecting one of our own.'

The fault for the crime always lies with the perpetrator. Still, Hoyle's comments nag. *Could I have done more? Could I have foreseen this happening?* He briefly gives his DI a review of what they've got so far.

'Rattenbury? You're sure? Then get him in. Bloody make him squawk. His dad'll be bloody giving us awards, he wouldn't want one of his doing this to Stokes. Don't be caught napping again, detective sergeant. Get on with it.' Hoyle cuts the connection.

It would have been good to have had a proper discussion about the next step, *but not with Hoyle.* Theo doubts Bert Rattenbury would do anything other than stand by his son. *And, in reality, the link we have, a van registration, is with his daughter, Felicity. Could she have done this? Mrs Stokes said a man. Could she have been wrong? Confused? I arrest Felicity I get to look at the van.* It's a good first move. *Have I got enough to arrest Phil? He could run rings round us if not and then we'd have to let him go.* But leaving him out there could mean dangers for others. *If Phil is capable of this,* Theo glances at the house. *What could he do to anyone who's a threat to him? Like Caroline Peer.*

Chapter 27

Thursday 27 May

The plum-coloured skin of the sky is peeled back to reveal the orange flesh. For a moment the scene is stabbed through by lobster hues, the first clawings of the sun's chelipeds on the horizon. It adds a tinge of unreality to what is happening. For a breathless moment. Then the shouting and the banging crashes in.

As well as taking Shilling with him, Theo has mustered a modicum of back-up. It's not like the Tactical Assistance Unit he was used to in Manchester, but one man in a stab-proof vest with a stout tactical entry ram. Plus he has Trench (stationed in the lane at the back of the terrace) and another PC who will also do the follow-up search of the house. In the end, no force is required, only a great deal of hammering on the door and shouting for it to be answered. Felicity Pritchard is dishevelled from sleep, a towelling dressing gown over a cotton nightie, her feet bare. Her face, pasty and loose-skinned around the eyes, sets when she sees who is assembled on her doorstep, her pale lips clamped into a thin line. She declares she is not going anywhere with them and is not letting them in. She waves away the warrant Theo holds out to her, 'I don't care, d'you hear me?' She would have closed the door if the paltry TAU hadn't positioned himself to prevent it. 'I'm going to phone Dad, he'll have something to say about this,' she says defiantly.

Theo agrees she has the right to a phone call and suggests Shilling goes in with her while she gets dressed and then makes it.

Felicity stands for a moment, clutching the edge of the white uPVC, maybe calculating her options, then she lets go and shouts, 'Whatever,' as she stomps off down the hallway.

An hour later, Theo is sitting across the scratched table from Felicity in an interview room. Beside her is Reggie Harvey, immaculately turned out with his trademark dicky bow which today is pin-striped in fuchsia. He had been summoned by Bert

Rattenbury who had arrived in reception shortly after his daughter had been brought in.

Bert had demanded several times to see the 'man in charge', asserting loudly 'our Fliss has done nothin' wrong' and this would never have happened back when 'you lot' (addressing the PC behind the desk) 'were more 'n pen pushers'. Bert was finally persuaded to quieten down, by a uniformed sergeant. They knew each other of old, regarded each other like two fighting cocks. The sergeant asked Rattenbury the whereabouts of Phil, to which he received a shrug, 'He finished a job yesterday morning. He's got the rest of the week off, he's old enough to decide what to do with his time off 'iself I reckon.' However, before convincing Bert to go home to take care of his wife, as 'he was doing no good here', the sergeant had extracted a mobile phone number Rattenbury said belonged to his younger son. When tried it went to an automated message telling the caller the person they are trying to reach is unavailable and to ring back later.

Phil Rattenbury is unaccounted for, proving hard to find. As is Mrs Peer. Theo had learnt from a phone call with Marta that Caroline had gone out early, possibly to meet 'the money-man'.

Theo holds himself steady, showing Felicity any disquiet would hand her the power. He wants all the anxiety to be on her side. He has opted for a PC to accompany him in the interview, having instructed Shilling and Chesters to continue the investigation, and especially to keep him updated on the forensic examination of the van. Felicity had reluctantly directed them to where it was kept, in a local lock-up, and had handed them the keys. 'Ms Pritchard, are you clear on why you've been arrested?'

'Encouraging burglary and an aggravated burglary? Conspiracy? Assisting an offender? I understand the words, but I don't know what they have to do with me.' Her voice is laced with irritation.

Your default setting. 'Could you tell me where your brother Phil is, please, Ms Pritchard?' She'd already been asked this when it became obvious he wasn't in the house with her, but Theo hopes her arrest may persuade her to give a different answer. It does not.

'I told you. I don't know for sure. He went off for the day, on his motorbike, he likes to do that when he's not working. He'll be off over the moors somewhere.'

'And he left when?'

The first time she'd been asked this, at her home, she'd hesitated for a fraction. Now she responds immediately, "Bout half an hour before you lot arrived, I reckon.'

You've got your story straight now.

She continues, 'Am I going to have to repeat everything twice?'

'Tell me what happened yesterday evening and last night. And remember you are under caution.' He's aware of the tightness in his torso as he focuses, and of the anticipation, the thrill even, a hunter finally getting a glimpse of his quarry.

'Nothing much.' She glances briefly towards Reggie. He pauses in his note taking to smile encouragingly. Theo can imagine the advice he's given her, 'Appear helpful, but don't actually be too helpful.' Theo wonders if Felicity is up to the balancing act. She replies staring at a spot somewhere in the centre of the table, 'I got in from the university about five. Phil was already home, he'd finished his job early. He, he'd cooked, pasta. He's a good cook.' The hint of a smile and the softening of tone are testament to the bond between the twins and give Theo a benchmark for when Felicity is telling the truth. She continues to detail an evening in front of the TV with a couple of tinnies.

Mrs Stokes said her assailant smelt of lager. 'What did you watch?'

'The *Star Trek* movie, you know the prequel, when they're all young?' Her gaze flits up and then away again. The window high in the wall shows a blue sky, it might as well be a painting.

'And then?'

'There was a documentary, about the history of the novel, BBC4, I watched it. Phil went to bed.'

'What time was this?'
'Nine-thirty. He was tired, from the job, from driving.'
'And you?'
'I watched the news, went up after.'
Ten-thirty. 'Then what?'
'Then what? Then what nothing,' the irritation is back. She clasps her hands on the table top. 'I slept didn't I? Till you lot gave me my alarm call.'
'And Phil?' He is careful not to change his stance, however he feels his whole attention leaning forwards, the trail is leading to a trap.
'I told you, went out 'bout half an hour before you got there.'
'How do you know?'
'I heard him.'
'I thought you said we woke you up.'
'OK maybe I was already awake, waking up, you know.'
The stuffiness in the room is becoming more evident. 'And before that, did Phil go out during the night?'
'No.'
'How do you know? You were asleep.'
'I would have heard him.'
'Sure about that?'
She glares at him, 'Yes.'
No you're not. He can smell something sharp, acidic underneath her copious layer of perfumed deodorant. He sits back, skims over the notes he has on his pad in front of him, considers which tack to take next. 'Retired DCI William Stokes and his wife Pauline, do you know them?'
'Dad does.' Her hands unclasp and clasp, they leave a damp imprint on the surface they are leaning on.
'Their house was trashed last night and Mrs Stokes was attacked.'
'You said when you read out all them charges. I don't know nothing about it.'
'And Phil?'

'He wouldn't hurt no one.' The words are spaced out. She slumps back in her chair.

Reggie says mildly, 'You're asking my client to speculate, DS Akande. Let's keep to questions of fact.'

'Did Phil have keys to your van?'

'The keys were kept in the house, on a hook in the kitchen, for us both to use.'

'Did you use it much?'

'Not really, I bought it for him. He wanted to start his own business, gardening, handyman.'

And the rest. 'And you got him work?'

'When I could.'

'Like for Dr Hal Denver?'

She nods tentatively. Her fingers are still now.

She's on alert. 'What other jobs did you get him?'

She shrugs.

'Could you say something for the tape, please, Ms Pritchard? Indicate what your shrug means?'

She shakes her head.

'No, you can't comment? No, you didn't get him any other jobs?'

'Don't badger, sergeant,' says Reggie easily. 'Ask a question. And then maybe we could take a comfort break.'

'Did you get him some work with Professor and Mrs Peer?'

She meets his gaze then. *Startled? Or fearful?*

'I said I don't know nothing about Harrison Peer going off.' Her voice is heavy, belligerent.

Definitely lying.

'Comfort break,' Reggie interrupts, before Theo can form his retort.

* * *

The plum-coloured skin of the sky is peeled back to reveal the orange flesh. For a moment the tangerine light lacquers the room.

For a moment, a breathless moment, and then it is gone. Hannah drags herself from a dream in which she is trying to find a corner to hide in a Perspex room. A familiar dream which never ends well. She doesn't want to return to sleep and, possibly, to dream. She lies still, trying to relax. Instead, unbidden, her mother's words from the previous afternoon begin to surface. 'You always was an ugly baby and difficult child. Always demanding. I could never get you to take your bottle nicely, not like Stephen, he was so easy. If one of those misses had taken, we'd never have bothered with you.' That her mother had miscarried before she'd had her was news to Hannah, the rest wasn't. *Wouldn't take my bottle nicely. Did you not think to wonder why, Mother? Or did you know and decide to ignore it? Me. Your ugly baby.* Hannah curls over on herself, a claw scraping at the inside of her stomach.

Val Poole had continued, 'Your stories, they're all fantasies, Hannah. We are a happy family, we always were, your dad took good care of you, of all of us.'

Hannah had been standing at the French windows in the kitchen gazing out. The silvery bark of the aspen was gleaming in the hazy sunlight, in amongst the grass at its base were the remnants of its catkins, white fleshy tongues cut off and discarded. *Stories, our way of making sense of the world. There's life as it is lived and then life as we tell it.* She'd read this somewhere. *There's truth in my fiction and fiction in her truth. More in both than she can allow herself to know.*

She remembers turning to look at her mother, and a quote from a Sayers novel came to mind, about seeing oneself in a distorting mirror. *What is the rest of it?* 'While the voices might have been one voice with its echo.' *I am not like my mother. Will never be like her.* It is this which finally propels her into the office, determined to occupy herself.

She turns on her computer and pulls Professor Peer's manuscript onto the screen. She's read it once and is now picking her way through it more carefully. Apart from the leaden prose, there's something niggling her. As she works on, it becomes clearer what the problem is. *Could this explain his disappearance? His suicide even?*

She wonders whether she should bother Theo with it and decides to check out her understanding with Lawrence first. It isn't quite 6 am. She hesitates. Not long ago, she'd have felt she could have called him whatever the time. The thought she no longer has this liberty temporarily flattens her. *He's been kinder recently, talking to my brother, he won't mind, as long as I don't mention ... it.*

Though it is Lawrence who brings 'it' into the conversation, obliquely. He responds to her call promptly, his voice immediately amiable, and he quickly confirms her suspicions. Then he tells her he'll do as she asked, 'Tell the whole story, of your father, but not just that, there's a much bigger story here.' He's talked to Pippa Wiltshire, Hannah can hear the excitement in his voice. She feels small, forgotten, ignored. *It only becomes valid when someone else tells it.* Still she rallies to assure him she's pleased, *I don't want to lose him again. And he's right, I do want the story told. The story? My story? It won't be my story.*

Trying to hold onto feeling pleased at her competence, *I was correct about Peer,* she creeps downstairs to make herself coffee. As she waits for the kettle to boil, her phone chirrups. A text from Maya. She reads it. *The bloody coat again.* She'd forgotten all about it. Out in the hall she finds a green Gore-Tex jacket she doesn't recognise. In the pocket is a scarf which she does – it belongs to her mother, who only the day before had been making a fuss about losing it. *She'll have shoved it in here by mistake.* Hannah pulls the scarf out of the jacket pocket and a piece of paper falls to the floor. She picks it up. The handwriting is neat, square, it's not one she knows. The word 'PEER' is printed next to several numbers. Immediately she connects this to the professor, *though I suppose it might not be to do with him.*

Her phone rings, it's Maya. Hannah tries to follow, 'What? Slow down. What's happening? Who's Phil?'

Chapter 28

Thursday 27 May

The comfort break has not brought Felicity Pritchard any. Her face is chiselled out of the hardened chalky crust of a volcano, points of lava have appeared on her cheeks. Her neck, shoulders and hands are taut. She's pulled her hair into a tight greasy ponytail.

Theo feels a modicum of compassion, then he concentrates on the job he has to do. The interlude has furnished him with more information. Slowly, he hangs his russet-coloured suit jacket on the back of his chair and sits. He asks again where Phil is and gets a sulky negative rejoinder.

'My client has already answered that one, several times,' says Reggie Harvey, he still appears unruffled, but there's a steely edge to his voice.

He wants this over and done with, soon. Maybe he's a swanky lunch planned, Theo thinks, not without rancour. Unhurriedly, he brings out some photos, 'Is this your van, Ms Pritchard?'

She's sitting back from the table and hardly glances up. She shrugs.

He reads out the registration number. She shrugs again. He says, 'It's registered to you.'

'Must be mine then.'

He pushes another couple of photos towards her, 'We found these clothes in a dumpster next to the lock-up where your van is kept. Are they your brother's?' Grey builder's trousers with sewn-in knee pads and multiple pockets. A black long-sleeve polo shirt and quilted gilet Theo had last seen over a toned physique. 'Take a careful look. These small patches here are blood.'

Despite herself, Felicity is drawn forwards, her eyes widening.

'Careful, detective sergeant,' says Harvey. 'You can't possibly know whose blood at this juncture.'

Sod him. 'Are they your brother's clothes, Ms Pritchard?'

She shrugs and slumps back.

'For the recording, Ms Pritchard indicates she doesn't know. Where were you the seventh of May this year, Ms Pritchard?' He heads off another lift and drop of the shoulders with, 'Think carefully, Ms Pritchard, it was a Friday three weeks ago.'

A glance from her solicitor elicits an answer, 'Out with friends. I stayed ova.'

That's it, give me a crumb, which you think is not incriminating. 'And Sunday the sixteenth of May?'

A slight hesitation, 'I was looking after Mum. Sundays I usually do, so Dad and Robbie can have a night off.'

'Yes, they went and did a spot of fishing and drinking in Whitby.' *Mostly drinking.* 'Does your friend from the seventh have a name? The one you stayed with?' This time the hesitation is longer before she gives up a name, the same one her niece had given when Shilling had spoken to her, the first time. *Not the second time around.* 'You're sure about that, Ms Pritchard? Only Robbie's girl has told us something different.'

The volcano erupts, silently, spilling heat into Felicity's face. Even so, she winds her arms around herself as if she is cold.

'We've been told that on both Friday the seventh and Sunday the sixteenth you were with Professor Aiden Haswell.' After some gentle prodding from Shilling, Felicity's niece's resentment at being left looking after Grandma one time too many came tumbling out. 'Her fancy man, Professor Haswell,' was how she'd put it. Theo continues, 'Then we spoke to Professor Haswell, he said he'd only seen you on the seventh. What were you doing on the sixteenth, Ms Pritchard?'

She takes a moment to form a coherent sentence, it comes out as a stuttering wail. 'I was at home, I needed time to myself. You don't know what it's like, Mum's dying. I needed a break.'

That much, at least, is probably true. Theo notices how bashed down the woman in front of him looks. For a moment, there's a conflict between his impulse to cut her some slack and his desire to know what really happened. Neither wins outright, his tone is mild as he pushes on, 'We have some CCTV of you at King's

Cross station on the evening of the sixteenth of May. You were coming off the train Professor Harrison Peer was booked on. Were you travelling with him?'

'I didn't see him.' She's tense.

Watchful? Anxious? 'We have further images showing you took the next train north. Why did you do that?'

'I, I like travelling on trains. It calms me.' If possible she has wilted further into the corner away from Theo.

'Are you certain you didn't see Professor Peer on the sixteenth?' She nods wearily. He continues, 'We're examining your van forensically, Ms Pritchard, it won't look good for you if we find something which links it to Professor Peer.'

Reggie appears about to issue a caution or maybe a reprimand to Theo, but Felicity bursts out, 'We were helping him, he wanted to get away, needed to get away, something to do with his book, he was going to get into trouble, big trouble, so we helped him. Phil took him to Hull, for the ferry. He left him there. I took the train with his ticket, to cover his tracks. We were helping him. I don't know anymore.'

'And the film, Ms Pritchard, why was Professor Peer's face in the window of the house at Knipe Point if he was on the ferry to Rotterdam?'

'Robbie's boy did it, my nephew, cut and pasted a photo in. Phil said it would throw everyone off the scent. Phil said Professor Peer agreed to it. Phil said the professor wanted his own back, on the others, his colleagues. Phil thought it a laugh.' She doesn't sound convinced. 'We were helping him, Professor Peer, and he texted his wife after the house went over.'

'You did that, Ms Pritchard.'

She shakes her head. 'No it was him,' she says in a small voice. 'We were helping him.'

You're lying.

'I think,' says Reggie slowly. 'Ms Pritchard has answered everything satisfactorily. She has an alibi for the burglary on the seventh. She and her brother were merely assisting Professor Peer in his machinations ...'

'Which could have led to fraud,' butts in Theo. *His wife collecting on her trust fund.*

'You'll have a hard job proving Ms Pritchard was aware of any fraud on the part of Professor Peer,' says Reggie, as his client shakes her head despondently. 'And last night Ms Pritchard was at home with her brother. I see no reason to hold her further.'

The solicitor looks like a man expecting to get his way, *he must know Felicity is going nowhere while we've still got time left to question her and before the forensics from the van have come in.* 'There's one more thing you can assist us with, Ms Pritchard. Did Professor Peer pay you anything for helping him?'

Reluctantly she says, 'A bit.'

'How would you define "a bit"?'

'Expenses, paid for my return ticket, some petrol.'

Her tone suggests to Theo that she's telling the truth. *But then why? Why help someone you didn't like for little reward? Unless it helped someone you do care for.* Phil is the obvious answer, only it's the image of Clare Shrimpton at her most stunning which comes to mind. Hannah's words re-occur to him: *'A strange threesome.' Stick to what we've got,* he cautions himself. He pulls out another photo, of an evidence bag full of notes, 'Five thousand pounds is a lot for expenses. We found this in your brother's room.'

Again she is drawn to lean forwards. 'Must have been for a job, a building job,' she says quietly. 'Or ...'

Or bootleg brandy? Or burglary? Or GBH? Or maybe some heavy-duty gardening? A knock at the door interrupts them. Theo swears mutely, but leaves Felicity, a smidge slack-mouthed, staring at the photo. He finds Shilling in the corridor, Hannah is here. His immediate reaction of an irritated 'What does she want?' is silenced when he is told she has news of Phil Rattenbury.

He returns to collect his files and close down the interview. As he watches Felicity being led away by the WPC he thinks, *You have a little think about the money. No one likes to be double-crossed by a brother, especially not by a twin brother.*

CHAPTER 29

Thursday 27 May

Theo is vaguely aware of the benign May day outside the police station: the warm air tickled by a light breeze; the sun in the blue sky, its arc now clear of roofs, causing windows and windscreens to sparkle. He has summoned up Chesters, Trench and his TAU officer. They are in the other unmarked car a short way behind. If Hannah is right and Phil really has 'got' Maya, they don't want to spook him, but, equally, they need to be prepared. It's possible Phil's capacity for violence goes beyond using his fists.

Hannah has insisted on coming with Theo in his car. 'I know exactly where she is, it'll be quicker than explaining.' Sitting tense beside him, she explains about Professor Peer's book.

As Theo drives rapidly across the Valley Bridge and then left onto the Esplanade, he clarifies, 'You mean when an extract from another book is used, permission has to be given by whoever wrote it originally?'

'The person who holds the rights, it could be the author or maybe another publisher. It can get a bit tedious sorting it out, I've done it for Lawrence's books in the past. I don't know if Professor Peer was being cavalier with his referencing or forgetful or ... I don't know what the word would be, deceptive, I suppose – appropriating the inventions, the creations of others, and passing them off as his own.'

'Is it serious if the permission isn't sought?' He has to slow to allow a dog and its owner, both equally stiff-legged, to reach the pavement.

'It can be. The rights holder could potentially bring a civil case which would cost money. But it's more that this could be plagiarism, pure and simple, and that would be disastrous for both Professor Peer and the publishers in terms of reputation. I wonder what led him to even contemplate ...' She glances to the side, 'Stop, we're here.'

He pulls the car in to the kerb. All he can see are leafy tree crests beyond the railings at the top of the cliffs which fall from the roadway to the sea. Hannah is reaching over to let herself out of the car. Theo clamps his hand on her arm, 'You're going nowhere. It's not safe.'

She tries to shake him off her, 'I still need to show you where, then I'll hang back, let you get on with it.' Her green-flecked-with-gold eyes hold his gaze steadily. He lets go of her. He barks some instructions into the radio; tells Chesters to follow, discreetly, keep them in view. Theo is led by Hannah through an arched gateway in the balustrade down several steep rickety paths, right, then left, then right again around over-grown plots. With the luxuriant bushes and the beeches with the girth of an adult elephant's limb, the cliff gardens offer plenty of hiding places. *Too many.* The adrenalin keeps Theo's blood pumping, his muscles and his senses primed.

Crack! A twig snapped in half, perhaps under the heel of a boot, then three pebbles bounce erratically down from the path above. Theo halts in the lee of a bush. He pulls Hannah back towards him. He listens. All he can hear is Hannah's ragged breathing. He has his arm wound round her shoulder and across her chest. He can feel the heightened pace of her heart. A slight tremor judders through her frame and he is reminded of her fragility. 'It's OK,' he mouths into her ear. He tries to extricate one sound from another: Hannah's exhalations, now slowing; the shu-ush of waves on the beach; the breeze rustling the leaves. *Is there something else? Someone else? Is there?*

Crack! Another twig is snapped. More dislodged pebbles and grit. Theo readies himself to spin round, his clenched fist set for smashing across Phil's jaw. Then a branch in the hebe beside them bends erratically and a squirrel launches itself to land spread-eagled against the trunk of a nearby tree, looking down at them nervously as it clings on with its four claws.

Hannah releases a quiet snicker as she leans into his embrace. 'You OK?' he whispers.

She nods, 'Come on.'

Without discussing why, they both move slowly, quietly, crouching over slightly for several more metres, then Hannah pauses and points forwards. Before them and below is a sun-drenched emerald dell shielded on all sides by wind-sculpted hawthorn, blackthorn and rowan. At the grassy centre is the body of a young woman, stretched out on her back on a blanket, honey-coloured flesh exposed by the bikini top and shorts she is wearing. In the seconds it takes for Theo to compute the scene, Hannah has slid beneath the railings and onto the grass, calling out, 'Maya, Maya.' *No, stop … Rattenbury could be … Hannah, wait …* None of the words quite make it out of his mouth before he realises the injured, possibly dead, body is sitting up, stretching, is fluidly getting to her feet.

'Have you got it?' is the first thing which issues from her pert lips.

'For fuck's sake, Maya!' Hannah berates. 'I thought you were in danger, I was really scared for you and you're lying here fucking sun bathing!'

'What have you brought him here for?' The last time they'd met, Maya had been seductive, she's not bothering now, she looks sulky.

'I thought you were in danger,' says Hannah. 'Phil Rattenbury. You sounded scared.'

'I can handle Phil, I just need me bloody jacket. Where is it?' Maya's voice is harsh, she drags the blanket around her.

Like she doesn't want eyes on her body. This once. 'I've got the coat, Maya, it's evidence. Now you can tell me where Phil Rattenbury is.'

She turns on Hannah, 'You gave him the jacket? What you want? You want me fucking dead.' She lets go of the blanket and lands a hefty swipe at the side of Hannah's head, who staggers backwards, swearing.

'OK, OK, enough.' Theo grabs Maya and pinions her arms down. He's aware of Chesters arriving with the others. *The cavalry*, he thinks, finding an essence of comedy in what's happening. He indicates to them that he can handle the situation, tells Trench to check on Hannah and administer first aid if necessary, then positions the youngster he is holding so she has no option but to look at him. 'Right, Maya, I will keep you safe, but I want you to tell me where Phil Rattenbury is and I want you to tell me now and without any more argument, do you understand?'

She squirms, even tries to kick out at his shins, and then seems to lose energy, tears collect in the corners of her eyes. *Real tears?* They roll down the side of her nose which is also beginning to dribble. *Yes.*

* * *

At what point did I think this was a good idea? She could have been taken back to the station with Maya or gone home. *I could have been having a cuppa.* Instead her eye socket is beginning to ache. *The bitch has given me a shiner.* And she's skulking around on the top of an exposed cliff at Knipe Point where the breeze is brisker. *I could have been warm. And safe.* The moment in the gardens when they had stood together, Theo at her back, his arm around her, and they had seen the squirrel and shared the joke, had made her brave. *Too brave. I wanted to show I could be brave.* She isn't feeling brave anymore. She wedges herself into the corner formed by the metallic corrugated wall of a caravan and the wooden steps going up to its door. There is no one at home here nor, it appears, anywhere else on the site. She knows Theo, Trench, Chesters and the other officer have spread out and are slowly, methodically, searching for their fugitive.

A fret is beginning to roll up from the sea. A massive white paw is anchoring itself onto the cliff in preparation for pulling up an opalescent giant from the deep. Hannah begins to shiver robotically, she has to grit her teeth to stop them from chattering. Soreness digs into the side of her face.

The giant's fingers let loose two figures. One is a man, tall, muscular, fair, striding forwards, confident. Stumbling beside him is an equally tall woman, long-faced, her grey hair cut short. Having escaped the giant, it could be the man is guiding the woman to safety, or maybe he has her elbow gripped to prevent her from escaping. Hannah cannot tell. She can hear an otherworldly careening. Is it the woman or the giant? She is drawn out of her hiding place towards the couple, they might be puppets performing, the fret some theatrical effect. She moves closer. She hears her name being called from behind her, but maybe it is a quirk of the atmospherics. Maybe it is the man who is summoning her. She's almost there.

Hannah sees more clearly now, the brutality in the man's face, the terror in the woman's. She stumbles again. The man drags her to her feet. Again. He sees Hannah. Halts. They are hardly two arm-lengths apart. He takes a dull-looking flat handle from his pocket. He holds it out to Hannah. *A gift?* She's about to take hold of it when it acquires a blade. *No, no I mustn't.* The sharpness slicing her skin, it is too enticing. She steps back and back and back, not daring to turn and run. From somewhere she gathers inside herself and then volleys forth a bellow. It echoes inside her throbbing skull. It stuns the man for a millisecond. It's loud enough to scatter the molecules of the giant's hands.

* * *

'He's got a knife,' Hannah had screamed. Only there is no sign of it and Phil surrenders without a fight. When Theo begins the litany of charges and then rights, Rattenbury grins, 'I was only trying to help Mrs Peer, she'd got lost in the fret, couldn't see the edge of the cliff, she'd have gone over without me being here.'

Theo fastens the handcuffs behind Phil's back, ignoring the other's cheery, 'No need for those mate.' Theo says quietly, speaking very close to Rattenbury's ear, 'I've been having a nice little chat with your sister this morning. She's quite a talker when she gets going.' Then he lets Chesters lead Phil away, enjoying the slightly perturbed glance thrown back at him by the arrested man. *Chew on that.*

'Theo.' Hannah is at his side.

He turns to her, 'You OK?'

'Not really, but I'm more concerned about Mrs Peer. She's wandered off that way.'

They walk quickly. The mist is thinning, however they still can't see clearly. Theo recognises the path and the abandoned bungalow, they are approaching where Denver's house went over. Theo remembers the yawning gape of the cliff edge, the soft earth forming a steep, continuously shifting ramp to the rocks below. 'Mrs Peer?'

A few paces more and they see her, perched on the toothless lip. *Too close.* He checks his impetus to go forward and grab her, and puts his hand on Hannah's arm to bring her to a halt. 'We don't want to startle her into slipping,' he says in an undertone. 'We need to assess what's going on for her.' He senses Hannah's acquiescence rather than sees her nod, as he keeps his attention on the woman perched on the edge. 'Mrs Peer, it's DS Theo Akande, how about you step over here?'

Caroline is wearing a light-coloured pullover and slacks, she melds with the fret. She has her arms wrapped round her flat chest. She speaks to the horizon, her voice taut, 'It's my fault, all my fault, what a fool I've been, losing all our money, then borrowing and borrowing and losing it all again. Trusting Phil Rattenbury. Now he wants what he calls interest, said I tried to dupe him with those diamonds. Said did I think he was that stupid? Though Harrison paid him the five thousand we loaned. What a fool I've been. We had plenty, more than enough, and now we have nothing. It's all my fault. Harrison's gone and it's all my fault.'

Theo feels Hannah shift her balance forward, he tightens his grip on her, she stills. He continues conversationally, 'It doesn't look very comfortable over there, Mrs Peer, how about you come over here and we talk about it some more?' He calculates and recalculates, each time the same conclusion, *too much ground to cover and the edge is too soft to risk both me and her.*

'What's the point? Harrison's gone. I might as well join him.'

'Then you'll need a ferry,' Theo keeps his tone light. 'Felicity told me Professor Peer took the ferry from Hull.'

'She's wrong, deceived by her brother like the rest of us. I'd know if he was still alive, he'd have been in touch with me, somehow. I know he would. Harrison's gone and it's all my fault.' She totters slightly, a few bits of grit and stone tumble down the cliff.

Hannah tenses. 'No, Mrs Peer,' her voice is raised.

Briefly, Theo fears this may unintentionally shove Caroline backwards. He prepares himself to launch into a type of rugby tackle in which he could grasp flailing arms and legs while not following her down the incline. Then it is as if curiosity gets the better of her, she snaps, 'Who's that?'

Hannah takes a deep breath, steadies her tone, 'It's Hannah Poole, Mrs Peer, remember me? I'm working on Professor Peer's book. Why don't you come and join us, over here?'

Mrs Peer is now looking inland.

Good. OK, just move towards us and I can come and get you.

'You miss him, Mrs Peer,' Hannah continues quietly. 'You miss your husband, of course you do. You love each other very much. He wouldn't want you hurting yourself. And there are people here who would miss you. You know how painful it is when you miss someone. You wouldn't want to inflict that kind of pain on anyone else, would you? Come over here and let us take care of you. I bet you'd like to be taken care of right now.'

Well done, Hannah.

'I don't deserve it,' Caroline's sounding uncertain.

There's a pause before Hannah speaks again, then she says gently, 'I understand you feel that way, Mrs Peer, but just maybe there were other reasons why Harrison went. Had you thought there could be?'

Caroline's heels loosen soil which falls the 150 metres to stones being churned by the incoming tide. 'Explain,' her imperious tone is back. It prickles at Theo's spine.

'His book. He knew he could never get it published. After all his work, it must have been very hard for him.'

'You're lying.'

'No, Mrs Peer, I am not.'

The silence stretches. The two women watch each other, an invisible tether between them, one which might be strong enough, or might not.

'You know, Mrs Peer, Professor Peer would not have chosen to leave you unless he had very good reason. There was only one thing which could take him from you.'

'His book,' Caroline says quietly, sadly. 'I knew he was having problems writing. He once told me he didn't think he could do it anymore, write. But then he was writing, I thought everything was OK.' She pauses. 'I knew it wasn't.'

'His book, his life's work. It wasn't your fault. Now please, Mrs Peer, come here, come and join us.' Hannah treads tentatively towards the other woman, hand held out.

Mrs Peer's feet stride away from the cliff edge, only they find no purchase, no traction. She screams.

'Shit,' Theo leaps forward. Hannah is at his shoulder. They are both too late.

CHAPTER 30

Thursday 27 May

Having spent most of the day with Stokes, DI Hoyle is subdued. To Theo's surprise he'd invited him to his office for a share in a takeaway Indian. 'Must keep your strength up lad. What with Mrs Peer going off like that, there'll have to be an investigation, paperwork.' As the daylight faded, they shared delicately spiced pakoras and chicken in a chilli-infused sauce washed down by a couple of beers straight from the bottle. The atmosphere was one of closeness, mateyness. It brought forth some news which Hoyle shared as if it were a personal confidence. A tip-off, 'anonymous' (Theo could almost see the speech marks dangling in the air), had taken police officers based in Whitby to an old kipper-smoking shed owned by Bert Rattenbury. It was where he kept his fishing paraphernalia, along with, through a trap door under some matting, boxes of what purported to be fine brandy, Courvoisier Connoisseur Collection. At present, Rattenbury senior and his two sons are staying tight-lipped. *Who will implicate whom?* Theo wonders. 'We'll see who bleats first,' says his DI, mopping a dribble of crimson sauce from his chin with his handkerchief.

Now the aromas of cardamom and coriander hang about them in the dusky light. Theo does feel better for having eaten. Hannah had held it together until Ben had come to pick her up, then she'd become agitated, blaming herself for Mrs Peer's death. It rubbed salt into Theo's own guilt, *could I have done more?* Ben had held her close, until finally she quietened enough for him to suggest he take her home with him, 'Aurora says she'll check in on your mother.' As they were leaving, Ben gave Theo a hug, 'And don't you go taking this on yourself either. Come round after you're done here, doesn't matter the time.' Lawrence had said much the same, 'Ring when you're finished up, no matter the time.' It had been a balm of sorts.

Hoyle flicks on the ceiling light, the sudden stark brightness dissipates the unlikely cosiness which has developed. He wants an update. Before being collected by her mother, Maya had given a statement. She'd identified the green Gore-Tex jacket as Phil's and Theo is sure the digits noted down in its pocket will match the combination of the Peers' safe. Maya had also said she'd heard Jayson and Phil talking about the burglaries, one real, the other staged.

Hoyle is unimpressed. 'There'll be an argument over whether any of this is admissible,' he grumbles. 'Not to mention the young lady's reliability as a witness. What about the knife Ms Poole said she saw?'

'Hasn't been found.'

The DI has his chin on steepled arms and fingers, 'Another one who any defence will demolish if it ever comes to it, her previous as a victim of a knife attack won't help.'

Theo can't disagree. Though he'd seen a resolution in Hannah today which he'd not observed before, by the time they got back to the station, she was already undermining herself about the knife.

'It's the attack on Stokes,' growls Hoyle. 'I want him for it. The younger generations, no sense of allegiance.'

Under pressure from Theo, Maya had also repeated, with some embroidering, what she'd told Ben and Hannah about Professor Aiden Haswell's dislike of Stokes. Now Theo says, 'Felicity's relationship with Haswell gives a link between Phil and the attack on Mrs Stokes.'

'Maybe, but is there any hard evidence? Those spots on his work clothes?'

'Not from Mrs Stokes. A filial match to Bert's which we have on file, so probably Phil's, but we need a test from him to be certain.'

'He injured himself at the scene?'

'Nothing found there as yet.'

'All we have then, is the sighting of Ms Pritchard's van a few streets away?' Hoyle leans back in his chair, it creaks under his weight.

Theo nods, weariness seeping in. Over a couple of hours, he had taken Phil through everything step-by-step and had not gained an inch. With an endless supply of charm, Rattenbury had stuck to his story. He hadn't even been in town for the burglaries and when the bootleg brandy was being touted. He agreed he'd done the bit of gardening for Denver and had 'helped out' Mrs Peer with a bit of cash, but he'd been working away on 16 May, the day the house went over. Even hearing what his twin had said about Peer's disappearance didn't faze him, he agreed with it, saying, 'It's not a crime to give an old bloke a lift, is it, detective sergeant?' He'd been adamant he'd spent the previous evening in front of the TV with a couple of tinnies, his words precisely echoing his sister's. *Too precisely.* Then Reggie Harvey's elegantly suited female colleague had called time, though her client was the only one in the room not flagging.

'I want him, DS Akande,' repeats Hoyle.

'And your advice is?' says Theo tetchily.

His DI swoops forwards, the empty foil cartons rattling as his elbows once more land on the desk, 'Break the woman, lad. Break the woman.'

A more complete forensic report on the van has been sent over. Before he goes back into the interview room, Theo skims through it to see if there is anything new. There is.

Felicity is looking ragged, especially next to the solicitor, who must have somehow found time for a shower since sitting in on Phil's interview, as she is smelling of a fragrant shower gel. She tries to persuade Theo that there are no questions left to answer, but she is less persuasive than Reggie and more easily derailed.

Theo tries to look Felicity in the eye, only she is staring at the table top, her skin tone is almost as grey. 'Have you anything further to add to what you have already stated, Ms Pritchard?'

She shakes her head jerkily. A loose tendril of hair hangs lankly by her cheek.

'We've found adulterated brandy in the cellar of a shack belonging to your father. Have you anything to say about that?'

Again the negative twitch of her head.

Theo taps the buff folder in front of him, 'We've found blood in your van, it matches the professor's. Plus there's signs of the passenger door and footwell being cleaned with a high-grade detergent used specifically for biological stains.' Theo can hear her nerve ends jangling. He can see the nails have been bitten and the cuticles are raw. 'Did Phil not tell you? Perhaps he cleaned it up and you never knew?' *I'm giving you a chance here. Say something.* She doesn't. 'I'm asking you Ms Pritchard, what happened, what really happened to Professor Peer?'

Her reply comes out as a moan, 'I don't know, I don't know.'

'But you did know about the blood? You cleaned it up?'

She flinches, her head still moving from side to side.

'Is that a no, Ms Pritchard?' *It's a yes, I know it is. You've known all along something happened to Peer. Or did Phil persuade you it was nothing serious or an accident?*

'My client is shaking her head, detective sergeant,' the woman solicitor says quietly. 'Very well.' He takes a sip of water. 'Let's talk about Mrs Pauline Stokes.'

'I didn't do nothing,' is delivered between clamped teeth.

Should I point out your double negative? 'You wrote letters to retired DCI Stokes. Threatening letters.'

'I did not,' her denial, like her brother's to the same accusation, has the indignation of truth.

'And you arranged for your brother to go to the Stokes's house last night, so he could trash it and beat up Mrs Stokes.' He pulls out some photos of the damage done and of Pauline's bruised face, 'Look at them, Ms Pritchard. Look at them.'

She doesn't, instead she finds some defiance, 'Why, why would I?'

'Because, Ms Pritchard, you are having an affair with Professor Haswell and he has a score to settle with Stokes. You were helping him out, the way you were helping Professor Peer out. And now you're protecting Haswell, like you're protecting Phil. Your loyalty would be admirable if it didn't lead you into doing the reprehensible and ...' he pauses for effect. 'And if those you are devoted to were faithful to you.'

She's silent and motionless. The hands on the clock behind her head click on again.

This is my last chance. He sits forwards, says gently, 'Your niece told my DC you were with Haswell on the sixteenth. Now, DC Shilling is always very thorough. As you know, she checked with the professor and he said it was not the case, and then you said you were on a train down to London. However, my DC didn't stop there, she also checked up on Haswell. Do you know what she found out?'

Felicity can't look away from Theo now.

'Come on, DS Akande,' the solicitor breaks in crossly. 'Stop playing games.'

Theo nods, 'Professor Haswell wasn't alone on the night of the sixteenth, he was with Dr Clare Shrimpton, all night.'

It takes a moment for his words to filter through, then Felicity searches wildly around. 'No,' she breathes. 'No, no,' her voice gets louder. 'It's not true, it's not true.'

'It is true, Felicity. I am not lying to you. Both of them were quite open about it. Now tell me what you and Phil agreed to do for Professor Haswell.'

Felicity's eyes are glittering, her hands reach to her ears as if she wants to cover them. She breathes out a raw sob.

'Tell me, Ms Pritchard. Did Professor Haswell ask you to get your brother to turn over DCI Stokes's house and attack his wife?'

'She wasn't meant to be there,' Felicity says miserably. 'Ade said she wouldn't be there.'

For a couple of seconds Theo feels triumphant. It doesn't last. Hoyle may get off on breaking women. Theo does not.

Chapter 31

Thursday 27 – Friday 28 May

After the initial breach, Felicity quickly dams up her defences again. Her statement reiterates that she and her twin had helped Professor Peer disappear and as far as she knows he is alive and well somewhere pondering his options. She agrees she and Aiden had discussed causing minor damage to Stokes's house and she may have mentioned it to her brother. However, she returns to her story that they'd spent the evening together, Phil had cooked pasta and they'd watched a DVD.

Phil remains implacable, he denies having anything to do with the attack on Pauline Stokes. And as for Professor Peer, 'I took him to the ferry, like I said.'

'And the wedding ring we found on the beach?'

He doesn't miss a beat, 'I threw it ova, he told me to, it was business, purely business.' Theo picks up on a sense of entitlement, it reminds him of a merchant banker failing to defend a million-pound bonus. *You did all this for money, the money you could squeeze out of the Peers and you killed because you didn't like being screwed over with fake diamonds.*

In the end the Crown Prosecution Service agrees to only one charge, against Bert for offences under the Licensing Act. 'I want Phil for Stokes,' Hoyle repeats as all the Rattenburys are released, only one facing an indictment.

As the morning shift comes into the station, Theo heads home to sleep fitfully for a few hours. Then he is back at his desk going over and over the reports and statements from the previous day. *There must be something.* Both Lawrence and Ben phone telling him to go back home, get some rest. But it is Suze who finally persuades him to leave, saying truthfully, 'You're no use to anyone in this state, DS Akande.'

Even so, on his way back to his place, he calls in on Professor Haswell. Finds him with two substantial suitcases in his hallway.

'Going on holiday?'

'A short break. Can we make this quick, I've a plane to catch.' Some of Haswell's varnish has been rubbed off.

How Theo would love to scotch the professor's travel plans. He begins leisurely, 'Retired DCI William Stokes and his wife Pauline. Do you know them?'

His blue eyes in his smooth tanned face do not flicker. 'Define know.'

I thought you were in a hurry. I can play games all afternoon. 'What contact have you had with retired DCI Stokes at any time in your life?'

He speaks slowly, maybe considering his words, 'I believe he was amongst the officers who were brought in to break up the strike in the mining village where I grew up.'

You believe? 'You told Maya Short you still hold a grudge against Stokes for his actions?'

He smiles. 'Maya is an enchanting young woman with a vivid imagination.'

'What about recently, what contact have you had with Stokes recently?'

'None. Now if you'll excuse me ...'

'You wrote threatening letters to him.'

He laughs, 'I did not.'

Then who did? Theo has run out of guesses. 'You spoke to Felicity Pritchard about your grudge against Stokes and asked her to arrange for her brother to turn over the Stokes's house and attack Mrs Stokes.'

Haswell crosses his arms, 'I did not and it's outrageous of you to suggest such a thing.'

From a folder he's brought with him, Theo pulls out the photos of Pauline Stokes's bruised face. 'This is what's outrageous, Professor Haswell.'

Fleetingly his eyes widen, he swallows hard.

'Fine in theory, eh Aiden, not so nice in practice.'

Haswell shoves the images away from him, 'I had nothing to do with this. Now I really must ...'

Theo reveals Mrs Stokes's bashed-in face again, revs up his tone a notch, 'Your argument was with Stokes, but this is Pauline Stokes, she didn't deserve this. Look at her.'

He does so briefly, a flinching glance as if it were him being hit. Then he takes a step backwards, leans a shoulder against the wall, runs fingers through his dark rakish curls before his folded arms buttress his chest. 'I know nothing about it. And if you had some evidence you would have arrested me. Since you haven't any, I'm telling you to leave.'

Theo knows he doesn't have a choice. He takes his time, however, to put the photos away, say goodbye, thank the professor for his time and start to walk out the flat. As he does so, Haswell's mobile rings, he answers it, 'Yes Clare, I'm on my way ...' Theo doesn't hear any more, the door is closed firmly behind him.

Chapter 32

Friday 28 May

She hears whispering, outside on the landing. Then a baby crying. A baby choking. Maybe it's a dream? Maybe it's all inside her head? She can't tell anymore. She buries herself under the duvet and returns to sleep.

It's much later, she can tell, as it's dark and quiet when she eases herself out of bed and onto her feet. She finds her fleecy cardie and her leggings to pull on over her bedshirt and creeps downstairs. Ben's spiralling iron steps are icy on her feet. The ground floor is always shaded, the kitchen window is a frame for a night sky hammered through with tarnished nails. She hardly registers the outside through the glass, she is intent on finding something sharp, the paring knife from the drawer will do. She sits on one of the wooden chairs, reveals the flesh on her left arm. *This will help, it will let the pain out, the poison out. Go on, do it. Do it.* The words rattle around and around her mind; a train of commands following the same old looping track. To cut would halt its repetitions. *Bring some peace.* She grips the handle of the knife. *One cut. See the blood. Then wipe it away. And it's done with. It's all so easy.*

She's still sitting there half an hour later. Cold now and stiff with it. She hears the creak of floorboards above, of someone coming down the stairs, saying her name, halting as he surveys the scene.

'I didn't do it, I didn't,' she says softly, not daring to look up. She lets the knife fall, its unblemished blade skitters across the tiled floor.

He puts his arms around her shoulders. 'Do you want to tell me about it?'

She manages to articulate some of it: the foreboding, the despair, the weeping, gagging baby, the whispers.

'It was Aurora who came round, with Oli, he was snivelling, had a bit of a cold.'

'He was choking, suffocating.'

'No my darling, Oli is fine.'

Then she remembers clearly why she needs punishing, on top of all her other faults, 'And Mrs Peer, I let go of her.'

'You never had hold of her, Hannah, you couldn't have saved her.'

'I feel so bad.'

'I know, and you're not bad.'

She is on her feet, unsteady, 'I should go, you don't want me anymore.' *I don't want you to see me anymore, you're too close.*

'Stop, stop running away.'

'You hate me.'

'I don't, I love you.'

It's too much to hear. Love is a slippery word, not to be trusted. She begins to walk towards the stairs.

'Please stay.' He touches her shoulder. She flinches away. 'Hannah, it's me Ben, you know me, I won't hurt you.'

Won't you? Reluctantly she allows herself to be led to the sofa and wrapped in a blanket. 'I'm damaged goods. I'll never be any good.'

'You're fine, as you are.'

She reaches over and pulls him to her, kissing him, trying to push her tongue into his mouth. He gently holds her away from him. *There, you don't want me, you don't love me.* 'Come on, it's what you want me for, isn't it?' She reaches for his crotch. She's shrinking to a skinny kid next to his bulk, the aniseed breath hot on her face. *No, no get away from me.* The child crying now, it's her, suffocating, 'I don't want it, I don't want it.'

'Hannah, stay with me. These are old memories, only memories, it's not happening now. Come back to me here.'

It's maybe a second or several minutes, or years, before his voice infiltrates to her. When it does, she becomes aware of the blanket scratching her neck, her toes numb, the ache in her shoulders. She lets her breath go. She leans back against the sofa arm. She closes her eyes. 'I'm sorry.'

'It's fine.'

'It's not fine. I put you through this all the time and it's not fair on you.'

'It's not all the time, it's less and less. And I choose to stay with you.'

She's suddenly afraid he might choose to leave instead. She grabs his hand.

'I'm not going anywhere.'

I won't make him promise, promises are broken. She is angry. With herself.

'What's the matter?' he reacts to her tensing.

'After all these years of therapy, of training, and I'm still fucked up.'

He smiles, 'I think we can all say that. And you're less fucked than you were.'

'I almost did it, I nearly cut myself again.'

'And you didn't cut. Yesterday was very upsetting, shocking, would have distressed anyone. And still you didn't cut. I'm proud of you.' After a moment, he stands, stretches, 'Do you want anything?'

'A whisky.' She sees his face tighten. 'I'm joking. Something warm would be good.' As she listens to him clatter about in the kitchen, she grows back into the contours of her grown-up body. She begins to permit his words to soak in – maybe even take root: *I'm proud of you Hannah.*

Chapter 33

Saturday 29 May

Following a long bath, Theo finally sleeps, deeply and late into the following morning. He has a leisurely breakfast and then sets out for Hackness. If there'd been anything new, he'd have got a phone call and he can't face going into the station if there is no progress. Not yet anyway.

Many shades of textured green – from the bluey pines to the jade grass – collage the valley he is driving through. They soothe his battered spirits a tad. The cerulean sky arches overhead, with cirrus clouds raked thinly across in uneven furrows. The air is fresh and warm. Getting out of the car, he pauses to sup it in, rid his lungs of the breath of others made fetid by their warped motivations and self-justifications. *In some ways, even these two were architects of their own demise.* He looks up at the house, admiring again its Georgian elegance and the path bordered by roses which are just coming into bloom. He imagines these ruby, pink and yellow flowers were Caroline's pride and joy, their scent heavy and luscious. *Their jauntiness is almost an insult.* Despite this it continues with the lifting of his mood.

There are suitcases in the black-and-white-tiled floor, hardly more substantial than Professor Haswell's. 'We have to go,' explains Marta, sounding regretful. 'There's no money.'

Hasn't been for a while. Theo wonders how long Marta and her husband stayed on with the promise of wages soon and then remained out of loyalty, *or because they cared.* Marta's tawny skin has darkened with the sun, yet there's something sunken about her sculptured cheekbones and the corners of her eyes are reddened. 'We shall miss it here, we miss the professor and Mrs Peer.'

Perhaps the only people to grieve, the beneficiaries to the will are nephews and nieces who haven't visited in years, so Theo has heard. *Though presumably they'll have to wait until the professor can be declared dead, and they may not get much once the debts are paid.* Marta takes him through to Harrison's office, untouched since he last saw it, and they open the safe using the numbers which had been written on the paper found in Phil's jacket. It is useless as evidence, but is somehow satisfying. There is an envelope inside marked for Marta. She opens it, finding a card and drop earrings encrusted with what could be diamonds. Theo wonders if they are real. Marta is concentrated on the card, tears spill over and dribble down her face, 'Poor Mrs Peer, she made mistake, but she was a good woman. She didn't deserve to die in the way she did.' She hides her eyes behind quivering fingers and a sob is wrenched out.

Theo rests his hand on her shoulder, 'No, she did not.'

It is a moment before Marta composes herself enough to straighten and dab at her tears with a handkerchief retrieved from her pocket. 'But they are together, she's with the professor. It's what you say, isn't it detective sergeant? You say they are both passed?'

He nods, *what if I'm wrong? What if Phil did take him to the Hull ferry?*

'He wouldn't have gone without her, not anywhere in this world. Maybe he took her by the hand and led her down the cliff.' This thought appears to comfort her.

Outside again, Theo has two messages on his phone, one from Shilling, *a breakthrough at last,* and one from Stokes, he wants to meet.

Pauline Stokes has refused to return to the house where she was attacked and is staying with their daughter while planning a move to Malton. However, Stokes has told Theo to come there. It has been tidied up. Inside, what's left of the furniture has been shuffled into the centre of rooms and covered in sheeting ready for the decorators. 'Maybe when she sees it all done up she'll change her mind,' Stokes says quietly. They're standing in the garden overlooking the field. 'I've had enough of upheavals.' Then he continues more bumptiously, 'Well lad, who'd have thought we'd have them to thank?' He indicates the horses tranquilly cropping the grass. He hadn't needed to be told by Theo about the manure found on the soles of boots belonging to Phil Rattenbury, plus on the hems of the trousers found in the dumpster. 'Puts him at the scene.'

Just about.

Stokes lets out a spurt of coarse mirthless laughter. 'Shit, he stepped in it and now he's up to his neck in it.'

'Would be better if we could remove his alibi.'

'The lass'll cave, on the stand. What about Haswell?'

'He'll be a witness, for sure. I expect he'll use the opportunity to grandstand.'

'I'm bloody sure he will.' Bill Stokes sighs, 'How much more harm can he do? And if he goes too far, he'll learn more than he wants to about his sainted dad. There were no angels them summer days. We were all working for someone else's agenda.'

In that minute, Theo sees Stokes's intelligence and why he was promoted beyond Hoyle.

The older man slaps Theo on the back. 'You've done a good job, lad. Hoyle said you were the one to sort it for me. So what is it I can do for you?'

Theo's sense of well-being is still fragile, it takes a knock. 'I've done my job as well as I'm able, it's good enough for me.'

'You want me to guess? Hoyle's job?'

'I'm applying for Hoyle's job, I'll go through the correct channels.' Fatigue is suddenly descending. He forces himself to stay focused, *Maybe there is something you can help me with?* He needs to remain cautious, 'You knew about Shilling's photo on Facebook before it happened. I don't need to know how ...'

'But you've got your own ideas?' Stokes tone is gravelly. 'If you had to speculate?'

Theo doesn't like this game. However, if he has to, 'Chesters? An offer of a remarking of his sergeant's exams.'

'I couldn't promise that.'

'No, only Chesters is naive enough to believe you could.' He inhales the dung-spiked air, *it's now or never.* 'You know why your old buddy got left at DI level, he didn't move with the times, believes women like DC Shilling should recognise their place, which isn't much above making the tea. Maybe you agree with him, but you know that kind of thinking has no place in the modern police force.'

Stokes grins, parrots Theo's tone as he repeats, 'Modern police force.'

Makes me sound officious, up myself. Maybe I've pitched this all wrong.

Then Stokes says gruffly, 'Just tell me what you want lad.'

'What I want you to do is persuade Hoyle to expunge any mention of it from Harry's record. And while you're at it, tell him to back off.' Theo can hear the nickering and stamping of the horses in the field.

Stokes steps back into the shadow of the house, the sun has brought sweat to his brow, 'And if I don't?'

'Haswell might not be able to do any more damage, but he's pointed the way and I can do some digging. I can ask questions. Remember, it's what I'm good at.'

Stokes shrugs his tensed shoulders. 'OK, I'll see what I can do.'

Should I push it?

As if noticing his hesitation, Stokes says, 'And nothing for you lad? I hear your record isn't unblemished anymore after the Dr Greene case.'

'I can look out for myself,' Theo growls. *No way I'm going to be beholden to you.* 'DI Wiltshire, on the other hand ...'

Stokes interrupts abruptly, 'We none of us like those who do that sort of thing to kiddies, even if it is one of our own. Wiltshire's safe and so is her investigation.'

'Then we're done.' He makes to walk away.

Stokes holds out his hand for a handshake. 'Aye lad, we're done.'

Chapter 34

Monday 21 June
This has been the best birthday ever. I am enjoying myself. These two thoughts cause a fizz of excitement which gains strength as it rises inside Hannah, an internal firework rocket which breaks into an umbrella of multicoloured stars against the dark heavens. Only four of them have gathered for the midsummer ceremony at Rose's – Hannah, Aurora, Ben and Rose herself. Hannah is relieved, the others who normally come are nice enough, but she feels the closeness of this group. *They're my family now*, this pops up in her brain.

    She looks round at them. Aurora's dark skin and long hair look luxuriant against her white organza dress. It is ankle length, as is Rose's more robust cream cotton one. Rose has a large round bronze pendant hanging around her neck. She has allowed Aurora to tease her grey hair into curls which soften the edges of her square-chinned face. Ben has on a dark-green cloak, the gold sun on the back sending out rays around his waist and over his shoulders. As usual they have created their sacred circle in what is essentially a large shed at the bottom of Rose's garden. Though the decoration of candles and verdure of the season hides its essential shed-ness. They have invited the spirits of the four compass points and the lord sun and the lady moon to join them. It is the vanquishing of the lord, the father, the sun. From now on the female power of the moon will be in ascendance, its blurred imprint on the mackerel sky outside is coming into fullness. At this moment of transition, they bring their focus onto their own strengths and how they might be harnessed. They call upon the divine powers and the spirits to help them in their endeavours and to bring peace, sustenance and health to those they love, to the community and to the wider world. Hannah adds some silent blessings for Caroline Peer, *I'm sorry I couldn't hold you.*

    Then they go outside, where Ben and Rose have contrived a way for a wicker wheel stuck with sparklers to drop from the shed roof, a feral Catherine Wheel which spits into the cool of the evening. They hold hands and throw their wishes up to the gathering dusk. From behind closed lids, Hannah catches the step and scent of a fox. She is beginning to understand that it will come to her at every observance. Tonight she hears in the snap of its auburn tail the words, *be brave, little one, be brave.* A bubble of joy bursts inside her.

The ritual is over. Normally they would eat together at Rose's, but they have joined Lawrence, Theo and Max on the beach for a picnic. The sea lies peaceably, flatly reflecting the veins of pink and yellow which streak the sky as the sun slips behind the crumbling cliffs.   The friends have chosen the beach by the old lido. Away from the main drag, pools glint in between the brown-seaweed-covered rocks, a crab cautiously feels its way across the lion-pelt sand.

As the warmth of the day dissipates, Theo, Ben and Max build a fire, gently ribbing Lawrence for his protests that it must be illegal, and this brings them closer together. They've all, except for Hannah, had several servings of Rose's fine homemade elderflower wine, it fuels their laughter, their chat. Aurora tells Hannah she's heard Haswell won't be returning to Scarborough, is planning an extended research trip to Brazil to explore judicial corruption. Clare is also on the move, to Bristol University. She has her book deal. Hannah has agreed to be her proofreader. *I need the money.*

Later, they watch the flames catch, not speaking. Ben puts his arm around Hannah, resting his warm hand on the centre of her back. She takes a sip of her fruit punch, silently making a toast to each one of the people gathered around her: *you all help me in your own way to hold the pieces of myself together.* The fire cracks and spits. A bat flits down from the undergrowth of the South Cliff gardens and into the orange glow, picking off a dozy insect, then flits quickly away again. The waves are undulating, expelling the softest of sighs.

* * *

After the party, Theo goes to put Mrs White's bin out. She'd been taken into hospital several weeks previously, before Trench could get a statement from her. It's possible she won't be returning home as it's likely she will need twenty-four-hour care. Theo'd told her the fraudster with the white van would be prosecuted and did not correct her assumption that it would be for his crime against her.

He lets himself into her house, it has a mouldering air now she is not there to dust it every day. He checks round it as he had promised to do. Mrs White's daughter had phoned to say her mother was concerned her bedroom window wasn't shut tight. Theo enters the floral, eau-de-rose sanctum to find the window firm and locked. As he turns he notices the Bible on the nightstand. It's old and well thumbed. He picks it up, it is bookmarked at Romans 1:18, a now familiar quotation. After a moment, he replaces it.

As he makes his way into the kitchen through the lounge, his gaze settles on the photos. Their stories are clearer to him now. He recognises Aiden Haswell as a young boy, with his curls, sharp nose, tanned skin and (even then) engaging smile, crouched on the sand with a younger version of Mrs White's daughter. 'Ade' – Mrs White and Felicity had both used the diminutive. It had been for Haswell that Mrs White had bought the bootleg brandy. Not for her son, as Theo had supposed. The son literally torn out of a family's story because he chose to work against his father's wishes. *Another legacy of Stokes's violent intervention into the strike.* The sole picture of Mrs White's boy, now a grown man with his family by a lake, Derwent Water, in Cumbria, is maybe evidence of a tentative healing of the estrangement.

Theo goes through to the back of the house where Mrs White collects her recycling. There's at least several months' worth stacked up, it seems she hadn't managed to clear it by herself and hadn't been able to ask for help. He picks up a pile of newspapers.

He doesn't have a good hold of them and sheets fall away to the floor. They are lace made of paper. Words and letters have been cut out of them. He studies them for a moment. It's easy to deduce what words are missing from the headlines and how they might have been put together to make phrases such as, 'You're a dead man 4 what you did.' Then he gathers them up and goes out to shove them into his neighbour's blue bin.

Thank you

Thank you to you the reader for spending time with my story. If you have any comments, please send them to AvenuePressScarb@talktalk.net.

Thank you to all those who supported me in this endeavour, gave me advice and encouragement; especially Lesley, Felix and Kate and my many writing friends. Thank you to those who represent the very best in therapy and helped me know myself better, especially Annie. Thank you to my husband, Mark, for his unstinting love, sustenance and backing, which has got me through the hard times and much, much more.

Thank you to my copyeditor extraordinaire, Charlotte Cole, http://charlottecoleeditorial.com, and my equally wonderful proofreader, David Powning, www.inkwrapped.com. Any mistakes which remain are entirely my own.

If you have enjoyed *The Art of Breathing,* you may like to turn the page to find out more about the others in the Scarborough Mysteries series: *The Art of the Imperfect* (long-listed for the Crime Writers Association Debut Dagger Award 2015) and *The Art of Survival*. Both from Avenue Press Scarborough.

The Art of the Imperfect **by Kate Evans**
Scarborough Mysteries #1
Long-listed for the Crime Writers Association
Debut Dagger Award 2015

The death of the renowned psychotherapist Dr Themis Greene in Scarborough sends storm waves through the intertwining lives of three of the small seaside town's residents. The murder in the town perched on the edge of land and sea pushes Hannah Poole, Aurora Harris and DS Theo Akande to the borderlands. They are forced to explore the edges of reason, understanding, justice and love. What they discover gets them through but is far from perfect.

This isn't gritty crime, this isn't cosy crime, this isn't police procedural. This is poetic storytelling which peels back the psychological layers to reveal the raw centre.

The Art of Survival **by Kate Evans**
Scarborough Mysteries #2

Little girls lost. DS Theo Akande is investigating the disappearance of eight-year-old Victoria Everidge. Her mother, Yvonne, is a desperate woman. What is she capable of? Eminent journalist and newspaperman, Stan Poole, dies leaving a filing cabinet full of secrets. As these leak out, his daughter, Hannah, begins to question her own girlhood. She is losing her way. Her best friend, Lawrence, newly an item with Theo, finds it hard to remain supportive. Instead Hannah clings to her work as a trainee counsellor and to her client Julia. Julia is apparently no little girl lost, but appearances can be deceptive. Then a body is found. The intertwining stories unfold against the wintery backdrop of a seaside town in North Yorkshire.